No place in the Sun

www.noplaceinthesun.com

ALSO BY JOHN MULLIGAN:

Dancing on the Waves
published by Collins Press, 2004

*Following in the Footsteps of the
Four Famous Flannerys*
published by Connaught Telegraph, 2007

NO PLACE IN THE SUN

John Mulligan

ORIGINAL WRITING

www.noplaceinthesun.com

978-1-907179-05-1

A CIP catalogue for this book is available from the National Library.

Published by Original Writing Ltd., Dublin, 2009.

Printed by Cahills, Dublin.

For Una

ACKNOWLEDGEMENTS

As with any publication, this one didn't get written on its own. A lot of people helped me with this project, and several good friends were involved in turning a disparate collection of rough chapters in to the finished book that you now hold in your hands. David Rice of the Killaloe Hedge School first showed me that maybe I had the germ of an idea that needed nurturing, and he gave me the techniques that helped me to turn the outline idea into a draft novel. Kate McMorrow, Brian Rogers, John Breen, Joe McDermott and Joe Fahy all read the draft and made useful suggestions that shaped the final version of the book. Isobel Creed of the Writers Consultancy was always encouraging while at the same time being critical of things that needed criticism. In hindsight, she was right about almost everything.

My brother Frank is my best sounding board for my work; he is always my first port of call when I need something to be read and critiqued. His encouragement from the first chapters encouraged me to keep going and write it to the end, and his suggestions as always were sharp and have shaped the final product.

Last and not at all least, my partner Una encouraged me to write the book and gave me the space and support to allow my creativity to flow unhindered. She was the one who kept me going when the muse deserted me, and who stood back and gave me plenty of room when it was all going well.

INTRODUCTION

A few years ago I was invited to a small gathering in a city in another country, both of which shall remain nameless; indeed this all happened in what now seems like another era altogether. Most if not all of the people who were there on the night were working in the property business at various levels, primarily developing and selling foreign property to Irish and UK buyers. They were all there; the big developers, the lawyers, the builders, the people who sold the furniture, people from the international marketing companies, and even the few 'bottom feeders' – the small time operators who made a living on the fringes by inserting themselves into deals and getting small slices of the action. The drinks were flowing, times were good, and it would have been fair to say that pretty much all of the guests were making a good living from the business. I certainly wasn't aware that anyone I met that evening was struggling.

The big money had been made in tried and trusted markets like Spain, Portugal and France, selling largely good quality property to buyers at prices that were fair, for the most part. The buyers were getting nice holiday homes, the builders were making modest but adequate profits, and the agents were making a good living as long as the volumes remained steady. There was no need for anyone to get greedy; it would have spoiled things and 'killed the goose.'

There was much discussion about the emerging phenomenon of Irish and UK buyers re-mortgaging their own houses and using the money to buy foreign holiday homes, and increasingly, investment properties. While many of them were making shrewd investments, an awful lot of them appeared to be throwing themselves at the mercy of agencies that were usually reputable, but sometimes less so. We talked a lot about the opportunities in this new market, as well as the responsibility of protecting some of these naïve buyers from their own recklessness.

One agent told us that he had started to sell property in Bulgaria, and he had a plan that he thought might be of interest to anyone thinking of doing the same. He was pre-booking cheap apartments from Bulgarian developers, adding obscenely large margins to them and persuading UK buyers that they represented great value in comparison with property in the South of England or on the South Coast of Spain. He had what he reckoned to be a killer sales ploy; he was adding two years rent to the price of each already over-priced property and persuading buyers that he could give them two years rental guarantee with each apartment that they bought. They were 'walking out the door,' as he put it. He didn't mean, as I initially thought, that the buyers were walking away from such a blatant scam; this overpriced garbage was selling like the proverbial hot cakes.

I told him in no uncertain terms that what he was doing was crooked and that apart from the rights and wrongs of it all, he was bound to get caught and his reputation would be ruined. His attractive and heavily bejewelled wife had been listening to our conversation; she laughed as she took a long swig from her glass of champagne. She put a conspiratorial arm around my shoulders and gave me a more than slightly drunken smile. The words she slurred over have stayed with me, exactly as she said them on that night.

'Life is too short,' she said. 'Put your fucking conscience back in your pocket and make yourself a few pounds for a change.'

Looking back on that evening and on all that happened since then, I reckon that that was when I realised that it had all started to go terribly wrong, that the lunatics were starting to take over the asylum. I began to wonder what might happen if people like that ever got to be in charge, if they got a chance to pull the wool over everyone's eyes. This is how I think that it might have turned out; this is their story.

CHAPTER ONE

'I hab a pleadin pun in the pag, ged dowd on de four.'

The young man was dressed in a pair of navy tracksuit bottoms and a white hooded sweatshirt; the hood was pulled up over a cream coloured baseball cap and he had a red football scarf wound round his mouth. A pair of extra-large sunglasses completed the picture. The youngster was wearing the brightest whitest pair of trainers that Tom had ever seen; he looked at him in amazement.

'I hab a pleadin pun. I'll pleadin ude it.'

'He has a gun in the bag and he'll use it, that's what it sounds like.' Walter put his hand on Tom's shoulder. 'I think he wants us to get down on the floor.'

The youth lifted the scarf away from his mouth and screamed at them. 'That's what I bleedin said, I have a bleedin' gun in the bag, get down on the bleedin' floor.' He waved the brown paper bag in the general direction of the two salesmen.

Tom lowered his lanky frame flat on to the floor of the shop, no sense arguing with the guy, he might be on drugs or something. He lay flat on his stomach and said nothing.

Walter got down slowly on one knee and put his hands on the floor. 'Take it easy, son. We only work here, we'll do whatever you say, no need to point that gun at us.' He put the other knee on the ground and then slowly stretched himself out until he was lying on the carpet tiles beside Tom.

'Wherd the manader?' The youth lifted the scarf from his mouth; 'where's the bleedin' manager?'

'There isn't a manager as such, there's just four of us working here.' Walter raised himself up on his elbows to speak to the raider.

'Four of yous, where's the others so?' The youth angrily pulled the scarf away from his face and stuffed it in the pocket of his hoodie. 'Get down on the bleedin' floor, I said.'

'Robert doesn't come in until this afternoon, and Andrew will be coming through that door in a minute. He's the nearest thing we have to a boss.' Walter nodded his head towards the swing door leading to the canteen.

'You better not be bleedin' shitting me, I have a bleedin' gun.' The youth waved the bag menacingly at the Tom and Walter.

'Like I said, son, no skin off our noses, we're not shitting you.'

A youth in a green hoodie peered round the front door; he had the front of his hood pinched in one hand to conceal his face. 'Hurry up, Macker, there's an old dear coming.'

The raider strode nervously up and down the aisle between the washing machines and the vacuum cleaners. 'Shite, fuck, tell her it's closed, tell her the gaff is closed.'

The youth stuck his head back into the shop. 'She wants to know when it'll be open, she wants to buy a washing machine. She said her old one is broke.'

'Fuck her and her bleedin' washing machine; tell her to come back in an hour, tell her the electric is fucked or something.'

Andrew chose that minute to make his entrance through the swing doors. He marched across towards the small appliances counter, coffee in hand. He looked around for Tom and Walter but couldn't see anyone except the youth with the paper bag.

'Good morning, sir. My apologies, I thought my colleagues were out on the floor; how can I help you?'

'He wants to rob you, Andy.' Walter carefully raised himself up on his knees from behind the row of vacuum cleaner boxes. 'He has a gun, but he promised not to use it if we cooperate, so don't panic.'

The raider waved the bag at Andrew. 'Hand it bleedin' over.'

Andrew stood in shock, his mouth opening and closing but no words coming out. He wordlessly handed the paper cup of coffee towards the youth.

'Not the bleedin' coffee you stupid queer, the bleedin' money, where's the bleedin' money, open the fucking safe or I'll blow yous all away, I'm not kidding yous.'

The other youth poked his head around the door and spoke from behind his hands. 'Hurry up for fuck's sake, Macker. I have to go to the jacks.'

'In a fucking minute.' He turned to where Andrew stood rooted to the spot. 'Open the bleedin' safe, now I said!'

'It's not locked, but there's nothing in it, we just opened the shop an hour ago.'

'There has to be bleedin' money in it. This is a big fucking gaff; yous must have loads of bleedin' money in the safe.' The youth was losing some of his bluster.

'Honestly, it's here under the counter, and it's open; come and look.' Andrew was white faced and trembling.

The youth raced over to the counter and pushed past the terrified salesman. He pulled the empty cash box and the book of gift vouchers from the safe and threw them on the ground. He kicked the cashbox away and rounded angrily on Andrew.

'There has to be bleedin' money here somewhere, I'll kill ya, ya fucking queer ya.'

Andrew was shaking; he put his cup of coffee on the counter to stop it from spilling.

'Really, honestly, there's no money here. We nearly never have money in the shop; it's all hire purchase and credit cards anyway. Please, you have to believe me.'

Walter stood up slowly and carefully and dusted himself off. 'He's telling you the truth, son, there's no money here. There was a time when we'd have a few bob in the safe maybe, not much, but a few bob. Since that Whitebox place opened across the way we have less and less.

Tom pressed himself up from the floor. 'It's true; business is very bad here since that Brit place opened. Why didn't you rob them? Waste of time coming here.'

The raider was calming down a little; he held the bag by his side and had stopped waving it around. 'They have a bleedin' security man, and you can't get near the bleedin' place with security fucking cameras. Have yous no bleedin' money at all?'

'No, not a cent.' Walter shook his head.

The other youth poked his head around the porch door. 'Come on, for fuck's sake, Macker, I'm burstin.'

'I'm coming, I'm coming; they have no bleedin' money.'

'They must have fucking money.'

'They fucking haven't.'

'Get something so, get playstations or something.'

The youth pointed the bag at Tom. 'Hey, ya big ginger fuck, I told ya to get down on the floor.'

'The carpet is dirty, it's destroying my suit. Don't worry, I won't move from here though.' Tom sat on a low stack of microwaves at the end of the row.

'Gimme a couple of playstations so and I'll go.'

'We don't do playstations; Miltons only does white goods and tellys and computers. You'll have to go to Whitebox for the playstations.'

'What else have yous? Any phones?'

'We don't do phones, but we have kettles. Do you want a kettle?' Andrew held up a box with a plastic kettle in it.

The raider swiped at the box, sending it spinning to the ground. 'What would I want a stupid fucking kettle for? Who'd buy a fuckin' kettle, you can get them for nuttin off the social. Stick it up yer fucking hole, will ya? This is bleedin' mad, so it is.' He moved towards the door. 'Stay where yous are for ten minutes, don't call the bleedin' coppers or I'll come back and kill yous. I will!'

Walter walked carefully towards the door and peered out. 'They're gone, no sign of them.'

Tom came to the door and looked across the car park. 'We're ok, should we call the cops, or should we bother?'

Andrew was sitting on a chair by the computer desk. 'Oh my God, this is the worst day of my life; I thought I was going to die.'

Walter picked carpet fibres from his suit. 'I doubt if he had a gun, if he did he would have taken it out of the bag, but you can't take a chance. I reckon there's no point in calling the cops.'

'But we have to, don't we?' Andrew looked worried.

'Walter is right.' Tom took off his jacket and brushed it off. 'They didn't get anything, and if the cops come they'll close us for half a day, no commission for us and a lot of lost business for your uncle Maurice; he won't be too pleased, Andrew. I'd say just carry on, forget about it.'

'Ok so, you're right I suppose. But I won't be the better of this for ages.'

***

'I wouldn't fancy a repeat of this morning's caper.' Tom put the drinks on the table by the window. 'It wasn't too bad at the time but it's a bit scary looking back at it.'

Walter picked up his pint and took a long swallow. 'I still think he didn't have a gun, I'd say it was just a bluff.'

'I'm still shaking. It took me completely by surprise. When I walked out on the floor I assumed he was a customer. I couldn't see you guys, I thought you were in the stockroom.' Andrew spun the ice around and around in his gin and tonic.

Tom put his change back in his pocket and sat down at the table. I'm not going to worry about it, it's over and nobody got hurt.'

Walter laughed. You're right, Tom, there was no harm done. Do you know the worst thing about it?'

'Yeah, having to lie on that dirty carpet. It looks clean until you have your face down beside it.'

'Not that, the fact that there was no money in the till at ten o'clock on a Friday morning; I remember a time when there would be a dozen cash sales made at that time of the day.'

'That's a fact.' Tom hadn't thought about it, but it was true enough. 'Between the robbery and this wet weather and the sales for the last few weeks, I'm fed up with it all. The job isn't the same lately.'

Walter shrugged his shoulders sympathetically. 'We're all in the same boat since the Brits opened, but we have to keep going the best we can. I'm well down on last month and it's getting worse every day.'

They pondered their problem silently. It used to be easy to sell washing machines and fridges, but since the competition opened it was getting tough. The basic wage was no use on its own; you had to be making a lot of commission to make it worthwhile.

Andrew gathered the empties from the table and went to the bar for another round.

Walter looked at his departing back. 'It's all right for fairycakes there, he doesn't have to worry.'

Their colleague stood to inherit the business when his elderly uncle passed on, which wouldn't be a minute too soon as far as Andrew was concerned. He often joked with the others that the old man was looking poorly, and that they would all be out of a job when he sold his inheritance and moved somewhere where the boys had dusky skin and the sun shone all day.

Andrew put the fresh drinks on the table. 'Cheer up, lads. At least dear Uncle Maurice isn't worth any less after today.'

They laughed at his attitude. Both of them knew that there was no love lost between their friend and his uncle. Andrew just humoured the old man to avoid being cut out of the will.

'You'll just have to invent a few new tricks for parting the customers from their money, Tom.' Walter didn't always approve of Tom's methods for closing a sale.

'The punter is the enemy, don't you know that? You need all the tricks you can think of to beat them.'

'Like telling them that the machine they are looking at is the same as the one you have at home.'

Tom laughed. 'Come on, every salesman uses that trick. If the punter thinks you bought the same model, they're happy.'

'That's all right as a last resort for closing a tricky sale, but you do it to them all.'

Andrew laughed along with Walter. 'I wouldn't mind, but you're renting that flat, you never bought a washing machine in your life.'

'Come on now, be fair. I'm not the only one that uses a few tricks to make a sale.'

Walter joined in the ribbing, the strain of the morning's events almost forgotten. 'First you tell them that they are buying the most reliable machine in the shop, and then you sell them a guarantee, in case it breaks down.'

Tom laughed. 'Guarantees are good. For commission anyway.'

'True enough, but you don't have to push them on every old lady that buys a kettle.'

Tom shook his head. 'Come on, Walter, you're missing the point. You can't go around telling the truth if you want to sell stuff; that would never do.'

Walter laughed and slapped him on the back.

'I have to hand it to you, Tom; you'd sell shoes to the footless. You'll go a long way if they don't catch up with you.'

***

It was cold in the canteen after the weekend, and the vending machine was acting up. Eventually Tom managed to get it to produce a cup of coffee and he joined Walter and the other three salesmen at the table. These monthly sales meetings were a nuisance, coming in an hour early on a Monday was nobody's idea of fun, but on the other hand it was good to find out how the month had gone and what products might carry an extra commission.

Milton sipped his tea and looked around at his staff. They talked about the attempted robbery for a while, and then he opened his file and started what Walter always called his state of the union address.

'Well done to everyone for a good effort, but we are hurting badly since our English neighbours arrived.'

They nodded in agreement; there was no doubt that the competition was having a major impact.

'Walter, you topped the league again, well done.' Walter was a shrewd old goat, a long time around and able to thrive where others would die. He had pulled in a big sale of television sets to the new hotel down the road, more because he played golf with the manager than anything to do with his selling skills. Still, a sale was a sale and you had to hand it to him.

'Tom, you did very well, number two slot; good work even if you had to make a lot of small sales to do it.'

Tom smiled, he had hoped to top Walter's score but never mind. Next month would be different.

'Andrew, good steady performance, I know it's hard to do big money in small domestic appliances but you did very well indeed. Well done.'

Andrew smiled and went back to his daydream.

Milton turned to young Robert, the computer specialist who had been paraded as the great white hope when he had joined the firm a year earlier. He shook his head sadly.

'What happened to you this month?' he asked the hapless teenager. 'Not a single computer sale. What on earth were you doing, young man? Do you think we can run a profitable computer department just by selling a few ink cartridges?'

Robert tried to stammer a few words in his defence, but it was obvious that the computer department was not doing the business. Whitebox had a sister company with a worldwide reputation for computer sales, and they had opened a few weeks earlier just two doors away. Blackbox computers was sucking up all the computer business for miles around, with their special offers and heavy television advertising. It was impossible to compete, and everybody knew it, but Robert was feeling the heat. He muttered something about having a lot of hope for the next month, but it was clear enough that he didn't believe his own words.

Milton didn't pursue the matter and Robert relaxed a little, the focus off him for a while at least. They were getting to the interesting bit, the bonuses and the list of stock that needed to be cleared and that would carry extra commission.

'Walter, good month for you, just over fifteen hundred commission; excellent!'

Walter smiled, that was slightly better than he had expected.

Tom, one thousand two hundred, you're catching the old fellow. Well done to you both, good result in bad times.'

He pulled out another page and perused it. 'Walter, you should be doing better on the extended guarantees. You failed to sell them in around sixty percent of cases compared to Tom's closing rate of seventy percent, he only dropped three in ten customers. I know that they are a bit of a nonsense from the buyer's perspective, but you need to forget that and push them harder; they are difference between profit and loss on a lot of items.'

Milton never discussed Andrew's commission at the meetings, and this month it was clear that he wasn't going to mention Robert's zero sales any further. He shuffled the papers in the file and drew out the list of appliances that had been de-listed, replaced by new models. It was essential that these were moved quickly before the public realised that they were obsolete, and the extra commission made sure that the salesmen focussed on this old stock. He passed around this list of dead stock to all the team.

Tom studied the list carefully. There were some good ones in it this month, brand leaders that would be easy to sell. He was already doing a mental tour of the store, taking in all the items that he would be trying to offload before Walter found customers for them.

The list seemed longer than usual this month, but then he realised that there were a lot of computers on it. Still, that was Robert's department, no point in thinking too much about those.

It was Robert who spotted the problem first, and he spoke out in astonishment.

'I don't understand; are we de-listing all the computers in the store?' he asked incredulously.

'Got it in one, my boy.' The old man tidied up his papers to signal the end of the meeting.

Robert was red faced.

'But what are we doing with.....' his voice trailed off as he realised that he had just been publicly sacked and humiliated. He got up and left the canteen quickly, leaving a stunned silence in his wake.

Milton was preparing to leave. 'Ok, team, let's get stuck in and take the fight to the Brits. This is a tough business, lads; we're fighting for survival.'

Tom dropped a couple of coins into the vending machine, but nothing happened. He thumped it angrily and swore. Walter stepped up beside him and caressed the reject button; the cup rattled into the holder and the coffee trickled down, filling the room with its rich aroma.

Walter spoke quietly. 'Keep the cool, don't sweat the small stuff. If the place goes under, we get a few quid and we move somewhere else. That's life, son, don't worry about it.'

Tom shrugged his shoulders; maybe it was time to think about a move. For now though, there was a list of appliances to shift, and the chance of a few extra quid on the guarantee racket. Time to face his public. He stirred the sugar into his coffee and kicked his way through the swing doors, clicking on the lights as he passed the bank of switches. Walter threw the main switch to turn on the rows of television sets on the back wall, and Andrew pressed his thumb on the button that opened the shutters. The store was coming alive, wakening from its Sunday slumber. Milton's was open for business.

***

Tom rapped on the steel door with a coin. It was early, time for a coffee before the store opened, and a chance to read the paper in a bit of comfort. The look on Walter's face caused him to stop short.

'What's up?'

Walter shook his head. 'Go in and ask Andy. He's not in his usual sunny form I can tell you.'

In the small canteen it was clear that all was not well with Andrew. He sat at the end of the table, and he had been crying. His usually cheery face was streaked with tears and he looked older than his thirty years.

'What's up, Andy?'

For once, Tom avoided the temptation to give his colleague a ribbing. This looked a lot worse than the usual saga of one of Andrew's boyfriends moving out and leaving him lost for a few days until he found a replacement. He felt sorry for the poor bugger really, despite being the first to pull his leg on these occasions. Andrew was a harmless enough fellow, living for his clubbing and his flamboyant social life, and he enlivened the tea breaks with his jokes and banter.

Andrew sniffled noisily. 'He is marrying a woman! She's a lot younger than him too, bloody gold-digger.' He started to sob uncontrollably.

Tom put a protective arm around his shoulders. He figured that one of Andy's boyfriends had gone straight, and he could understand how that could upset the poor fellow. 'Never mind, lots more fishes in the sea and all that.'

Andrew's sobbing got worse; Tom found it hard to understand the words that escaped between the sobs. 'No, no, not that, uncle bloody Maurice, he met a young bitch, getting married. Selling the place and going to Spain.' He slumped over the table with his head in his hands.

Walter put three cups of coffee on the table. 'Looks like we're going to be out of a job, son. Seems like the old lad found himself a new woman and he's selling out to a British outfit.'

'No way, he isn't, is he?' Tom looked at Andrew for confirmation of what he was hearing.

Andrew took a couple of swallows of the coffee and seemed to calm himself. His voice steadied.

'He asked me to come round this morning for breakfast and he told me everything, I knew he'd been seeing the woman from the golf club but I thought he was just fond of a bit of company.'

Tom was starting to get the picture. 'Old Milton has a woman?'

Andrew nodded and sniffled again. 'He'll have a closing down sale starting tomorrow, he's already sold the store and the warehouse and they are going to retire to Marbella and play bloody golf.' He started to sob. 'She put him up to this, bloody bitch, I know she did, he was happy working in the business.'

The enormity of what was happening began to sink in, Tom looked at Walter. 'So we're on the fucking road so. Just what I need with a car loan and the fucking bills I have.'

Walter shrugged his shoulders. 'I have a mortgage and a wife and child; I need this like a hole in the head, but I'm not going to panic about it. You and I will always get other jobs, son; anyone who can sell as well as us can sell ourselves to another employer. We're the best, Tom. We'll be ok. I feel sorry for our friend here though, he has lost a lot more than a poxy job.'

Tom stopped and thought, it was true, poor Andrew had just seen his inheritance disappear over the hill to the Costa del Sol. There wasn't much future for him; he had only survived up to now because of his uncle's patronage. Being the boss's nephew could have its downside.

He put an arm around Andrew's shoulder. 'Cheer up Andy' he said, with as much conviction as he could muster, 'there's always work for good men.'

Andrew's sniffling continued long after they had moved out to the shop and opened the shutters to start another week. They would have to sell a few kettles today; the usually chirpy Andrew was in no state to stand behind the smalls counter for a while.

The day started well, they each collared a couple of good sales with very little effort, then things quietened down and they drifted over to the couch in the television viewing area.

Walter turned down the sound on the sports channel. 'So, what do you think? Should we walk away and get other jobs right now, or hang on to the bitter end?'

Tom sighed. 'I don't know, in one way I feel like getting out of here now, but then again there could be an easy bundle of commission here with the closing-down sale, and we must be due redundancy or something. He must have got millions for this place, so it's not like he's short or anything.'

'I reckon there'll be damn all redundancy. I think it's only paid on the basic, not the commission, and you can be sure that Milton won't kill himself that way. I mean, he has no reason to be generous or anything, he won't need us again and why should he give us anything over and above what he has to?'

Tom hadn't thought of it that way, but as usual Walter was right. Milton would try to get out of this whole deal with as much money as possible, same as always, and there was no point in having big expectations. The old bastard hadn't even bothered to tell them himself about the closedown, just left it to poor old Andy to break the news.

Walter gestured back towards the canteen; Andrew hadn't emerged all morning. 'Jesus I feel really sorry for poor old fairycakes, imaging getting a kick in the hole like that. He always thought he was the heir apparent, who would have thought that the old guy would have a bit of life left in him? The curse of the Viagra generation.'

The younger man shook his head. 'I never would have figured Milton as having an interest in women. I mean his wife must be ten years dead and he never talked about women or anything, just golf and money; that was all I ever heard him on about anyway.'

Walter was suddenly angry. 'Fuck Milton. I'm more concerned about myself, and you should be too. I reckon that if another job comes up I'm off, I'm not waiting round for this place to empty out, it would be too bloody depressing.'

Tom didn't know what to do, being faced with losing his job was a shock. 'I suppose that's the way to go, but it's hard to call it. Depends on what's on the table I suppose, if he's offering a lot of money I'd stay on, otherwise I'll go to the best offer I can get.'

A young woman walked in and started to mooch around the cooker section. Tom got reluctantly to his feet and walked over to intercept her. 'Good morning, madam, can I help you?'

'Just looking, thanks.'

Tom turned and walked back to the couch; any other time and he would have persisted and tried to get a sale, but today he just wasn't in the humour.

Walter was smiling again. 'Losing your touch, son. Not like you to let one off like that!'

Tom sighed; it might be time to start looking around right enough.

***

Milton appeared just before closing time, all business as usual and looking at his watch pointedly as Tom rolled down the shutter a couple of minutes before six. The old bastard would never change, make you listen to his spiel on your own time and not waste a second of selling time.

Old habits die hard, thought Tom to himself, as he walked back to the canteen to hear what was happening.

The boss was his usual brusque self. 'Well, Andrew told you the bad news?'

They nodded silently.

'I had no choice really, since those people moved in we were just pushing water up a hill. You guys are the best in the business, but we can't compete with their buying power.'

He outlined what would happen next, the morning paper would have a big advertising spread and they would try to clear all the stock from the warehouse and then from the shop floor in about two weeks. On the last few days they would have further reductions on the display stock for take-away customers only.

'There will come a point where the remaining stock will be worth less than the cost of staying open for two days. At that point we'll close the door and leave it there. Everyone clear on all that?'

Tom couldn't wait to ask a few questions. 'What about us? Do we get a severance payment of some kind?'

'Tom, Tom, always thinking about the money.' Milton was his usual sarcastic self.

'Hang on now.' Walter came to Tom's aid, 'that's what has us all here. What about the money, what have you in mind?'

'Well, you will get your full month's basic, along with any residual commissions and you get statutory redundancy on top of all that. That goes without saying; don't I always pay you for what you do? Have I ever left any of you short?'

Tom was angry; they were being pushed out without an extra penny, after the effort they had made for the old bastard. 'It's not fucking good enough.'

Milton reddened; he wasn't used to being spoken to like that. 'Mind your tone, young fellow' he said angrily.

Walter moved in to calm things down. He spoke quietly. 'I agree with Tom. To be fair, we could leave now and you would have to shift a warehouse full of stock on your own, and you know that you need us to do it. We need to be looking after our own interests, to find another job and all that, so if you want our continued loyalty you will need to make a reasonable gesture or I'm out of here, for one.'

'Me too.' Tom backed up his friend.

Milton sat back and folded his arms defiantly. 'Andrew and I can sell the stock. We don't need you two if that's what you want to do. I can give you your money in the morning and you can go, I really don't mind.'

Andrew sniffled in the corner and said nothing, but his demeanour spoke volumes. He hated his uncle at that moment; Andrew wouldn't be killing himself to sell a warehouse full of cookers and fridges.

Milton was angry and flustered; he got up and walked around the small room. Walter stood up too, not wanting to give him any psychological advantage. Eventually the older man sat down and calmed a little.

'Ok, ok, fair enough, you need to be given some recognition for hanging on to the finish. I propose a loyalty bonus of a thousand each on the day we close the doors. How is that, that's very fair isn't it?'

Walter held his hand up to stop Tom from saying anything. 'Make it two grand each, and pay us our salary and redundancy and all our commissions the week before, at the end of the month, then you have a deal.'

He looked at Tom for confirmation; Tom nodded assent.

Milton shook his head. 'I can't possibly. It isn't in it, you know; small margins on most of this stuff, lads. Be fair now.'

The two salesmen sat with arms folded, saying nothing.

'Ok, ok. I'll pay you all that's due at the end of the month, then the two thousand on the following Friday when we close.'

Tom sat forward. 'Or on Thursday if we sell out by then?'

'Of course. Goes without saying. Are you coming, Andrew?'

Walter walked to the car park with Tom. 'He'll never pay us the two grand on the last day. That's why I wanted our normal money and the redundancy paid the week before. As soon as I get that, I'm fucking gone. He'll leave us short, I know the bastard too well.'

Tom was surprised. 'To be fair, he never left us short a penny, ever.'

'Of course he didn't, he wanted us to come back the next week, but this is a different kettle of fish. I'm looking around, starting right now, and I advise you to do the same.'

Tom drove home slowly, Walter might be right, but at the same time the old guy had made a deal in front of three people, surely he would stick to that? Walter was probably right, it was time to put the CV together and see what was out there.

He envied Walter at a time like this; he could go home to his wife and talk it over with her. Not that that would make a lot of difference, but it helped to have someone to share a trouble with. Somehow if you could talk over a situation with another person, it made it all seem easier. This bachelor living was all very well, but it had its downsides. For a moment he thought of calling his father, telling him what had happened and asking his advice, but he immediately thought better of it. That would be just what the old bastard would like to hear, that his younger son was out of a job, a failure, just like he had predicted.

No, this was one to fight on his own, just deal with it and move on.

CHAPTER TWO

It was surprising how quickly the word spread, a closing down sale was just the thing to draw the punters in, and they came in their droves. It wasn't as if there were great reductions, but just the idea of a place closing gave people the idea that there were bargains to be had. Walter marked full recommended retail prices on all the goods, then slashed through them with a black marker and added in the normal prices. The public couldn't get enough of it, and by the end of the month the warehouse and stockroom had been all but cleared and all that was left was what was on the shop floor.

It had been a tough few days, and Tom and Walter called into the Willows on the way home. The older man got the drinks and led the way to the corner by the front window. He took a long swallow from his pint and sat back in the soft seat.

'That's it, I'm not going back there on Monday, but keep that to yourself.'

Tom looked at him in surprise; he hadn't really believed that Walter would do a runner as soon as he got his money.

'You reckon that he won't pay up the two grand then? You're taking a long shot, bud, I mean we might be closing the door by Thursday and you would have earned two grand for four days work.'

Walter leaned forward. 'I'm too long in this game, son. And I know too much about human nature. How about we have a bet, say the usual?'

Tom raised his pint in salute. 'You're on so, and it was great working with you by the way.'

Walter lifted his drink. 'Mutual. I'll let you know how I get on anyway; I think I have a job with an estate agent on the south side. There is a bit of a stir in the property business and they need someone to show houses, good commission and mileage but a miserable basic as usual.'

'That's good news; do you want another pint?'

'Thanks, no. Pamela wants me home, we have a babysitter and we're going into town for something to eat.'

He put down his empty glass and headed for the door. 'Adios amigo. I'll meet you here Friday night to collect my tenner.'

Tom laughed. 'That was my line. I know he'll pay up; I'll wring his scrawny neck if he doesn't.'

***

Tom was still angry on Friday evening when he pushed his way into the crowded bar. It wasn't the losing of the bet that annoyed him; that ten spot had been passed over and back between Walter and himself so many times that he had no idea which of them was ahead at this stage. It was more the fact that he had failed to see that that pompous old goat might have screwed him like that. Who could have imagined that old Milton would be such a greedy bastard, after all he had done for him?

Walter put the ten euro note on the bar and ordered two pints. 'Hate to say I told you so' he laughed, 'but why would he pay you? The game was over at that stage.'

Tom smiled wryly. The way it was done had taken him by surprise; he couldn't have foreseen it in a hundred years. They were low in stock by close of business on Thursday and Milton had clapped him on the back as he closed the shutter.

'Well done, Tom. You played a great game this week, and all on your own as well. I won't forget that. I reckon we can probably call it a day tomorrow, maybe stay open a bit late, but there won't be much left by then at this rate.'

Tom arrived in early the following morning, anxious to be done with it and to get his two thousand euro bonus and start looking for a job, but his key wouldn't work in the lock. Must be stuck, he thought, and he banged on the door.

'Yes mate.' The Englishman answered his knock. 'I'm afraid there's no one here, the place is closed.

Tom was startled. 'It can't be. I work here, I'm working today.'

The man at the door smiled. 'Not unless you want a job sweeping up; we took possession last night and we're starting to gut the place now. The fit out has to be ready for our people in six weeks.'

'But the rest of the stock.....?' Tom was still shocked at what he was hearing.

'No stock here, lad. They cleared it all out last night, the old guy and his poofter friend were here very late, Polish fellow with a truck, we nearly had to throw them out but they got it all into the lorry ok. Nothing left, lad, not a sausage, come and look if you like.'

Tom followed the stranger through the empty canteen, not even the coffee machine remained. He walked through the swing doors and out on the shop floor, where a team of builders was removing ceiling panels and lifting the carpet tiles. Two big electric platform hoists trundled around the floor, warning sounders bleeping and amber lights flashing, as the electricians removed the old lighting units. The emptiness of the place stunned him and he looked around in amazement.

'Fucking bastard. What about my fucking money?'

The foreman shook his head sadly. 'How much did they stick you for?' He asked kindly.

Tom just couldn't believe what he was seeing. 'Two fucking grand. I'll kill the bastard.'

The Englishman kicked a length of ceiling trim out of his way. 'Same old story, I see it everyplace we go. Companies close and leave fellows hanging. Forget about it, lad, and move on. Be wiser the next time.'

Walter smiled sadly as he took a swallow from the pint. 'Hate to say I told you so, son, but the odds were always against getting that bonus.'

'But old Milton, mister fucking pious churchgoer. I never thought he would screw me.'

Walter wiped the beer froth from his moustache. 'They're all the same, Tom; you have to keep yourself covered all the way.'

'I was fucking caught rightly, wasn't I? What a bastard, I never saw that coming. I must be fucking thick; I should have listened to you.'

Walter played with the beer mat, flicking it over and over. 'It looked likely enough to me; he gave in too easy when I pushed him for the bonus. I just had an instinct that he wouldn't deliver, just a feeling, kind of thing that has kept me out of trouble up to now.'

Tom chugged down half his pint and called for two more. 'So how is the real estate business then?'

Walter brightened. 'Easiest money I ever made, to be honest. When you spent your life selling washing machines and cookers, it's very easy to sell a house. You have a buyer who wants a house, and one house is much like another when you think about it. All you have to do is push them a little bit; just close a sale like you would in a shop.'

Tom was suddenly interested. 'Making money so?'

'A lot more than I made in Milton's. These lads haven't a clue about selling; they just show the punter the house and step back. What I do is just what I always did, stop the buyer from thinking about the next place and focus them on the one I'm showing. I'm selling as much as the other four put together, and the commission is damn good.'

'So any chance of a start for me in that place?'

Walter hesitated. 'Not at the minute, but I'd say I might get you in there in a few months. If I keep outselling those guys there's bound to be a bit of pressure on the others, and I'd say one of them might cave in and leave. You should find something to keep you going, and I'll watch the space for you.'

Tom was still deflated from his experience that morning. 'Not too much out there when you start to look; all the Brit places just use English managers and loads of part-timers, students and stuff, no real salesmen at all.'

Walter agreed. 'That's how it's going in that game. They throw bodies at it in busy times and then send them home if it's quiet. Not like it used to be.'

They sat in silence for a while, and then Walter had a thought.

'You could always go and work for your dad. The building business is getting busy and I'm sure he has plenty of room for an extra man.'

Tom laughed. 'Can you really see me working on a site? Anyway you know we don't get on; we haven't spoken since I left home.'

'I know that, but isn't it about time you mended a few fences in that department? You were young and foolish then, you're older and wiser now.'

'No, we'll continue to agree to disagree. Anyway he has plenty of help from Michael, mister fancy college boy.'

'Ok, sorry for sticking my nose in your business.'

'That's all right, no offence. I just don't want to have any dealings with my old man or my brother. The old boy would just love me to come crawling back looking for a job, and I can just imagine

Michael smirking if I arrived home like a loser. No, I don't think that's on at all.'

'You're not a loser Tom; this kind of shit happens to the best of us, so stop putting yourself down. You're a very capable young fellow and you were doing well in Miltons. This was just a bit of bad luck and you'll rise above it no problem. Just give it a week or two.'

'Not much sign of a lot of work out there though.'

'There's always something. Did you ever think of selling cars? I was in City Auto today to see Kevin, the fellow that owns the place. Thinking of getting a new car. He was asking me if I wanted a job, heard Milton's was gone. Told him I was fixed up. Good bloke Kevin, Welsh fellow but he's here years, bit hooky but all right really.'

Tom perked up. 'I might drop in to him on Monday. I used to sell cars for a while a few years ago, when it was harder. You had to tell some serious porkies then, a lot of the cars were dodgy enough. Not like now, they're all fairly reliable.'

'Tell him you were talking to me. I play golf with him on Sunday mornings usually, there's six of us that play together on and off, know them for years. I'll mention it to him Sunday if you like.'

Tom raised his pint. 'Here's to a life after Milton. Maybe he did us a favour; maybe we'll make our fortunes in cars and real estate.'

Walter smiled sadly. 'Or maybe not, but we'll give it a good try anyway, son.'

***

Tom tapped on the door of the portocabin; City Auto didn't spend a fortune on facilities, stock had priority around here. Kevin stood up and gave him a welcome handshake.

'Walter tells me you are the best around, apart from himself of course. So do you think you can sell cars?'

Tom immediately felt that he was meeting a fellow salesman, someone who liked to sell.

'Not a problem. Did it before, can do it again. If you can sell washing machines to some of the old bitches around here, you can sell a few cars to the local young lads.'

Kevin laughed. 'It's not that easy, but if you're a good enough salesman to start with, I can make you a car expert in a few hours.

Just a matter of sounding like you know what you're talking about, whether you do or not.'

Tom was enjoying the exchange. 'Same as washing machines so.'

Kevin slid a thick book across the desk. 'That's the bible, every make, every model, every year. You need to know it by heart where it refers to any car in the yard, no point in looking it up when you are in the middle of a sale. You need it in your head.'

He pointed to the yard and the serried ranks of cars. 'Let's go for a bit of a walk, see what you know. If you're as sharp as I hear you are, you'll pick it all up fast.'

They strolled around the gravelled area where the cars were lined up for sale, each with the price displayed in big vinyl letters in the windscreen. The front row had roof banners that had the usual clichéd descriptions, car-of-the-week, reduced-for-quick-sale, low-mileage.

Tom had seen it all before. 'Everything is negotiable I suppose?'

Kevin laughed. 'Of course, but only top prices get top commissions. If you want to give away my money, it will cost you.'

Tom thought it might be time to talk about earnings. 'How much of my wages would be commission then?'

Kevin looked surprised. 'Didn't Walter tell you? All of it. We don't do basic here, you'll be self employed; if you don't sell anything, you don't earn anything. I'm not running a fucking charity. That's fair enough isn't it?'

It wasn't what Tom was expecting.

'On the other hand, you can make some serious money of you're as good as I hear you are. I'll pay a hundred and fifty a car for full price, a hundred for the coded price, and unless you want to pay me money you won't sell below that.'

Tom was dubious. 'Doesn't sound like a lot. I expected a basic to be honest, you know, for being here to keep the place open when it's quiet and all that.'

Kevin was showing some impatience. 'Look, that's how I do business; it's not up for discussion. But look, the last guy was making five hundred a day some days. Still would be if he could keep out of the pub and the bookies. I expect you to be here when you're supposed to be here.'

'Five hundred a day? Is there that amount of business in it?'

'It's up to you. If you can really sell, you know, be ruthless about it, this is the place to make serious money, a lot more than Maurice Milton could ever pay you. I'll pay you in cash every Friday, or every day if you want. The taxman will never know how much you got, and I won't leave you short either. Have we a deal?'

Tom looked him in the eye; this might be good. He held out his hand. 'Deal.'

***

Tom was surprised at how easy it was. He had worked part time in a used car lot about eight years earlier, when he left school, but his experience in the intervening years had fine tuned his selling skills and given him the ability to close sales where he would have been less confident in the past. It wasn't exactly easy money, but he found that if he kept his concentration and stayed focussed, he could make a very good living. Maybe old Milton had done him a favour by closing down.

Sometimes he wondered about what he was doing. If he stopped to think, looked back on the day and ran the sales through his mind, it could get inside his head a bit more than he would have liked. Some of the punters were really thick, they knew nothing about cars and it was easy to sell them some really slow movers at high prices. Some of them were smart enough, knew their stuff, and he tended to steer them to the better models. The easiest ones were the guys that talked as if they knew all about cars, but really knew very little; these were the ones that could be milked for the highest prices and the best commission. Still, apart from these occasional doubts, Tom was making some decent money and he was very satisfied with the way things were working out.

Kevin was happy too; his new salesman was letting very few buyers leave the yard without a car and he was managing to shift the rubbish along with the better stuff. The previous guy had tended to steer buyers away from the duds, but Tom had a lot less scruples when there was a commission to be earned. If Kevin was paying an extra few quid on a particular slow mover, Tom would have it shifted before the end of the day.

They stood at the back of the yard watching the driver unload the latest crop from the big transporter. Kevin bought in bulk from trade suppliers and from leasing companies, the five and six year old models that the main dealers didn't want on their forecourts. Every so often he took a big batch of cars from the car rental firms, as long as they were registered to an anonymous company and didn't have a record of being hired to tourists. These were big profit earners, they described them as one-owner cars and Willie cleaned them up well in the big shed at the back of the yard.

'Who sent me that piece of shit?' Kevin couldn't conceal his disgust at the bright yellow Volkswagen that was rolling off the top deck of the truck.

Tom could barely hold back the laughter. 'It kinda stands out all right.'

'Looks like a fucking builder's jacket. Get it round the back and out of sight before anyone sees it, we'll be a laughing stock.'

'I wonder does it glow in the dark?' The more Kevin got annoyed, the more Tom could see the funny side.

'There's yellow and there's yellow, but that's the worst colour car I ever saw in my life. Fucking diarrhoea yellow. It's like the back of a shagging ambulance, nobody will buy that thing.'

Tom looked inside the car when it was parked up. 'It's not in bad shape though, really low miles and very clean.'

Kevin was sarcastic. 'Would you buy a car that colour? Who would be interested in that thing? I'll kill McGuire for dumping that on me.'

'Maybe we might find a colour-blind customer for it.'

'Let's see you sell it, smartass. Let's see how good you are, an extra hundred if you shift it by Friday.'

They went through the rest of the cars. Kevin was in a bad humour from the fluorescent yellow VW, and the rest of the load didn't help his mood either.

'Ah Jesus, look at the clocks on these wrecks.'

Tom looked at the car in question, the Toyota had nearly a hundred thousand miles on the odometer. 'Looks clean though, should go back all right.'

Kevin cheered a bit, but he still wasn't happy. 'Myles has to be paid his cut for clocking it though; all comes out of the profit. I'm getting sick of McGuire short-changing me.'

He stomped back to the office and slammed the door. Tom took out his phone and called Myles.

'Can you call over this evening and adjust a few for us?'

'How many?'

'Nearly all today's batch, about ten, all high numbers but look good otherwise. We need them done tonight though before customers see them tomorrow.'

Tom made two cups of coffee and left one of them down in front of Kevin. 'Myles is on his way.'

'Thanks boyo. Can you do something for me on the way in to-morrow? I need a letter dropped off at the test centre, ask for Roger Hall and wait for an envelope from him and bring it back. It's some paperwork that they didn't have for me last week.'

Myles arrived just as they were turning off the lights.

Kevin waved his arms at him. 'For God's sake, don't leave that fucking Jeep out front, someone will see it. Bring it round the back quick.'

Myles drove around and into the shed. Tom shook his head. 'For such a smart fellow with his computers and all, he hasn't much sav-vy. Why does he have to have his name written on the Jeep?'

The offending vehicle had a bright sign on each side that told the world that it was owned by 'Myles Back', a play on the owner's name and the nature of his business. The smaller print advised that he was in the business of recalibrating speedometers, a legitimate business need when a garage replaced a broken speedometer with a new one and the mileage had to be brought up to the correct level on the new instrument. While he might get the occasional job of that nature, Myles made most of his money by 'clocking' cars for unscrupulous dealers.

Kevin sighed resignedly 'he's a bit thick that way, but he comes when we want him and he's cheaper than the others by a long shot.'

Myles looked at the yellow car in astonishment. 'It'll take more than a bit of clocking to make that one sell. Where did you get that thing?'

Tom motioned to him to shut up; Kevin was in a bad enough humour without upsetting him further, but Myles kept rubbing salt in the wound. 'You could put a 'Follow Me' sign on it and sell it to the airport; they could take it out on really foggy days.'

Kevin retreated to the office and slammed the door.

Myles was still laughing at his own joke. 'What's up with him?'

'Don't mention the war. He's not too happy with today's batch, and that thing just added insult to injury. Let's make a few home improvements, cheer him up a bit.'

'That's one ugly car, mustn't be a standard colour, I never saw one in that yellow before.'

'It was one of two specials for that radio station that started up and only lasted a few months, do you remember, Mellow Yellow FM, played a lot of oldies?'

'Oh yeah, crappy music, no wonder they folded.'

One by one, they drove the cars into the shed and closed the doors. Tom popped the bonnet on each car and Myles connected the lead from his laptop to the service port and made a few quick adjustments on the keyboard. In an hour all the cars were a lot more saleable.

Myles closed his laptop and packed it away in the case.

'Is that the lot, Tom?'

'That's all, I'll just finish putting on the new rubbers on the clutch and brake pedals and then we're done. We're going for a few beers, do you want to come?'

'No, I'll pass on that, see you next week.'

Tom and Kevin retired to the Willows for a well-earned pint. Walter was sitting at the bar; they motioned him to join them at the corner table.

'You were right about this lad.' Kevin clapped Tom on the back.

Walter smiled. 'Told you he could sell, nearly as good as me, maybe better for your game.'

'Sand to Arabs, coal to Polacks.' Kevin was back to his old self.

Walter had heard a bit of news. 'I hear you weren't the only one to be screwed by Maurice Milton.'

Tom was surprised. 'What did you hear?'

'He never paid the guarantee money over to the insurance company, not for the last year or so, put it all in his pocket and said nothing. He must have been planning to make an exit for longer than we thought.'

'I had that old bugger figured all wrong.' Tom was shocked that the old man had turned out to be such a crook.

Walter had more. 'That's not the half of it. None of the suppliers were paid for the stuff that we sold from the warehouse. We were selling stolen property for the last couple of weeks.'

Kevin swallowed the last of his pint and got up to leave. 'All this talk of dishonesty is upsetting me, I'm heading home. Don't forget the letter in the morning.'

Tom tapped his jacket pocket. 'I have it here, see you about ten o'clock.'

Tom looked at the envelope on the breakfast table; it was addressed to Roger Hall and marked 'private' in large letters. Why would Kevin be sending private letters to the clerk in the test centre, he wondered, and why the insistence on delivering it by hand to Roger Hall?

He snapped on the kettle for another cup of tea, turning the letter over and over in his hand. Finally his curiosity got the better of him and he slit the envelope open; he could always put the letter in a fresh envelope and reseal it, Roger would never know.

He pulled out a sheet of A4 paper with a short note typed on it, and a bundle of cash, five hundred euro in total in hundred-euro notes. The note listed the registration numbers of ten cars; at least one of them looked vaguely familiar. He copied the numbers into his notebook and put everything back in a new envelope and addressed it to Roger hall.

At the test centre he called Roger aside and handed him the letter. 'Kevin asked me to drop this in to you. Said you had something for him, do you have it on you?'

Roger took the envelope and slipped it into his inside pocket. 'Give me a minute; I have a letter for Kevin.' He disappeared into his office.

Ten minutes later he reappeared and handed Tom a large white envelope. 'Pass that to Kev; tell him thanks.'

Tom was intrigued; he threw the envelope on the passenger seat and headed back to the yard.

Kevin was busy with a customer when he arrived back, and a young man was wandering up and down between the rows of cars.

Tom dropped the envelope on his boss's desk and went outside; there was money to be made. 'Can I be of help?'

'I'm looking for a nice low mileage Japanese car, not too expensive to insure, what have you in that line?' The young fellow was well dressed, shirt and tie, probably worked in one of the local offices, or maybe a clerk in one of the law firms.

Tom switched into selling mode; he gave the customer his warmest smile. 'You couldn't have timed it better, we got a couple of beauties in last night, miles in the mid fifties, well maintained, super cars, come and have a look.'

He walked to the back of the yard where three of the cars that had been clocked by Myles had already been cleaned and polished by Willie. They looked great; he knew they would look nothing like high mileage cars once they were given the clocking treatment. 'You're lucky, these haven't been brought out front yet, just in, but any one of them would be ideal. Low insurance as well, how old are you?'

The customer was excited at getting ahead of the pack on these desirable models. 'I'm nineteen, still on a provisional license, I'd love something a bit bigger but I suppose they would fleece me on the insurance.'

Tom sensed a chance of a killing, maybe get the full commission and even sell this guy the finance as well. 'Hang on here until I get the keys for these, we'll start them up and see how they sound.'

He headed back for the office to get the file sheets for the cars; these would show him what Kevin had paid and what the sticker price would be, as well as the lowest price that Kevin would allow him to accept. There was a lot of information on these sheets, in a simple code, and they were essential before getting into negotiations.

He detoured slightly to catch Kevin on the way back; he spoke quietly 'Have any of the new ones got test certs?'

Kevin was trying to close a sale on a slightly down at heel Passat. 'All of them.'

He walked back to the young buyer as quickly as he could, a bunch of keys in hand. 'Which one do you fancy? The silver one is probably the best one; it has the lowest mileage as well. Let's take her for a drive.'

They drove around the block, Tom keeping up the patter. 'This is a beauty isn't it, only fifty thousand on her, you were just lucky you came in when you did, this one would be snapped up as soon as it went on sale.'

The young man was excited at driving the car, 'I like it well enough, but how much is it?'

Tom flicked through the sheets. The code was 000053/000015/000065, that meant that Kevin had paid three and a half thousand for it, you just read the numbers backwards and dropped a few noughts. The lowest price he would take was five thousand one hundred, and the price that would go on the windscreen was five thousand six hundred.

Tom waited until they had parked the car. 'He wants an even six grand for it, but if I approach him the right way I think we can do a bit better. The way I see it, you're young, so even if we make nothing off you on this sale, you'll come back to us again for your next car, and maybe the one after that. So maybe I could drop it a bit, say take two fifty off?'

The youngster was delighted, but was trying not to show it. He wanted to drive a hard bargain. 'The most I would give would be five and a half; I can get that much from the Credit Union.'

Tom smiled to himself, the kid was offering was close to what he needed to get the top commission, but he held his nerve.

'Couldn't do that I'm afraid, that's less than we paid for it, but I'll try to get a few quid off it for you. Could probably get him to drop three hundred, say five seven. How does that sound?'

'I might go to five six.' The kid was wavering, 'but I'm not sure if I'd get the money.'

Tom could smell an opportunity; there was another hundred in it for him if he could persuade the buyer to arrange finance through a hire-purchase company.

'Don't worry about the money, if you are working you can get the money no problem, we can recommend you to a finance company that will give it to you, we could sort it out over the phone in ten minutes.'

The youngster was nearly wetting himself. 'I'm working full time in the call centre down the road; do you think you could arrange the money, really?'

'Of course, we do it every day.'

Tom reached out his hand. The ball was on the penalty spot, and nobody in the goal. He tapped it towards the line. 'So do we have a deal at five seven? I'll be sacked for giving this one away, I'd advise you to grab it before the boss changes our minds for us.'

The youngster shook his hand. 'Ok, yes, I'll take it.'

Goal! They went back to the office to do the paperwork.

***

Kevin spotted her first; you couldn't miss her, to be fair. Skinny legs, short yellow skirt and yellow boots, and a fluffy yellow jacket and matching handbag. She looked about twenty, although it was hard to tell. She was wandering around the front row of cars, peering at stickers. He nudged Tom.

'Look at what the cat dragged in. Day-old chicken.'

Tom looked at the girl as she wandered among the cars. 'Good looking girl, forget the colour sense, she's pretty.'

'She's like fucking Big Bird from the telly, that kids programme. Must be colour blind, very fond of yellow anyhow.'

Tom jumped to his feet and dashed out to intercept his quarry before the penny dropped with Kevin. He slowed to a stroll when he got close to her. 'Good morning, madam, can I be of assistance. He tried to keep the grin off his face; this girl was really a vision in yellow.'

'I'm just having a look; I want to buy a car.'

'Any particular kind, madam? I'm sure we have something to suit you. I'm Tom by the way.'

'Amanda.' She held out her hand. 'Something nice, not too big, but it has to be reliable.'

He was itching to go for the kill, but he needed to pace himself. 'Haven't I seen you before somewhere, maybe on TV, are you a model or an actress?'

Corny as it was, flattery always worked. She gave him a huge smile. 'No, I'm not a model, I'm a nail technician.' She extended two manicured hands with much decorated nails, glossy and speckled with a yellow design. This girl was nuts about yellow.

Tom opened the door to a bright red Clio. 'Sit into that one, see how you like it.' The car was one of the cleaner ones in the row, and girls liked the Clios, especially the red ones. He could see she was impressed.'

'That's nice, I like the colour, is it a good car?'

'One of the best, but maybe I have something even better. Would you like to come this way?'

He led the girl towards the back of the lot where the bright yellow car was parked, out of sight of the office where Kevin didn't have to see it from the window.

'This one came in yesterday, really good car, low mileage and a very reliable machine. Really stylish too, just the thing for a stylish lady.' He opened the door to the VW, trying not to smile at the combination of yellow clothed girl and bright yellow car.

She sat behind the wheel and gave a cry of delight. 'Omygod, omygod, omygod. Oh it's so beautiful; oh it's perfect, omygod, omygod omygod.'

She got out and danced around the car. 'This is so beautiful, this is my dream, I love it, I love it, I love it. I'm taking it.'

Tom smiled at the sight. 'Don't you want to know how much it is?'

She stopped for a minute, crestfallen, 'maybe it's more than I can afford?'

'Depends on how much you can afford.' Tom was playing with her now; the fish was on the hook.

'I can't go more than nine thousand.' She was starting to look worried. 'Oh I hope it's not more than that.'

Tom looked at the sheet; the sticker price would be nine thousand exactly. He could take eight four at a pinch. 'Nine and a half, how does that sound to you?'

'Maybe I could do it, but I don't think so.' She looked at him pleadingly. 'Is there any way it could be a little cheaper?'

The image of a day-old chicken and the words 'a little cheeper' just got to Tom, and he had to turn away to hold back the laughter. 'Let me talk to the boss for a minute' he spluttered.

He called Kevin on the mobile. 'Do you think we could let the yellow VW go at 9k? This is a very nice lady and she can't rise above 9k.'

'You jammy bastard.' Kevin was enjoying the joke. 'Day old chickens can't rise above anything, their wings aren't developed yet.' He howled at laughter; Tom hoped that the girl couldn't hear the exchange. He was doing his best to keep a straight face.

'I see, boss. So can I say that that's a deal so?'

'Sit on her before she lays a fucking egg, get her feathered ass into the office and get her name on the docket before she runs away on you.'

Tom turned to the girl. 'Well, Amanda, it looks as if this is your lucky day, he's in a good humour and he's agreed to all your demands.'

'You're all so nice here; everyone has a smile for me.' She counted out the money from the yellow purse on to the desk.

'It's because Easter is coming up, we'll be opening our eggs in a couple of weeks.' Kevin was shaking with laughter.

Tom was doing his best to hold it together. 'Sign here and here, and here.'

'Don't let that fellow ask you for a date.' Kevin was almost hysterical. 'He's too old for you, he's no spring chicken.' Tears were running down his face and he had to go outside and walk across the yard to calm down.

She gave Tom a kiss on the cheek. 'Don't mind that crazy old fellow, I think you're a lovely guy, and thanks for finding me that beautiful car.'

Kevin plonked two mugs of coffee on the desk; he was still shaking with laughter.

'That was the best laugh I had here in weeks. I have to hand it to you for thinking about the yellow car when you saw her, if I had been a bit quicker off the mark I'd have made the sale myself and I wouldn't have had to pay you a bonus on it.'

'I'd have nearly done it for nothing; did you ever see such a fashion statement?'

'Definitely colour blind. Not a bad looker if she lost some of the yellow though, a real cracker.'

Tom agreed. 'Needs a bit of a makeover, but she's gorgeous, I wouldn't mind at all.'

'Rule number thirty two, never date the clients.' Kevin wagged his finger at Tom. I'm outa here, can you lock up?'

Tom was still sorting out paperwork; it had been a very busy day. 'See you Monday so.'

It had been a tiring shift, but he would prefer to get the adminis-tration out of the way and not have to face it on Monday. He filled out all the forms and stamped the envelopes for posting on the way home; it had been a good day and he had made some serious money to boot. He stretched himself and called Walter.

'Are you going for a pint? The Willows, yeah?'

He noticed the envelope as he was turning off the lights. It lay on Kevin's desk, torn open where the boss had given a cursory look at the contents. Tom couldn't resist a peep; he picked it up and pulled out the papers for a look. It was nothing of interest, just a bunch of test certs from the car test centre.

He was about to replace the certs when he noticed the registra-tion number on the first one; it was the same as the one he had just processed, the small car that he had sold to the young guy from the call centre. He rifled through the others, they all belonged to the cars that had just come into stock a couple of days before. Tom was stunned.

'I don't believe this. Certs for cars that weren't tested. What the fuck is going on here?'

He pulled out the notebook where he had entered the numbers from Kevin's letter to the guy in the test centre; the numbers were the same as the certs in the envelope.

He was shaking as he replaced the papers. This was serious stuff, this was beyond a joke, you could go to jail for this. The clerk in the test centre must be taking cash to provide Kevin with bent test certs. Clocking cars was dodgy, but everyone was doing it. Mucking about with the paperwork in a government test centre was a differ-ent story.

His head was swimming as he got in the car and headed out to meet Walter. Should he tell Walter or not? Walter knew Kevin for years, played golf with him most weekends. Maybe Walter knew all about it, he did say that Kevin was a bit hooky; maybe that was what he meant.

Walter was in sparkling form, he had continued his winning streak of sales and he was high on it all. He spotted Tom's dark mood immediately.

'Why the long face? You look like a man that needs a drink.'

Tom decided to say nothing; you never knew who you could trust in this kind of situation. He switched on a smile and decided to forget about what he had seen for the moment.

'Just tired, it was a long day, but let me tell you a good one.'

He filled Walter in on the saga of the girl in yellow, and the sale of the fluorescent yellow car.

Walter was soon laughing along at the story. 'Opening your Easter eggs, how did you stop from cracking up? Kevin is a panic when he starts.'

Tom agreed. 'Any light relief in your place, anything like that happen with the guys you work with?'

'Not a chance,' Walter shook his head regretfully, 'they're too straight-laced, take themselves too bloody seriously. That's one thing I do miss, do you remember the fun we used to have when we did a double act with a sticky customer. We used to play it like a football match, keep passing the ball back and forth until there was a clear shot at the goal.'

Tom remembered 'Giggs to Rooney.'

'Rooney back to Giggs.'

'He plays it up the left wing.'

'Here comes the cross. Rooney is there.'

They raised their pints in a toast. 'He shoots, he scores. Goal!'

Walter put down his empty glass. 'Another one?'

'No thanks, I have the car. Talk to you next week.'

CHAPTER THREE

'Answer the phone, answer the phone, answer the phone.'

The sound seemed to be part of his dream; Tom was out for the count, slowly coming up from a deep sleep. That stupid ring tone was driving him nuts, should have turned the bloody thing off last night. He reached out and slapped the mobile until it stopped.

He gradually became aware of the bells, church bells that were loud and close by. Must be Sunday, don't have to get up, he thought to himself.

He suddenly snapped into wakefulness. I don't live anywhere near a church, he realised, where the fuck am I?

He opened one eye slowly, he was lying face down in a bed; a bright yellow glow seemed to fill the room. It wasn't a light, he realised; the pillowcase was yellow. He opened the other eye and raised his head slightly. The sheet and the duvet cover were yellow too, and sunlight was breaking in through the yellow curtains. He suddenly remembered the night before; he felt around beside him and touched another body in the bed.

He raised his head and focussed on the blonde head on the pillow beside him. She was still sleeping; she looked completely out of it, must have drunk as much as he had, maybe more.

His head throbbed, and his mouth felt dry and raw. He gradually remembered everything, dancing in the club, then the girl who tapped him on the shoulder when he queued at the bar.

'Remember me?' He turned quickly.

'Amanda! How could I forget?' It was hard to forget someone who dressed entirely in yellow for God's sake.

'It's been ages; I didn't know if you'd remember me, you must meet loads of people in your job.'

'I never forget a face,' he lied, no point in telling her she stood out a bit. She was really pretty though if you ignored the colour scheme.

'Same in my job, I remember every face, or their hands, I'm not great on names though. It's Tom isn't it.' She was shouting to make herself heard over the noise.

The girl stirred in the bed, turned over and snuggled in beside him. It was all coming back to him now, the beers, the lines of shots, and the conversation that descended into a suggestive flirty banter that continued all the way back in the taxi. He regretted his stupid behaviour, but at the time it seemed like a great idea, his desperate need to find out if her love of yellow clothing extended to her underwear.

He looked at the frilly yellow knickers hanging on the bedside lamp. This was a mistake; I must have been very drunk, both of us must have been out of it.

He stayed raised up on his elbow, wanting to go back to sleep but reluctant to take his eyes off the gorgeous blonde head on the pillow beside him. She looked beautiful as she slept, at peace with the world. It was true what Kevin had said, the girl was a cracker.

'Answer the phone, answer the phone, answer the phone.' The electronic voice started up again. He pulled the mobile towards him and squinted at the display. Why would Kevin be calling him on a Sunday morning? He pressed the green button.

'Yeah'

'Where the hell are you boyo?' Kevin sounded stressed.

'I'm not sure, with a friend.' Tom spoke quietly to try not to wake the sleeping girl.

'I was at your place, you weren't there, need to see you now. It's urgent, can't talk on the phone, can you get back there now? Bit of trouble, need to see you.'

Something in Kevin's tone brought Tom to wakefulness. 'Give me half an hour, see you there.'

Amanda was half awake, rubbing her eyes. 'What time is it?'

'Nine o'clock, sorry I woke you, have to go, urgent.'

'Do you have to? Do you not want breakfast?' She reached out sleepily and tried to pull him back to bed.

Tom disentangled himself reluctantly and rummaged for his clothes. 'Urgent bit of business, you get some sleep, I'll call you.'

He found his clothes all over the place, one shoe in the kitchen, another in the living room. A trail of clothes led from the front door to the bed, half of them yellow. God, I must have been really pissed. I wonder what's up; Kevin is hyper if he's worried about work this time of a Sunday morning. I thought he would be playing golf.

He let himself out and looked around; the area was unfamiliar. At the end of the street he called a taxi. 'Corner of Rathgar Road and...' he walked around the corner and looked up at the other sign, 'Frankfort Avenue.'

The taxi got him home in fifteen minutes; Sunday morning traffic was light. Kevin was sitting in a black Nissan Micra outside the flat. He got out of the car as soon as the taxi moved off.

'Inside quick,' Kevin propelled him to the front door of the apartment building.

'What's wrong? Are you in some kind of trouble?' Tom was concerned at Kevin's demeanour; he had never seen the boss looking like this. The man was red-eyed and unshaven; he looked a mess.

'We're in deep shit, they're on to us.'

'Who's on to who? Slow down and tell me what's wrong.' Tom put the kettle on and spooned coffee granules into two mugs.

'Roger Hall, the lad in the test centre, he was arrested last night. Big racket with bent certs. They came looking for me as well but I saw the car outside the flat and I didn't go in. Willie said they called to him but he sang dumb, told them you and I were away for a few days.'

'Good man, Willie.' Tom put the two mugs of coffee on the table. 'But what's the story, were you involved in a racket with Roger?'

'Just the odd one, but that's enough to do me.'

Tom knew he was lying; he had collected a lot of envelopes from Roger since that first day a few months ago, and he never let Kevin know that he knew what was going on. He had always had a concern about the caper but he had put it out of his mind; the money was rolling in, and it was time enough to worry about it when it happened. Unfortunately, it seemed to be happening now.

'How does this concern me? I didn't know what was going on.'

'Someone at the centre, the fellow that was investigating it, saw you collecting the letter every week. They were looking for you as well as me when they spoke to Willie, but he told them he didn't know where you lived or what your second name was.'

Tom sat down and pondered this turn of events. No harm done yet, but they were sniffing at his heels, what was the best thing to do? He turned to Kevin, 'what are you going to do?'

'I'm heading for Wales, today on the ferry. I'm outa here, boyo.'

'But the business, all the cars and the yard..?' Tom was shocked.

'There is no business, Willie owns the yard and I just rented it from him. The bank and McGuire own anything in the yard, I can walk away anytime. I always kept the business well hollowed out, never any assets and all that. Even the portocabin is rented.'

'But they'll follow you, if the cops are involved they can get you back from Wales.'

Kevin laughed, relaxing a little. 'Get back who?' I can go back to my own name when I get off the ferry.'

Tom sat down, stunned at what was unfolding. 'So you were using a false name, you're not Kevin at all?'

'I'm Kevin all right, but not Kevin Jones. That was a name I took on when I moved here, had a bit of trouble in Cardiff when I was a young lad, decided to leave it behind me, you know yourself.'

Tom was angry. 'I don't know myself, am I the mug here, will I have to take the rap for your dodgy dealings?'

'Now hang on a minute, you were doing very nicely for the last year, more money than you ever made in your life. Did you think it was all kosher? You were in on the clocking every week, yourself and mad Myles, well able to take the fucking money. Don't lecture me about dodgy dealing.'

'Ok, ok, but you were the one making the really big bucks, I know what you were making on the caper, twenty grand a day sometimes. I must have been thick. What am I going to do?'

Kevin pulled a roll of notes from his pocket. 'How much do I owe you for last week, roughly?'

Tom went through the sales he had made since Monday, adding the commissions in his head. 'About two grand, give or take, including the finance commissions.'

Kevin counted off bills from the roll. 'Here's the two and another five, get yourself out of here for a couple of months, lie low for a while and it will blow over. They'll just figure you as an employee; they'll lose interest after a while. Don't ever mention what I said about me having another name, ok?'

Tom was still in shock at the turn of events, and his head was throbbing from the effects of last night. 'What do you mean, where would I go?'

'I don't know, go off to Spain for a couple of months, take a holiday, lie in the sun and meet a few nice chicks, just keep out of here for a while.'

Tom pondered the situation, it sounded attractive in one way. He hadn't had a holiday in the year he had worked for Kevin, and the flat was rented, he could be out of there today, leave his stuff with Walter. Suddenly the day looked brighter.

'Ok, I'll do it, get a flight to somewhere in Spain and chill out for a while. The weather is miserable here now anyway, a change of scene will do me good.'

'Good man. I'm heading away on the next ferry, don't tell anyone you saw me, tell them you are off this week if you are stopped by anyone.'

He held out his hand, and he seemed genuinely regretful.

'Good luck, Tom, you're the best I ever saw, bloody great salesman, pure natural. I'm sorry it's all gone pear-shaped, but good luck to you whatever you do.'

Tom felt no animosity towards Kevin; at least he had paid him and not done a runner on him like old Milton. In fact he would miss the mad bastard and the excitement of working in the yard. 'Mind yourself, you daft Taffy bugger, and stay ahead of the posse.'

***

Tom slept late after a restless night; in the morning he went to a travel agency in the city and bought a ticket to Malaga. He caught a bus back to the yard and got off at the stop at the corner and then walked back to see if Willie was about. The gate was locked and he peered through the fence to see if there was any sign of life around by the shed.

He hadn't noticed the dark blue car parked by the kerb, and he jumped when the man got out and spoke to him.

'Tom, is your name Tom, do you work here?'

He knew immediately that the man was a cop; he had that clean-cut look about him. He shook his head.

'No, I was wondering if they were open, I want to buy a car.'

'No, they seem to be closed today. You don't work here then?'

'No, of course not.' Tom's legs were shaking. 'I need a new car, just thought I'd see what they had.'

The policeman looked him up and down, and then got back in his car. Tom could see that he wasn't fully convinced, and he just wanted to get out of there before the cop radioed someone for a description. He skipped quickly across the street between the moving cars and flagged down a taxi going back into town. A couple of blocks away he got out and crossed the street and caught another taxi going in the opposite direction, not relaxing until he was back in Walter's house.

He spent the afternoon watching television and declined Walter's offer of a trip to the Willows for a pint.

'No thanks, I think I'll stay in tonight if you don't mind.'

'Keeping the head down?'

'I just don't want to risk being seen. You never know.'

It was great to have such good friends at a time like this. Walter was a good mate, somebody who was there for you when you were in trouble, no questions asked. He had been very good, had given up his golf to help him pack his stuff into boxes and move it to his garage.

'It'll be fine there, son, no hurry about moving it, get back when you can. We never use the garage anyway, don't worry about it.'

Walter's wife Pamela was very kind too, making up a bed for him in the spare room, and taking a morning off to drive him to the airport.

'Imagine, Kevin being a crook, who would have thought? Look after yourself, young Tom, and keep in touch. Ring when you get there and let us know you arrived ok.'

***

'Cabin crew, ten minutes to landing.'

Tom woke from his nap, his head against the window. The Airbus was side slipping, dropping over the Sierra Nevada and heading out to sea to make a turn and face the runway at Malaga airport. It flew low over the Mediterranean and crossed the beach, skimming the vegetable plots and the highway and bumping lightly on to the tarmac. The engines roared in reverse thrust and it slowed and turned off quickly on to the taxiway.

They were all on their feet before the plane had even stopped, grabbing at bags in overhead bins and switching on mobile phones, anxious to be on their way and to get the most of their week on the beach. Tom let the tide of people pass by and got slowly to his feet, strolling down the steps to the blast of heat from the still strong afternoon sun.

The bus to the terminal was packed with holidaymakers, excited about being in Spain, and remarking on the heat. The runway shimmered and the sun glared back from the white façade of the airport buildings. He was first out of the bus and through passport control; the policeman took a cursory look at his passport and waved him on. Tom felt relieved that he had not scanned the document; you never knew who might be looking for you. He put the thought out of his head, he hadn't really done anything wrong, not really, it would be Kevin they were looking for and not him. They would really only have wanted to question him about Kevin's whereabouts. Willie didn't know anything about him either, not that Willie would talk anyway. No, there was nothing to worry about, just relax and enjoy a few weeks in the sun.

The car hire agent that Walter had recommended was waiting at the barrier with Tom's name in big letters on a sheet of paper.

'Senor Murphy, I am Juan, come with me please.' He led the way to the car park where the small Seat was parked, two wheels on the pavement. The formalities were completed on the bonnet of the car, rubbing the credit card docket with the cap of a pen to make the imprint, no fancy zip-zap machine here. Tom felt like he was on familiar ground, this operation reminded him of City Auto.

Juan went to the pay machine and paid the parking ticket, wished him a buen viaje, and he was on his way. Walter had written out the directions, and he glanced at the sheet on the passenger seat. Through the roundabout, ok, then pass the brewery, that must be it on the right, you could smell the hops, then join the highway. So far so good.

Hard to go wrong with these directions, right at the BMW dealership and join the motorway, then stay on it all the way. 'Keep the sea on your left' Walter had said, 'and you can't get lost.'

Tom had never seen such a clear sky; not a single cloud marked the perfect expanse of dark blue. The Mediterranean glittered like a blue mirror that had been sprinkled with a million diamonds, and Tom felt his spirits lift. He was here in this sunny paradise, money in his pocket and the sun shining. How much better could it get? The road ran parallel to the coast, uphill from the string of holiday resorts that seemed to merge into each other along the shoreline. For the first time since the call from Kevin, he felt a lightness in his heart, a feeling of being on holiday and the excitement of being in a new and different place.

The highway split in two, one branch going towards the coast and a toll road that bypassed all the towns. He kept on the tolled branch as Walter had told him, and followed the road that cut through the mountains and lost sight of the coast. He paid the toll and kept his eye out for the exit that Walter had told him to take. Avoid the next toll road, keep right and through the tunnel, follow the signs for San Pedro.

There it was, the road split and the tunnel went under the highway, just as he had described. He switched on the lights as he drove into the gloom, blinking in the glare as he emerged again into the bright sunlight. Second exit after the casino, there it is on the right, so far so good. He talked himself through the directions Walter had given him. Fair play to old Walter, knows his way here all right, there's the office.

The young woman was gorgeous, something about Spanish women with their sallow skin and the natural suntan.

'Hola, Senor Murphy. I am Carmen, follow me please.'

Tom followed behind the girl with her jangling keys. What a stunner; I wonder are they all like her? I'd follow her anywhere.

Carmen opened the gate and led him through a garden with a blue swimming pool, then selected a key from the bunch to enter a clean marble corridor that led to the lift. He was conscious of her attractiveness, tried to avoid looking directly at her but it was difficult to avoid the view of her slender figure with the mirrored sides of the lift. She caught his eye in the mirror and flashed a winning smile at him.

'We get a lot of Irish here, they like Puerto Banus. You have stayed here before, no?'

'No, I have never been here before, first time in this area or in Spain at all actually.'

'I hope you enjoy very much your stay.' She opened the door to the small apartment and showed him where everything was. He loved the way she pronounced English words, with a slight lisp that was very appealing. She made 'enjoy' sound like 'enhoy'; he could listen to her all day.

He started to call Walter's number, then remembered to add the country code and dialled again. Walter answered on the first ring.

'You got there all right so?'

'Thanks, found it no problem, great directions.'

'How do you like the apartment?'

'Looks good, not expensive either, I expected somewhere a lot more slummy for that money but it's actually brilliant.'

'They do good deals this time of year; we stayed there a few times, love the place. It's handy for the port too, and the shops are close by, just go out the front and turn left, then cross under the main road at the casino, you can't miss it.'

'Walter, I really appreciate this; thanks for all your help. I won't forget it.'

'That's what friends are for, anyway I feel a bit guilty; I introduced you to Kevin in the first place.'

'Not your fault, I reckon it will all work out well, I have a good feeling about it.'

'Mind yourself, Tom, keep in touch.'

'I will. Thanks again.'

***

The evening was warm, just weather for shirt sleeves still. Tom closed the gate and walked down to the main road, turning left as Walter had described. The traffic was heavy, not too safe to cross by the look of it, and he walked back towards the casino. There was no sign of an underpass and he was considering making a dash across the dual carriageway, but the security man at the front of the casino motioned him to the tunnel entrance, hidden in the shrubbery just inside the gates. Nice friendly people, he thought to himself, I'm starting to like it here.

The underpass was a clean white pedestrian tunnel that brought him into an upmarket residential area; large marble floored apartment buildings with doormen and a few fashionable clubs and restaurants. This looked like a hangout for the rich and famous, the place had the unmistakable stamp of wealth about it.

Puerto Banus was spectacular; a large yacht harbour had been created in the sheltered water that was enclosed by a long breakwater that curved around in a semicircle to end at a stone lighthouse. Every berth seemed to be occupied, with some serious pieces of the shipwright's art moored along the quay wall. Tom had never seen such boats; these were floating palaces, most locked up but a few with groups of people sitting on deck, enjoying drinks or tucking into food. The parking spaces along the wall were filled with Porches and Ferraris and all kinds of luxury cars; this place seemed to attract some very rich people indeed.

It was also a magnet for lots of onlookers who strolled along the promenade, admiring the boats and the toys of the rich. It seemed to Tom as if there were two kinds of willing participants in the show; the wealthy were blatantly showing off their possessions, and the tourists were staring open-mouthed at this orgy of conspicuous consumption. Tom loved it immediately.

This place must be a salesman's dream, he mused. So much money and so many people, I'd love to be selling boats, or anything. What a place to live! He wandered along the street to find something to eat. A lot of the places were expensive, but Picasso's looked promising and he joined the short queue outside.

The menu prices seemed like great value, much better than at home. Some of the other diners were tucking into giant pizzas, or pasta dishes, but Tom felt the need for something more substantial. He plumped for what looked like a hamburger and chips.

'I'll have the hamburgesa con huevo con patatas fritas,' he pointed the menu item out to the waiter. 'And a beer,' he added, 'a big one please, por favour.'

'Cerveza grande.' The waiter wrote down the order.

'Whatever.' Tom shrugged, he felt sorry he hadn't learned Spanish in school. He puzzled at the menu and the waiter's conversation. Not sure what that was all about, the meal looks like a hamburger and fries, no idea what 'con huevo' means, maybe it's a kind of sauce, sure we'll find out soon enough.

'It's 'amburgesa,' that's how you pronounce it. You never pronounce the 'H'.' The man at the next table leaned over to speak to him. 'On holidays then?' He sounded English.

'Yes.' Tom didn't want to appear too friendly, you never knew what a fellow's angle might be, but he didn't want to be rude either. 'My first time in Spain, not a clue of the lingo. What does....' He opened the menu and looked at the item he had ordered... 'what does 'con huevo' mean?'

The Englishman laughed. 'It's pronounced 'wave-oh', not 'hoo-ay-voh'. It just means 'with an egg.' Huevos are eggs, 'Jamon con huevos' is bacon and eggs. You'll get used to it quick enough. Irish?'

'Yes.' Tom laughed at his own innocence, of course 'huevo' was an egg, sounded like it when you pronounced it the way the Englishman had said it. 'Are you on holidays yourself?'

The Englishman smiled, 'no such luck, I live here, ten years here now, not likely to go back to the bloody rain.'

'Looks like a nice place to live.' Tom was warming to the helpful stranger, 'but I suppose everywhere has its good points, and maybe its bad points too.'

'You have to weigh it up, take the good and bad, but I prefer it here. Went back for a week after the first year and found it too bloody depressing, never looked back after that. They'll take me out of here in a box.'

The food arrived and Tom got stuck in to the hamburger and eggs; the food was tasty, just what he needed. The Englishman got up to leave.

'Enjoy your meal; contact me if you ever want to put roots down in Western Marbella. Henry Williams is the name, I'm sales manager for one of the biggest property agencies in this area, be delighted to help if you ever need to buy or rent a place.' He dropped a business card on the table and wended his way between the tightly packed tables to the street.

Tom finished off his food and leaned back, taking in his surroundings. The restaurant was open at the front, facing across the narrow street to the harbour. A constant parade of pedestrians strolled up and down, alternately looking at the boats and at the diners in the restaurants. The occasional luxury car detached itself from its parking space and squeezed through the throng of tourists. The background noise was overlain with a constant clanking of ropes against the hollow aluminium masts of the yachts in the marina, the babble of a dozen languages and the rattle of glasses and cutlery. It was a pleasant place to sit and consider a few options; it seemed a million miles away from the pressure of the sales yard and the troubles that had descended on his head over the last couple of days.

The best course of action was to enjoy the break and do nothing for a while; that was for sure. He owed himself a holiday, and he had plenty of money in his pocket and lots more in the bank. The last year working for Kevin had been lucrative, with a combination of long working hours and high earnings and little time to spend the money; he was now well ahead and could afford to do nothing for months. Even better, the rent here was less than at home, and the price of everything seemed to be a lot less if Picasso's menu prices were anything to go by. Puerto Banus looked like a good place to lie low for a while.

His impressions of the cost of living were borne out a little later when he paid his bill and wandered further along the seafront. The promenade came to an end at a small beach, and he turned inland, intending to make his way home and get an early night. A huge department store faced him on a corner, and he strolled through the supermarket section and bought the basics for breakfast. 'Wave-ohs' he commented to the pretty cashier as she scanned the half dozen eggs and added up his purchases; she smiled and made some unintelligible comment that he assumed was the total. 'How much?' he still didn't understand the Spanish answer. The pretty girl pointed to the digital display on the register and smiled, but it was a friendly smile and he didn't have any sense that she might be mocking his lack of language skills.

It didn't seem a lot for such a big basket of food, this was getting better and better. A ten minute walk should have brought him home, but a couple of minor wrong turns delayed him and it was another half an hour before he was walking through the small garden past the pool and heading for bed. Still, he mused, the only way to get to know an area is to walk, and to get a bit lost. If this is to be home for a while, I had better get used to the place.

45

**

Tom dived into the still water and surfaced, swam a few lengths and got out to dry himself. The pool was cold, just the job to wake a body up and to clear the head. The beer had been flowing the night before; the saxophone bar had been rocking and he had been drinking with the English gang who worked at the water park. They were a wild bunch, most of them just taking a couple of years out of their lives to party it up on the Costa del Sol, but they were good company and he enjoyed meeting up with them on Sunday nights. The park was closed on Mondays and they tended to party well into the night, but he had dropped out of the drinking games about four o'clock and made his way home.

He brought his breakfast out on to the balcony and rifled through one of the Irish Sunday papers; they were very expensive here but it was good to catch up on the news from home. Nothing new from the home front really, just the usual parochial stuff. When you looked at it, a lot of the so-called news was just quotes from politicians who were saying nothing new, it all seemed a bit irrelevant from this distance. The property pages showed an increasing amount of expensive houses that seemed to be getting smaller and smaller as their prices climbed steadily; it was great to be away from it in a lot of ways.

He folded the papers and poured another cup of tea. The sun was hot but his terrace faced West and was shaded in the mornings. He never tired of the view from his breakfast table; this morning the air was exceptionally clear and he could see the rock of Gibraltar to the West, counterpointed by the blue shadow of the Rif mountains just across the Straits in Morocco.

Three weeks gone. He stretched back and admired the deep brown colour on his arms and legs; he had been working on his tan and now he didn't look like a tourist, more like one of the expat workers in the area's tourist trade. Time I was looking at doing something other than lying on a sun lounger, he mused.

It was hard to know what to do; the local English language newspaper had lots of small adverts looking for staff, but most of them were for bar and catering staff, a euphemism for pot wallopers and kitchen porters, and he wasn't prepared to go there. Not yet, anyway.

46

A two-line ad caught his eye in the middle of a page. A car dealership was looking for an English-speaking salesman; he called the number and got an answering machine that advised calling to the garage during office hours. It was in Calahonda, not too far away if he remembered rightly. He shaved and put on his suit, might as well make the right impression from the outset.

The Owner was apologetic. 'Terribly sorry to have put you to the trouble, we filled that job last week but I forgot to cancel the advert. Really sorry, Senor, I apologise very much.'

Tom was annoyed, a morning wasted. Sure, he hadn't been doing anything anyway, but it was a bit of a pain coming all the way to Calahonda when the bloody job was gone. He was warm in the suit, and the car was parked a half a mile away, no parking anywhere near the bloody garage. He slung his jacket over his shoulder and started to walk back to the car park.

'Hello, sir, would you like to enter a free draw for a camcorder?' The girl was attractive, slim and blonde, neatly dressed and in her early twenties.

Tom wondered what the scam might be; nobody gave you anything for nothing. Normally he would walk on, but the girl's smile was open and warm and she didn't look too hard-bitten. If she was a crook, she didn't look it.

'How are you? Now why would a beautiful woman want to give me a present of a free ticket in a draw?' A bit of flattery might drop her guard and find out the truth faster than an antagonistic approach.

'It's a genuine offer, we are promoting some property in this area and we are giving tickets in a limited draw to anyone who views the project. We also give a free bottle of wine to anyone who attends a presentation about the project, no strings attached, just goodwill by the promoters.'

Tom still had doubts, but she seemed to be respectable enough. She proffered a brochure showing a very nice looking apartment complex with landscaped gardens with palm trees and a huge swimming pool. It looked good, but he was curious.

'So, what's the catch, are you one of those timeshare outfits?'

'Absolutely not, this is a respectable company with thousands of satisfied clients. We run a holiday club, a club made up of prop-

47

erty owners who benefit from cheap flights and low cost holidays when they swap their properties with other members worldwide. I'm Kathy, by the way.' She sounded like she might be Dutch, maybe German, but her English was perfect.

Tom still wasn't sure about the setup, but it seemed less threatening than he had first thought. 'Ok, give me a free ticket, maybe I'll win the camcorder and take pictures of you for all the model agencies.' No harm in laying it on a bit thick, it might get results.

The girl never stopped smiling. 'You must come to view the project, it's not far away. I have a car.'

'I have a car too, it's just down by the beach car park; I'll follow you.'

She was persistent. 'It's too easy to lose someone on the way, come on with me and I'll drop you back here after. Don't worry, I won't bite you or try to take advantage of you.'

Tom was wary. 'I might give it a miss this time, catch you another time maybe.'

Her face fell; the smile still there but forced. 'Please, I need you to go there or I don't get paid, there's no catch, it will just take only half an hour to walk around and look at the place, you don't have to buy it or anything. Please.' She was pleading now.

Tom felt sorry for her, he had been there a few times, trying to make a sale and losing it at the last minute. She was an amateur though, he never dropped his guard or resorted to pleading; you could never get a sale that way. You had to keep the pretence up all the time, to make the customer want what was on offer.

'Ok, I'll go and look, but I'm not buying anything, not today anyway.'

She kept up the patter all the way to the development, which turned out to be a lot farther away than he had expected. The road passed through a narrow underpass below the motorway and left the built-up area behind, winding is way uphill through a dry and barren landscape until they arrived at a recently built apartment block with the bare concrete shells of three other blocks just behind it. There was no sign of any building work going on around the other buildings, just half-used pallets of materials and piles of rubble and soil with weeds growing out of them. Tom was not too impressed, but he made no comment and followed Kathy into the foyer of the completed building. Two young men, dressed in standard salesman uniforms of black trousers teamed with white shirt and tie, jumped to attention when they saw the newcomer arrive.

The nearest of the young men stretched out his hand. 'Good morning, I'm Timothy.' This one was English, North of England, maybe Manchester. Sounded like a character from Coronation Street. Tom shook the proffered hand. 'Tom, I'm here to collect a camcorder.'

'Oh yes, very good.' The salesman smiled nervously, not sure whether or not he should laugh at Tom's joke; he got straight down to business.

'We'd like to show you the complex, and to explain how you can be a part of Pueblo Alto Blanco. First I need a few details.' He clipped a pad to a clipboard and clicked a pen, 'Name?'

Tom gave him as few details as he could, skipping things like telephone number on the excuse that he didn't have one yet. Timothy was persistent, 'do you have a home phone number maybe, or an email address?'

'Just moved house' Tom wasn't giving too much away. 'I still have to organise all that stuff.'

Reluctantly, Timothy closed the clipboard and showed Tom around the complex. The apartments were attractive enough, marble floors and small balconies, and good enough views down the hill towards the sea, which could barely be seen in the distance. 'Not sea views as such, we prefer to describe it as 'sea glimpses', but the important thing is the build quality, and of course the prices.'

'So, how much is one of these, then?' Tom was still trying to figure out the setup; it wasn't a timeshare, Kathy had assured him that it wasn't, so what was the score here?

Timothy seemed reluctant to get down to the details, there was more to see. They left the show apartment and he led Tom to a large room off the lobby, where a scale model of the entire complex took up most of the centre of the room. Four blocks were planned, as well as a large swimming pool; it looked much better on the model than it did if you looked outside.

'Impressive.' Tom wondered why only one block was finished. 'When will it all look like this?'

'Just two years from now, all units will be ready then, but if you get in now you only pay the launch price, it will go up when the

49

whole lot is done.' Timothy seemed happier now that he was back on a learned-off sales pitch. Tom could read this fellow like a book; not a salesman, he reckoned, just learned how to sell this project and nothing more. I'd lose him in a minute in a yard full of cars, or a shed full of washing machines for that matter.

'So, let's cut to the chase then.' Tom was in control of the situation and he knew it. 'What's the deal, how much are the apartments? Spill the spiel, Timothy.'

Timothy stammered and stumbled his way through the sales pitch. 'It's, you know, a club, that is you share into the ownership, just use the place when you want and let others pay for the other weeks you don't need, very good way to own a home in the sun for very little money.'

'So, how much? Give me a figure in euros, bottom line etc.'

Timothy was still evasive. 'Depends on how long you think you'd need it for every year, and what time of the year.'

Tom smiled to himself. Useless salesman if I ever saw one, bottom of the barrel stuff. So it is a timeshare racket, just dressed up as a club, probably to keep it legal. Fucking scam artists.

'Well, Timothy, if you can't tell me the price, I have to be out of here.'

'It's not that simple, it depends on various factors.'

Tom was losing patience with this idiot. 'A figure, Timothy, how much? Cut the waffle and give me a figure. Ok, let me make it easy, how much would it cost me to have this place for the first week in July every year from now till kingdom come?'

Timothy brightened and looked at a spreadsheet in his folder. 'Well, for a north-facing apartment, one bedroom, it would only cost you twelve thousand euros, including furniture and everything, down to the last knife and fork.'

'And how much for the last week in January?'

Timothy rifled through his folder again. Tom remembered Kevin's advice on the 'bible' back in City Auto, 'you need to know it by heart where it refers to any car in the yard, no point in looking it up when you're in the middle of a sale. You need it in your head.' This guy wasn't a salesman, he was just a puppet who had learned a few lines off by heart, wouldn't cut it in the real world.

'That would be six thousand, very little when you think of the price of hotels, you would spend that in a couple of years, this is a great way to invest for the future and save yourself thousands as well. And of course you can always sell your membership at any time.'

Tom made a few calculations in his head. 'So, average price is about nine grand a week, more or less?'

'That's about right, yes.'

'So, nine grand a week, that's near enough four hundred and seventy grand a year if you took every week?'

'Yes, I guess so.' Timothy wasn't clear where this was heading.

'Four hundred and seventy grand for an apartment that's worth what, seventy or eighty grand on a good day? I'd want to be nuts, wouldn't I?'

Timothy seemed to know that he was losing this battle, but he struggled on. 'Yes, but if you join this club you can swap your week for a week in any of our affiliate resorts anywhere in the world, and you get peace of mind, you know....' His voice trailed off, he knew he had lost this one somewhere along the way.

Tom headed out to the lobby, Kathy was dropping off a middle-aged couple at the front door and he waved to her and made a steering wheel motion with his hands. She held up both hands, fingers spread, he would have to wait another ten minutes to get a lift back to the coast.

Timothy was still vainly trying to get him to listen to some more of the sales pitch. 'If you would like to view a presentation in the conference room, we will send you on your way with a bottle of wine, it's only ten minutes.....'

An older man emerged from the conference room. Tom looked him over; he exuded an air of confidence and seemed to be in charge. In his forties, Tom reckoned, about six foot tall, solidly built with a tight haircut, looked like he might have been a rugby player.

The newcomer extended a hand to Tom; 'I'm Alan, MD of Pueblo Alto Blanco Holiday Club, thank you for coming along today.' His grip was strong and his smile seemed genuine, nothing like the two salesmen who were now descending on the bewildered looking couple in the lobby.

Tom recognised a fellow salesman; this fellow had closed a few deals in his time. It was time to stop messing around and get out of here. 'I'm not interested in your offer, or in this project, but my thanks to your colleague for showing it to me.'

Alan's smile never faltered, but he seemed to also recognise something in Tom that meant that this would be a wasted effort. 'I'm sorry you don't have time to view our presentation; I'll have Kathy drop you back to Calahonda.'

The young woman said little on the way back to the town. Tom tried to extract some information from her on the way but nothing much was forthcoming, she seemed to have clammed up completely and the friendly smile had disappeared. He wondered at the whole set-up, hard to see how anyone would buy what was on offer, maybe it was a credit card scam or something. He was glad to get back to his car and head for Puerto Banus.

**

The Saxophone bar was packed with locals and holidaymakers, and the gang from the water park were lining up the glasses for one of their drinking games. They waved Tom to the table in the corner but he shook his head; he would just have one beer and head home, he wasn't in the humour for a session. The holiday mood had left him and he wanted to get into a routine, to get a job of some kind so as to have something to get up for in the mornings. It was nearly five weeks since he had arrived in Spain and he was tired of the party; it was time to get real. From here on he would be in serious job-hunting mode, tomorrow morning he would do the rounds of all the job agencies and get something.

'Una cervetha grande,' he was getting used to the lingo, pronouncing the 's' as a 'th', a kind of a lisp. The problem was, it never seemed to come out the same way as if a Spanish person said it. The barmaid smiled at him, he wasn't sure if she was being friendly or if she was amused at his pronunciation. He took a swallow from the beer and waited for his change.

'Grassy arse.' Hard to tell if that was a real Spanish accent or if she was taking the piss. He turned away from the bar and bumped into the big Englishman.

'Hello mate.' The big fellow didn't quite recognise him, maybe thought he had seen him somewhere, but couldn't put a name on him.

Tom was still curious about the setup in Pueblo Alto Blanco; he wanted to find out more about it, and down here in the port he was on home ground and could ask questions in safety.

'We met at your office a couple of weeks ago. Your young lady Kathy brought me up to look at your project.'

'Oh Kathy, nice girl, not with us any more unfortunately. I remember you now; you weren't interested. It happens sometimes; not for everybody and all that.'

'I'm still not sure what you are selling.' Tom tried to keep it friendly. 'I would say one thing though, I'm a salesman myself, all my life really, and the guys you have up there wouldn't recognise an opening if they fell through it. Wouldn't have made it anywhere I ever worked anyway.'

Alan stood back and looked Tom up and down. 'Let me guess, cars mostly I'd say, maybe insurance now and again?'

Tom laughed. 'More or less on the button. Cars, electrical goods, a while selling mortgages, that sort of thing.'

'And you love it; love the excitement of getting one over the line?'

'Yes, of course, nothing like the buzz of scoring a difficult one especially. You know yourself.'

The Englishman clapped him on the shoulder. 'You're one of us, mate; let me get you a beer. Here, Carley, give us two more beers there, love; proper cold ones, darling.'

'Coming up, amigoth.' Jesus, a bloody Aussie, she was taking the piss all the time.

'Let's get out of the noise; it's bedlam in here, not as bad outside.' The big fellow led the way through the crowd to the outside tables where the sound was several decibels lower.

Four rounds of beer later and Tom was getting the picture. Alan Merchant was a salesman too. He had started his working life on his father's barrow in London's East End, selling everything from slightly imperfect shirts to tins of fruit that were dented and damaged. In his teens he had stumbled across the 'Dutch Auction' stroke; along with a mate of his, they had milked hundreds of pounds from people by selling them bundles of household and electrical goods, usually at several times the true value of the items. The law had moved quickly to cover the legal loophole that allowed these scams to proliferate, and Alan had progressed to selling double glazing in council estates where tenants had just bought out their homes from local authorities and where lenders were rushing to lend money to these new property owners.

'I wasn't long figuring out that I could make more by providing the finance for the windows than the windows themselves.'

'So you started selling loans?' Tom was getting the picture of how Alan operated.

'I suppose you'd call it moneylending; basically I borrowed money and lent it on at a profit, and I had a few guys collecting the repayments every week at the doors.'

'Is that legal in England?'

'Not really, but it goes on in every council estate and nobody passes any mind. My mistake was in moving it up the scale.'

'How do you mean?'

'I opened an office in one of the big estates, it was an empty corner shop that I bought cheap, and I ran the loans business from there. Had it done up like a bank, it looked brilliant. It was great for a while, a real buzz on Fridays when the collectors were coming and going with the money.'

'So what went wrong?'

'I suppose ego if I'm honest. I just couldn't resist putting a sign that said 'Merchant Banking' up over the shop; it was quite a feeling when I was still only twenty two to think that I owned my own bank.'

'I think I know how you might have felt, but wasn't that pushing your luck a bit?'

'Looking back, I should have known that I was asking for trouble. Someone complained and I ended up in court for running an unlicensed bank. No way was I paying that big a fine, mate, so I moved to Spain. Best move I ever made; great place to live, nice climate, cheap beer, chicks coming out of the woodwork. What about yourself, same story?'

'Not quite, but a few similarities. Kicked out of school at seventeen for running a bookie operation, had a big falling out with my dad over that and moved out of home. Worked in sales here and there, ended up in car sales for the last year.

'So are you back in touch with your parents then?'

'No, my dad and I don't get on. My mother died about fifteen years ago; I was only ten. Looking back, I'd say I probably started to go off the rails a bit after that. My older brother is an engineer and he's in business with my dad, they're builders. I never went back, don't intend to.'

'You should keep in touch with your dad, family is important. My dad passed away a couple of years ago but I bring my old mum out to Spain every winter, she loves it here.'

'You don't know my old man, he wouldn't approve of my career choices. We never really got on anyway, but the day I packed in my education, that was the end of it for him. No, we agree to differ.'

'So how did you end up in Spain?'

'Had a small brush with the law, not really my doing, the guy I worked for was a bit bent. Decided to come out here for a while to let things settle a bit.'

'Always the other fellow that's bent.' Alan laughed. 'But you were happy to take the few quid even if you had your doubts. Am I right?'

Tom smiled, he was right of course, it was obvious all along that Kevin was dealing in bent certs, and he had just ignored the fact as long as the money was rolling in.

'Up to a point, yes, you're right.'

'None of us is as clean as we might like to think, believe me. We all do what it takes for a bit of easy pickings. So, do you want to make yourself some serious money?'

Chapter Four

It was good to be going to work again, even if it wasn't clear what the job entailed and how exactly this outfit actually made money. Tom decided to play it by ear, to see what the story was and not to get too involved if the thing was dangerous or blatantly illegal. It would pass a few days anyway; maybe give him an insight into the world of work in Spain. The very least it would do might be to pay the bills for this week, bring in a few quid to counteract the non-stop outgoings. Spain wasn't too expensive a place to live, but you needed to have an income long term.

Alan took a look at him when he walked into the conference room. 'You look the part anyway, Tom; you suit up well. Question is, can you deliver the goods, mate?'

'I just need some background on the nuts and bolts of the operation, and then I can make a few sales no problem. The key to anything like this is to know it off by heart, not to be looking in a file for answers in the middle of a sale.' Tom had learned some good lessons from Kevin in the car sales business.

'Pull up a chair and have a look at this stuff.' Alan had several red folders on the desk, and he pulled some single spreadsheet pages out of each and slid them across the desk to Tom. 'What we do is to sell timeshares, but we never describe it as that.'

'I partly guessed as much. Timeshare has got a lot of bad press, hasn't it?'

'It's not just that, they brought in some laws a while back that have cramped our style a bit. Nowadays you have you give a cooling off period to buyers, let them change their minds for a couple of days afterwards.

'That makes it hard to make a sale stick then?'

'It does, but we figured a way round it, I'll tell you about that in a minute.'

'Sorry to have interrupted you, go on about the project.'

'Ok, we take a building project like this, one that isn't selling too well, and we do a deal with the developer to sell the place for him, but on a shared ownership basis. Actually we dealt with the receiver on this one, the banks had moved in before we could rescue the original guy. We break each apartment into fifty two weeks, hold back the best apartments until the end, and sell individual weeks for each apartment.'

That was more or less as Tom had figured it; it was a timeshare but just dressed up as something different. 'But what about the legals, how do you get around that?'

'That's the easy bit, we break up the sale. By law we can sell up to thirty six months as a holiday contract with no cooling off period, then we sell the rest as an open ended contract for the balance. We take the deposit on the short contract, so it's non-refundable, and if they want to cancel the long contract they lose the short one and their money as well. Beware the small print!' He sat back and smiled. Of course we never call it timeshare, we call it fractional ownership.'

Tom was amazed at the simplicity of it; you had to hand it to these guys. 'So you keep it just barely legal. Lambs to the slaughter, I suppose you could say.'

'We're selling dreams, Tom, extracting a few quid from people who can't afford to buy a holiday home in the sun. This way, they get to be able to say to their friends that they have a place in Spain, somewhere that they go to every year.'

'And do they ever get what they pay for?' Tom had a momentary vision of hundreds of disappointed buyers lined up outside the gate of Pueblo Alto Blanco, while Alan and his crew disappeared down the road in a cloud of dust.

'Usually, yes. The beauty of it though is that we are only the selling agents, we have a contract with the project owner that means that the onus is on him to finish off the place and deliver the apartments to the buyers. Usually the developers are so glad to find someone to sell places like this that they don't look at the small print too closely.'

'So the punters could lose their money?'

'I suppose in theory they could, but we pay a good price for these apartments, and there is always enough in the kitty for the builder to be paid. I wouldn't worry about it; life's too bloody short to be worrying.'

'But you must make a good bit on it too. What do you pay in commission for a sale?'

Alan smiled. 'Doesn't take you long to get to the point, mate; I can see we are going to get on. I'll give you five hundred quid for every sale as soon as the punter has swiped their credit card. How does that sound to you? Now you're really interested, aren't you?'

Tom was surprised at the level of commission; this was serious money. In theory, you could do three or four sales a day; even more maybe, you could do a lot more if you got a run of good clients.

A lot of pickings around here, he mused. 'I'm interested all right, otherwise I wouldn't be here.'

'Good stuff, Tom, I need a couple of good salesmen on this job, the ones I have aren't great. They still make a lot of money though; Timothy made five grand last week for instance.'

'So how much of it is sold so far?' Tom had the impression that very few weeks had been sold.

'Around a third of it, believe it or not. All in the second and third blocks; we have marked this first block as sold although it isn't sold yet, if the shit hits the fan we don't want people turning up to claim their apartments.'

Tom was amazed. So you've sold a third of the apartments, for all weeks?'

'Yes, more or less, we usually manage to do a clean sweep for all fifty two weeks for each unit, we raise and lower the price to suit, if all the August stuff is flying off the plans for instance we might push the price up a bit, maybe drop a few quid off a January week.'

'But how do you do that, surely if you quote someone a price and then one of their friends comes along and you have changed the price....?'

'We can tweak it a bit, charge more for south facing, or west facing, or whatever we decide really. It works anyway, don't worry about the finer points; I'll look after that side of things. You just sell the stuff and leave the detail to me.'

'So how about the girls that work on the streets, bringing in the clients? Who pays them?'

'I pay them twenty euro for every client, that includes a couple or someone on their own, whether we get a sale from them or not. As long as we are converting at least half them into sales, we are doing ok.'

'And what percentage of them turn into sales?' Tom was getting interested in the detail.

Alan pulled out a printout from another folder. 'As of last month, fifty eight percent, but that's been dragged down the last couple of weeks with bad conversion rate by those two outside. Do you think you can do better?'

'If Timothy can do the kind of level you say he's doing, I know I can do a lot better.' Tom was getting excited about the prospect of earning a lot of money. 'Just load me and point me at the enemy.'

* * *

The woman liked the place, but her husband was less sure. 'I'm not too happy about some things, I've heard a lot about timeshares and how they can go wrong, we saw a programme on the telly once about gangs ripping people off.'

Tom drew himself up to his full height. 'I can assure you sir that this is not one of these crooked timeshare operations. This is a very reputable holiday club with thousands of satisfied members; we wouldn't be able to stay in business if there was a shadow of suspicion about how we operate.'

The man apologised. 'I'm sorry, no offence intended, you just can't be too careful these days.'

'Of course, no offence taken, but you can understand that we are very proud of our reputation.' Tom didn't want to push him too hard, just enough to keep him on the back foot.

'If there are so many satisfied customers, can we talk to some of them, get an idea of how it worked out for them?' The woman was still a bit unsure.

Tom had his standard answer ready; this was going to be easy. 'I'm afraid we have an obligation to our clients not to divulge any of their details to anyone, standard Spanish law on data protection and all that.'

The man nodded agreement. 'Yes, of course.' He looked at his wife. 'That's true, dear, I see it at work nowadays, you can't be too careful about data, can't leave it lying around you know.'

Tom sensed an opening, time to push for a close. 'I can show you some emails from clients, but their details are blanked out.' He produced a bundle of print-outs of emails that he had written himself a few weeks earlier, all of them thanking the staff at Pueblo Alto Blanco for their help.

The couple were warming to the idea, time to tap the ball towards the net. Just one good straight kick, the ball was rolling towards the line and the keeper was distracted for the moment.

'Look, if you find in a year or two that you want to change your mind, you can always sell on your membership and get at least what you paid for it, probably a lot more, and in the meantime you and your family will have had some great holidays for nothing. You can't lose.'

The woman looked at her husband, the game was nearly over. 'It would be nice right enough, our own place in Spain, we always dreamt of it didn't we, dear?'

The man turned to Tom with a pleading look in his eye. 'We can't really afford this to go wrong, we don't have much money. Are you sure it's ok, that we're getting good value? Are you sure we will be able to sell it again if we need to get our hands on the money?'

Tom tried not to let his feelings show on his face. The man was right to be worried, these timeshares were impossible to resell, worth very little at the end of the day, and it was hard not to feel sorry for the punters at a time like this. It wasn't too bad with the pushy ones, they deserved what was coming to them, but an old couple like this who asked you out straight, that was harder. His instinct was to take them aside, to tell them to put their money away and go back to their hotel and forget the whole deal. Still, his job was to sell, and anyway there was another five hundred quid ready to drop into the bucket if this sale went through. He put his arm around the man's shoulders.

'Nothing to worry about, sir, this is a respectable company with hundreds of satisfied clients. Your money is safe.'

'Well, if you say so.'

'If you come this way we can arrange the few formalities.' They followed him meekly to the desk in the small office.

He shoots, he scores! Walter would love this place, he thought to himself. Five sales today, two and a half grand in the pot and the day isn't over yet. I love this fucking country.

***

Alan double-parked out front of Mesa Bella; the elderly head-waiter took the car keys and showed them to a quiet table on the raised area at the far end of the restaurant.

'I like this place, never got a bad meal here yet, one of the best places on the coast.'

Tom liked the look of it, good atmosphere and décor, with a cosy noisy background of clattering plates and the laughter of happy diners.

'Well, lad, I have to hand it to you, you can surely do the business. I'm sorry now I offered you so much money; you're making more than I am nowadays.'

'Hardly true, I know what you are making, about ten times what I make, but that's life.'

'I got overheads, costs, expenses.' Alan was smiling broadly; they both knew that he was making a lot of money, but Tom wasn't complaining either.

'Come on, Tom, I bet you never made so much money in your life. Twelve grand this week, forty grand in the past month, where would you get it, I'm just a fucking mug aren't I?'

'You made at least two hundred thou last month by my reckoning, even allowing for your bloody overheads, but I'm not bitter.' Tom was happy, it was Saturday night and they never worked on Sundays. All the tourist groups changed over on Sundays, no point in wasting time going after them. Mid-week was best, the punters getting bored with the beach and starting to look around the neighbourhood, ripe pickings for Alan's team of hustler girls who delivered clients to the salesmen at the Pueblo.

They ate in silence for a while, the starters were tasty and the portions generous.

'Any plans for later on?'

'Might meet up with the crowd from the water park; have a few beers, nothing else. How about yourself?

Alan shook his head. 'Early night for me, not able for the booze any more, doctor says I need to watch it a bit.'

'So, how are we doing on the overall total?' Tom was losing count of how many apartment shares had been sold, it was hard to keep track. In any case, he didn't concern himself too much about the backroom detail; his job was to sell, and he just kept a note of how many sales he made each week and the names of the clients. Alan never quibbled, just paid him in cash on Saturday evenings, and they usually retired to a good restaurant for a leisurely dinner before going their separate ways for the rest of the weekend. The bundle of notes rested comfortably in his jacket pocket right now; there was nothing like the feeling of being paid in cash at the end of the week and knowing that there was more to be made next week again.

'We're nearly through all of block four now, we'll be moving back to block one in about three or four weeks. Start trickling it out, one or two apartments at a time, pretend that they're cancellations.'

'We're going well so.' Tom was surprised at the extent of the sales. It was easy to forget the big picture sometimes; you just focussed on selling one apartment at a time, just zeroed in on one client and made the sale, then moved on to the next, head down, keep slogging away.

'Doing particularly well since you came on board. You're selling three to every one of Timothy's for instance, of course the rankings system is working in your favour as well.'

The rankings was a simple system, whoever was top of the list got first choice of clients as they came in the door. Alan wanted clients dealt with by someone who was likely to get a sale, so the other salesmen only got a look in if Tom was already busy. It created a bit of competition too; the others had to try to sell more to catch Tom, but they hadn't succeeded, so far.

'Time flies doesn't it, seems like you have been with us for years. It's been a good move for you hasn't it, coming to Spain?'

Tom agreed, it was almost too good to be true. Nearly nine months with Alan's company, well more than a quarter of a million in the bank; would never happen at home. Still, you would miss home sometimes; it would be great to be heading out on the town at home instead of down to the bloody port, week after week, with the same crowd of losers propping up the counter in the Saxophone bar.

Soon, he figured, he would quit this game and get an honest job, one where he would be happy to meet his customers on the street and look them in the eye. It was ok when he was busy and didn't have to think too much about what he was doing, but sometimes he lay awake at night and thought about some of the people who came through the offices at Pueblo Alto Blanco. Some of them could afford to lose the money, but then again a lot of them weren't very well off and it seemed as if they were spending most of their life savings on a useless timeshare on a dusty Spanish hillside. A part of him wanted to warn them, to tell them to go home and forget the whole deal, but the thought of the fat commission on each sale kept him from doing anything so stupid.

'Penny for the thoughts, Tom.' Alan broke into his reverie.

'You don't get my thoughts for that kind of money, I thought we agreed that.'

'You have a price on everything, Tom, but who am I to talk?'

Alan called for the bill, and the waiter brought the Bentley round to the front door. 'Drop you somewhere? I'm heading home, can't keep up the pace any more.' Alan sounded tired.

'I'll get out at the road down to the port; the stroll will do me good.' Tom felt bloated after the heavy meal. 'I'm not getting enough exercise lately, added a couple of inches to the waistline since I started to work for you.'

'It does you no harm; a big tall guy like you can carry a few extra pounds.'

'Yes, but as long as it isn't all at the front.'

'See you Monday, Tom.'

He set off to walk to the saxophone bar with the intention of meeting up with the gang from the water park, but when he got to the fountain at the entrance to the port he paused. Tom wasn't in the humour for a noisy night of drinking and having to shout to be heard above the crowd. He was getting tired of the constant partying in this sunny holiday resort; he remembered the nights at home, having a pint with Walter and Kevin in the Willows, and going on to a club and meeting the friends he knew from childhood. Tom was homesick; he turned and walked back towards the underpass and his apartment. An early night mightn't be a bad idea.

***

He was awake early on Sunday morning and walked around to the twenty-four-hour supermarket to buy a couple of Irish newspapers. The news from home was the same as usual, not much happening, but it was nice to catch up. The property sections seemed to have got thicker, their pages full of adverts for new housing and apartment developments. The economy seemed to be doing all right, some of the gloom and doom was missing from the news stories and he detected a slightly positive slant to a lot of the articles. Maybe it was a case of far away hills, an emigrant's view of home through rose tinted glasses; he dropped the papers on the table and headed out to get some breakfast.

It was a perfect morning for a walk, not too warm but with a clear blue sky overhead and not a speck of cloud to be seen. He loved to see the masses of purple flowers on the bougainvillea that spilled over the walls of the garden; the best thing about living is Spain was the year-round display of flowering plants that lifted the spirits on an early morning walk. He strolled through the car park of the Casino and crossed the small hill to where a small group of shops curved around the corner by the roundabout. La Paloma was open; a scattering of expat regulars already laying claim to the best tables on the terrace.

Henry Williams had already cornered a table, and he motioned to Tom to join him. The elderly English estate agent was a regular at the popular café, and Tom had breakfasted with him there many times since meeting with him on his first night in Spain when he was trying to decipher the menu in Picasso's.

'Tom, sit down, pull up a chair. I'd like you to meet another Irishman; this is Harry Corbett, plays golf with me in Valderama now and again.'

They exchanged handshakes. Tom hadn't seen the Irishman before, looked a bit pale to be a resident in the area, probably had a holiday home here he reckoned.

'So, do you live in Ireland or here in Spain?'

'In Ireland unfortunately, although that sounds as if I dislike the place, but when I see weather like this, I envy you guys that have this all the time.'

'So, how do you know this reprobate?' Tom enjoyed a friendly banter with Henry, he had found him to be a helpful contact since their first meeting, and the two were now good friends.

'He sold me my apartment a couple of years ago, and then he wound up having to show me where all the golf courses were. So now I come out for long weekends and keep him away from his work, drag him around the golf course and try to win back the commission he made off me.'

'So, you offloaded an expensive piece of real estate on a poor Paddy, have the English not stopped exploiting us yet?'

The Irishman laughed. 'It might have been expensive at the time, but it looks cheap now. I'm very happy to be exploited if I can make gains like that, believe me.'

Henry stirred his coffee. 'At least he didn't end up in Pueblo Alto Blanco.'

'True.' Tom was able to laugh at himself. 'That would have been a bad outcome all right.'

'So, what's Pueblo Blanco or whatever?' The Irishman was curious.

'It's a timeshare caper in the hills; our Tom here has sold his soul to the devil and is making a fortune flogging it to innocent tourists.' Henry was joking, but there was a little tinge of disapproval in his voice; he didn't like the way Alan Merchant did business and he never made any secret of it.

'It's a holiday club.' Tom shifted uncomfortably in the chair. The banter was light-hearted, but Henry's comments had stung a little.

'Club, timeshare, fractional ownership, it doesn't matter what you call it, end result is still the same, people end up disappointed. Anyway, we have agreed to disagree on it, Tom; what do you want for breakfast, wave-ohs?'

They laughed at the memory of Tom's early attempts at the language; he was a lot better now although his attempts to pronounce the 's' at the end of words as a 'th' were still a source of amusement to his Spanish friends.

'Tom is the best salesman ever to come out of Ireland, he has a natural talent for selling, but he doesn't discriminate between good and bad, sells everything that comes along. I have to work my ass off to sell a few good properties; he seems to be able to sell absolutely anything, never lets one slip. Wish he'd come and work with us, but he never takes me up on my offer.'

'You can't afford me.' Tom was smiling again, the ribbing about timeshares forgotten.

They breakfasted in the warm sun until Harry pushed back his chair. 'I have to be heading off, have to drop off the car and catch my flight, back to the rain and wind.' He reached for his wallet but Tom waved him away. 'Breakfast is on me, you can get me back in Dublin sometime.'

They shook hands. 'You can take me up on that, any time.'

Tom looked at the departing rental car as it headed down the slip road. 'Nice guy, what does he do in Ireland?'

'Not exactly sure, he has a small estate agency business but I think he makes most of his money from financial services, you know, mortgages and insurance and that kind of thing. Doesn't talk too much about it, when he's having a few days off he's having a few days off, if you know what I mean. Good golfer though, I enjoy a game with him.'

Tom called the waitress and ordered two more coffees. 'So, you think I shouldn't be working for Alan?'

The older man shook his head. 'It's not for me to tell you what you should or shouldn't be doing; I just think that fellows like Alan Merchant are bad news. He'll walk away if the shit hits the fan and your reputation will be on the floor. Has the building started on the other three blocks up at Pueblo Alto?'

Tom nodded. 'Yes, a contractor started at the beginning of last month, big crew on site now, looks like they mean business. It makes it a lot easier for us too; it wasn't easy explaining away an empty site and big piles of rubble.'

'So everyone will get their apartments, or at least their share of an apartment?'

'No doubt about that now, but it looked dodgy for a while all right.'

'And you still kept selling? Even when you thought that they might get nothing? Sometimes I worry about you Tom, do you not see the problem with operating like that?'

'Henry, they're all big people in a big world. It's my job to sell; their job to buy. I can't sit on both sides of the scales.'

'Tom, between me and you, do you never think about the effect your actions might be having on the people you are selling to? A lot of those buyers can't afford to lose that money.'

'I used to worry about it Henry, but nowadays I try not to. If I started taking everyone else's problems on board I wouldn't sleep at night. The way I see it, I look after myself and they look after themselves. That's the only way I can deal with it.'

'It's not as simple as that Tom, but there's no point in us arguing about it, we'll never agree on it anyway. Be careful whatever you do, don't end up in jail for any bastard, look after your own hide.'

***

The aircraft descended through the thick cloud and rain, and suddenly the sea was visible, not far below. Tom peered through the murk and could just make out a line of yellow street lights that marked the coast. It was a miserable evening and he wasn't sure of he had brought the right clothes with him; it looked cold and wet out there.

It seemed to take the pilot ages to put the plane down; it was buffeted by strong cross winds but the landing was reasonably smooth, and they taxied a long way to the end of the runway.

'Ladies and gentlemen, welcome to Dublin. Please remain seated until the aircraft has come to a complete stop and no smoking until you have passed through the terminal building.' The announcer droned on through her little speech; Tom waited until the crowd had rushed for the exit before grabbing his bag from the overhead bin.

As soon as he had passed through the passport control area he turned on his mobile and checked his messages. Walter was still at work, but he would be home in an hour. Tom joined the long taxi queue and shivered in the cold wind; hard to believe it was summertime, he had forgotten how cold it could get when a bout of stormy weather came through.

The taxi driver was talkative; he seemed to have an opinion on everything. Tom kept his answers to monosyllables; the driver seemed content to listen to the sound of his own voice as he ranted on about traffic and the price of petrol and how expensive everything was getting. Tom hadn't been paying too much attention to where they were going; the driver was making turns all over the place to avoid the rush hour traffic jams. Suddenly he realised that he was on familiar ground, they were on the street coming up to City Auto. He looked ahead to see what was happening with the yard, was Willie still in business or was it closed?

The streetscape had changed. The car park beside the pub was surrounded by a hoarding and a building was emerging from the ground, with a tower crane moving overhead and a lot of activity going on. City Auto was a bit of a shock; the portocabin was gone and the big shed demolished, and a hoarding surrounded the site as well; looked like the yard was going to be a building site soon.

'That place there, used to be a car sales place wasn't it?'

The taxi man nodded. 'All gone, the fellow that owned the place sold it to a developer six months ago. Got three million for it I heard.'

'Three million! That's a lot of money for a bit of ground around here.' Tom was surprised at the turn of events. Willie had done well.

'Same all over, any bit of land in the city is making big money. Apartments and shops, that's what they put on them. I don't know who'll live in all these places, but they keep building them anyway.'

'So, no more car sales around here?' Tom probed to find out more.

'No, and it's a pity, that crowd weren't the worst. You could get a cheap enough car from them, they weren't bad at all. It was a Scottish fellow that owned it I heard, done a flit over tax or something, well gone. He was only renting it from a local fellow, best thing he ever did was to go maybe, the Irish fellow maybe didn't know what he was sitting on all the time.'

Tom sat back in the seat. Who would have thought it, Willie a bloody multi millionaire? Funny how the world turns. He smiled to himself.

The taxi pulled up at Walter's house; the meter read fifty euros.

'Twenty five to you, skipper,' the driver was apologetic. 'I thought you were a foreigner when you got in, the colour of you and the foreign accent had me fooled. It's only twenty five, don't want you giving me a dig, you know yourself.'

Tom laughed and handed over thirty. 'Keep the change, and watch that dodgy meter.'

Walter arrived as he walked up the drive. The new house was

great, with a wide driveway and a new four by four parked in front of the garage.

'Doing well in real estate by the look of things?'

'Can't complain.'

Walter was in his usual cheery mood. 'Life is good, selling like crazy and no sign of an end to it. Are you thinking of coming back?'

'I hadn't thought of it, although I suppose I will some time. It's always in your mind when you're out there, but then you come back and it's pissing down it all looks different.'

'The weather is part of it I suppose, but life can be good here too.'

'It's good for you by the look of things, I like the new place.'

Walter looked around at his new home. 'We love it, just about settled in now, got it at the right price, one of the perks of working in the game, you get to spot ones that come up that have been priced too low. Sometimes the owners put the price on them, they know better and all that, but they might be better leaving it to us to value them.'

'You have it made, it's a great spot.' Tom envied Walter in a way, nice family, lovely home and doing well. Decent fellow though, and a good mate, deserved anything he had. He often thought that it would be good to settle down with a girl like Pamela and have a life that was a bit more stable than his own bachelor existence.

Dinner was a lively affair, Pamela had made a stew and they opened a couple of bottles of the wine that Tom had brought from Puerto Banus. The talk was of Miltons and of City Auto and of old times when they worked together to drive difficult sales through.

'Willie did well.' Tom wanted to know more about the sale of the yard.

'You heard? You're well up on all the news so. He got a great price for it, it was our lot that sold it, I meant to tell you at the time but it slipped my mind.

'Did he get out of the trouble all right so?'

'Ah yes, that blew over after a while, the fellow down at the test centre was in court only last week, just got a fine and the probation act. Lost his job though but he got off light. Willie just sang dumb through the whole thing, opened a main dealership out on the ring road, he's in the big time now. We bought Pamela's four by four off him, gave it to us wholesale. Same old Willie.'

Tom shook his head in disbelief. 'I used to think Willie hadn't a bob, working for wages for Kevin, but he seems to have come out of the whole thing very well, better than any of us.'

Pamela poured more wine. 'You've done all right too by the look of you, fancy shirts and a Rolex no less, you must be making a lot of money in Spain.'

'I can't complain really.' Tom put down his drink on the coffee table and sat back on the couch. 'Made a few bob the last few months, mining a particularly rich seam lately.'

'I hope it's all legal.'

'Of course, just well paid sales work.' Tom decided against telling Walter about the details of the timeshare racket, he knew that his friend wouldn't understand.

'Ever think of buying a place here? I could look out for an apartment; get you one at a good deal if you weren't in a hurry.'

Tom hadn't thought about buying a place anywhere, but Walter's idea made sense. After all, what was he going to do with all the money that was piling up in the bank in Gibraltar? He didn't live too much of the high life, that all tended to wear a bit thin after a while in any case, and the money was just sitting there, not doing anything.

'Ok, let's do that, you find me the right place and just let me know how much to transfer.'

'How much have you available, if that's not too personal a question?' Walter didn't want to pry too much but he needed a guideline.

'About three hundred grand in the bank in Gib, maybe a few more bob here and there, not too sure.'

Walter looked at him in astonishment. 'You've gathered up that much money since you left? Bloody hell!'

'Not all since I left, I made a right few bob working for Kevin as well. How much would a nice apartment cost me then? Something in a good area maybe?'

'You could buy a couple of places for that kind of money. I'd suggest you buy something here and buy one in Spain as well; our strategy guys are looking at Spain for big gains over the next few years. I can't believe you're still paying rent with all that cash in the bank.'

Tom was starting to realise just how well he had been doing over the last year or so. He had been so busy working that he hadn't really been looking at the end result, but when you converted the harvest into something tangible like bricks and mortar, you began to get a measure of the size of the pile. He was suddenly enthusiastic about the plan.

'Let's go for it so, you get me one here and I'll go shopping in Spain, I have a friend in the business over there who won't see me wrong, decent old skin.'

'All you're short now is a woman.' Pamela was teasing him.

'Do you want me to look around for a woman for you as well?' Walter joined in the ribbing.

'I can do that myself; don't worry.' Tom was able to laugh along with his friends. 'Although I'd have to admit that you did well in that department yourself.' He raised his glass in Pamela's direction.

Pamela laughed. 'So, have you a girl in Spain?'

'Not really. Well, sort of. I have an occasional girlfriend if you could call her that.'

'Is she pretty? What's her name?'

'She's called Carmen, works in the rental company, but we're not really serious about each other.'

'Is that what she thinks as well?'

'I don't know, never actually had that conversation with her to be honest.'

Walter laughed. 'Same old Tom. Did you ever hear from that blonde girl, the one you sold the yellow car to?'

Tom shook his head. 'Amanda? No, I never saved her number, I wouldn't mind catching up with her again though; she was lovely.'

'You should have written her details in your little book.'

'I know, I missed out there.'

Pamela smiled and raised a glass. 'Here's to the start of Tom's property empire, and to his search for a nice girl. May you live long and enjoy it all.'

Chapter Five

It was hot, even for this time of the morning. It was a rare pleasure to have a day off for a change, and Tom was looking forward to having a good breakfast at La Paloma. The street was busy with crowds of people heading for the market, and the police were blowing whistles and waving drivers on past the turn to the hill. Henry had managed to hold on to a table on the terrace, and Tom pulled up a chair and ordered his coffee and breakfast.

'So, you want to put down roots in Marbella. I knew you'd come round to it sooner or later.'

'Not roots as such, more like dropping anchor for a while. Have you come up with a few for me?'

Henry pointed to the bundle of papers on the table. 'Picked you out six possible ones, including a beaut in the complex you're in. Good time to buy, prices are starting to go up but a lot of owners haven't realised it yet.'

Tom looked through the sheaf of papers and pulled out one that caught his eye. 'This one looks good, what's the story with it?'

Henry looked over the top of his glasses at the brochure that Tom was perusing. 'Not mad on that one Tom, too near the main road, nice complex but might be hard to get rid of it again. Wait till we get the food inside us and we'll go through them.'

They tucked into the tortillas and croissants, washing them down with a couple of strong coffees. 'So, good trip to Ireland? Did it convince you to stay here in the sunshine or do you still miss the rain?'

Tom laughed. 'I had a great few days, met up with some old mates and had a few good nights out. Glad to get back to a bit of decent weather though, I couldn't imagine having breakfast outdoors in Dublin today.'

'That sums it up, lad, we couldn't eat it outside in Newcastle for that matter, so I'm definitely staying put in Spain. Was that what made you decide that you wanted to buy a place?'

'Not really. Walter, mate of mine in the estate agency business, reckons that Spanish stuff is now underpriced and that it makes for a good investment. I'm buying one back home as well; he's looking out for one for me.'

'Good thinking, lad; I heard that stuff was starting to move over there as well. Definitely there's an upwards move happening here; it's a good time to buy, especially when you know your way around the business.'

They finished breakfast and ordered more coffees. The café was thronged with tourists from the market, but the waitress was looking after her regulars and they got the coffees quickly. Tom gave her the money for the breakfast, and they went through the papers that Henry had brought along.

'Here's the one in your own block, looking for a hundred and forty but I know he'll take about one-ten. Top floor, extra big terrace. He's living in South Africa and not coming back, so he's out of touch with the market here now. It's furnished as well, but I'm not sure how much he wants for the contents.'

'That sounds like a possibility.'

'Even better, I haven't showed it to anyone yet, told the guy that we are finding it hard to get people interested in that development. Soften him up a bit; make him grab at any offer if we make him wait long enough.'

'I like your style.' Tom turned another page round to face Henry. 'What about this one?'

'That's on with another agency, in the complex behind your place, tidy property but I don't have as much info on it for obvious reasons. As well as that, the other agency has to get the full commission, so I can't split it with you like I could on the first one.'

Tom was surprised. 'I didn't expect you to split the take with me, I mean, we all live on commissions, I don't begrudge you your slice of the action on any of this.'

Henry held up his hand. 'Say no more, lad, there's no argument about it, I'll split the commission with you fifty-fifty, no more than you'd do for me.'

'Do you want to walk back to those two? The traffic is crazy with the bloody market.'

'I'm not as young as you, but I can manage it if you take it easy.'

Henry got up from the table and they headed back towards Tom's apartment complex. The street was still crowded with shoppers, and a very agitated policeman was trying in vain to stop cars parking on the narrow roadway. Every time he tried to stop one driver from abandoning his car, another one stopped further along, and he rushed frantically up and down, blowing on his whistle and doing a lot of arm waving.

'Crazy country in many ways, you wouldn't see a policeman losing it in England.'

'Not in Ireland either, they tend to keep the cool.'

'We can come back for the car after these two and go around to the others.'

Tom shook his head. 'No need. I like living where I am, and if either of the two down there is any good, we'll do a deal right now. I don't want to spend a week house hunting.'

'Fair enough, you know your own mind.' Henry was puffing a little as they crested the hill. 'Slow down, Tom, I'm not as fit as you are.'

Tom let them in through the garden gate and they took the lift to the top floor. Henry tried several keys, and eventually they opened the front door to the apartment. It was dark and smelled stale, nobody had been here in a while. Henry found the mains switch; several lights came on and the fridge shuddered into life. The shutters were motorised, and sunlight flooded the living room as Tom pressed the button.

'It's quite a place.' Tom was impressed. 'A lot bigger than the one I'm renting downstairs, the extra bedroom makes a difference.'

'Decent furniture too. He didn't cut too many corners when he was kitting it out.' Henry rubbed his finger along the edge of a heavy oak sideboard; this stuff was all quality, the owner had spent a lot of money on the furnishings.

Tom rapped his knuckle on the widescreen TV. 'Plenty of fancy toys too, that plasma wasn't cheap.'

They ducked under the half-open shutter and walked out on the large balcony. 'West facing, evening sun, just what I like.' Tom was feeling at home in this place.

'Do I get a feeling that you don't want to look at to many others? Like what you see?'

'I don't want to look at anyplace else, this place is ideal for me, just a matter of doing the right deal.'

'He's asking one forty, but I know he'll take one ten at a pinch. He'd want a reasonable price for the furniture though, he spent a lot on it, needs to get some of it back.'

'You said he lives in South Africa; will he be coming back to close a deal?'

'No, can't come back for some reason, not sure of the story, he has a lawyer here with power of attorney, the lawyer can sign the deal. It's a fairly new development as well, so the legals wouldn't take any length of time.'

'Can you get him on the phone? Offer him a hundred, close in seven days; cash up front, no messing with mortgages and all that.'

'I can't see him doing it.' Henry shook his head but he scrolled through the address book in his phone and called the owner of the apartment.

'Mister Haas, Henry here, I have a buyer with cash, interested in making an offer for your apartment. I'm afraid it's lower that we expected, but we are finding it hard to get interest in this development at the moment. He's only prepared to offer a hundred thousand, but he can close in a week, or less if necessary.'

Henry put the mobile on speaker so that they could both hear the response. He motioned to Tom to keep quiet. The seller wasn't happy. 'I couldn't possibly take a hundred thousand; I'm looking for one forty. Look, I know we discussed one ten at a pinch, try and get him up to that and we have a deal.'

'Leave it with me, Mister Haas, I'll call you back.'

'What do you reckon Tom, one five maybe?'

Tom nodded. 'Call him back and hit him with that.'

The seller answered immediately. Henry again motioned to Tom to keep quiet, and put the phone on speaker.

'I'm sorry, Mister Haas, he has offered another five, but this buyer has viewed other properties today and he intends to buy today, he's heading back to Ireland in a few hours and I'm afraid we'll lose him. That's as far as I can push him.'

The seller sighed resignedly. 'Ok, Henry, you're the man on the ground, I need to let it off. Go for it, but nail him down, get a deposit and see if you can make some of it back on the furniture.'

Henry turned off the phone. 'Congratulations, Tommy lad, that's a sweet deal. You could turn it tomorrow for another twenty five easily, we can't get apartments in this building; people go mad for them.'

'I think I owe you dinner, how about we go up to Benahavis later on and have a good nosh?'

'Sounds good.' Henry was smiling, happy at the outcome. 'Harry Corbett is over for the weekend, I'm playing a few holes with him after lunch. Do you mind if I bring him along as well? He wanted to meet you anyway, so kill two birds...'

'No problem, more the merrier. What did Harry want me for?'

'No idea, time will tell. Maybe he wants to buy a timeshare.'

'I don't sell timeshares, just fractional ownerships.'

***

They climbed the steep steps to the Barbacoa restaurant in Benahavis; the small mountain village above Marbella was a diner's paradise, with restaurants everywhere you looked. Tom liked the Barbacoa; the owners and staff were friendly and the food was always good. The smiling waiter greeted him with a handshake and showed him to a table on the terrace. 'Welcome, Senor Tom. Nice to see you.'

'Good to be back, Paco. You know Henry, and this is Harry, from Ireland also.'

The waiter took orders for the drinks and they browsed the menus.

'I heard you bought a place, you did well.'

Henry laughed. 'He did very well, bought a bargain. How much are you going to give him for the contents, Tom? I reckon he paid at least forty thou for everything in the place.'

Tom smiled and sat back. 'I thought you said he lived in South Africa?'

'Yes, Capetown.'

'Then why would I give him anything, I'll go for a quick close and wait until the last minute and tell him I don't want the stuff.'

'But it's quality stuff, best of gear.' Henry was puzzled at Tom's attitude. 'You should offer him ten thou maybe.'

Tom swilled the wine around in his glass. 'Why would I offer him anything? Is he going to come over from Capetown and move it? Maybe I'll give him grand at the last minute, just to confirm that I'll own the stuff.'

Harry shook his head. 'I wouldn't like to cross you, Tom, have you no conscience?'

'I'm a salesman Harry; I wouldn't have any use for a conscience.'

They ate in silence for a while. The steaks were large and juicy, and their table gave them a good view of the street below and the strolling tourists. A babble of voices drifted up from the promenading day-trippers; it was noticeable that many were English and indeed that quite a few Irish accents could be heard.

Tom commented on the new phenomenon of Irish people making their way to these lesser known places, away from the package holidays and a week spent close to the beach.

'That's what I wanted to talk to you about, Tom.' Harry wiped his mouth with is napkin and folded it carefully. 'I have a plan, and I want you to be part of it.'

'A plan? Me?' Tom was caught off guard.

'Listen to him.' Henry interrupted. 'Harry told me about it today on the golf course; I think its well worth looking at, right up your street.'

Tom looked at Harry. 'I'm all ears, curious as to what you've been planning for me.'

They listened as Harry told them of his idea. He had just negotiated a sole international agency agreement for a huge development down the coast. There would be a thousand apartments, two hotels, a golf course and a range of commercial outlets including a supermarket and several restaurants. This would be huge; one of the biggest projects on the coast and the launch prices would be attractive.

'I think that the time has come for Irish buyers to get on the international property bandwagon in a big way. I can see signs of it in my business; we are getting enquiries all the time now about Spain, and we're selling a steady number of apartments through Henry without even trying.'

'But what has this to do with me?'

'I hear it from Henry, and I can see it myself; you are one of the sharpest salesmen around, and you know this coast well by now. I want you to come back and work for me in Ireland; you're the key to making this happen if we move it up the scales.'

Tom was surprised at the proposal. 'I'm doing grand here though, and I like the place well enough. Anyway, I can't see myself taking a cut in earnings just to move back home.'

'Who said anything about a cut? I reckon we can both make a fortune on this. I'm having one last big throw of the dice before I retire, I want to put four or five million in the bank in the next two years, and you can do pretty well out of it too. Probably a lot better than you're doing now, and selling stuff that you can stand over.'

'Nothing wrong with the stuff I'm selling now.' Tom was indignant at the inference.

Harry held up his hands. 'Sorry if I offended you, but you know yourself that real property is a step above the myths that your friend Alan is peddling. Anyway, maybe the money will tempt you, I honestly believe that you can earn a lot more than you're earning now.'

Henry had been staying out if it, but he turned to Tom. 'I looked at the figures on Harry's projections, if he hits the kind of sales that he's expecting you'll both make a fortune.'

Tom was all ears now. 'How much are we talking about?'

Harry leaned in over the table and spoke quietly. Work it out for yourself, a thousand apartments, we have first pick at them before anyone else, so in theory we could sell them all in a year, prices about a hundred and twenty upwards, and we have eight percent of that from the developers.'

Tom did a quick calculation. 'Eight percent? That adds up to a lot of moolah. How much of that would be mine then?'

'I'll do all the advertising, I reckon on going down the exhibition route, works well in the UK. Bring in the punters in their hundreds to a big venue, loads of good display material, the usual, like you see at the big shows in London. You flog the stuff off; we can break the development into phases to stop flooding the market, maybe get to raise the prices a bit on later phases. I reckon we can easily sell twenty or thirty places any weekend, maybe more than that if you get a good run at it, and I'll give you at least a grand a pop for every sale closed. One percent of the sale price to be exact. If you give it one good year, you should earn at least a million.'

Tom absentmindedly stirred his coffee. 'This is all a bit sudden, but I like the numbers anyway. Can I think about it for a few days?'

'Don't think too long, I need to get moving on this. I have an exhibition booked for three weekends from now, and I'd need you back in Dublin in less than two weeks.'

'You should go for it, Tom; you're wasting your talents selling timeshares.' Henry looked at the young salesman. 'Chance of a lifetime, lad; Harry is all right and you'd be better off away from Alan Merchant, he'll be trouble in the long term.'

***

'You are leaving, I know you are.' Carmen was crying.

'How do you figure that out?'

'Last evening you bring to the bins much garbage, many trips over and back, and now there is nothing left in the apartment, no food, no personal stuff. I know you are leaving.' She hugged the pillow to herself and wept bitterly.

'I was going to tell you, but I didn't want to hurt you, didn't know where to begin.'

'You could begin by telling me always the truth maybe? You are one fucked-up person, Tom, you know that? You have no emotion, nothing, nada.'

She got out of bed and dressed quickly, throwing pillows and cushions around angrily as she looked for her clothes. 'You Irish, all the same, you want to sleep with Spanish girl but you no want to stay with her.' She slammed the door as she ran from the apartment.

Tom sighed; it was a pity about Carmen. She was a decent sort, had helped him move from the rented apartment up to his new place, and had made sure he got back his full deposit from the place downstairs. She was right though, he was never going to be serious about her; there was something about an Irish girl that was so much more appealing. There would be plenty more fish in the sea, and there would be time enough for fishing when he got back there.

The plane was less than half full and he slept for much of the way. The announcement from the captain woke him; they were beginning their descent, only half an hour before he would be back on Irish soil. It felt good in a way, especially now that Walter had managed to find him a great apartment that would be ready to live in before the end of the month. In the meantime, Walter and Pamela had invited him to stay with them.

It would be good to live in a proper home for a while; this bachelor living could be a bit boring sometimes. A part of him wanted to settle down, to find a nice girl and make a proper home with her, but maybe that would happen now that he was making the move back to his native city. The apartment in Puerto Banus would keep; it would make a useful base for any time he had to come to Marbella on business, and his capital would be appreciating a lot faster that it would in the bank in Gibraltar.

It had all happened quickly after that dinner with Harry Corbett in Benehavis. They had driven out the following morning to the site at Playa Verde and met with the developer and the marketing manager on site. The project was huge, and the excavators were busy moving truckloads of earth around to create the landscape that would merge the golf course with the buildings that would surround it. The sales manager pointed out the location of the various blocks, as well as the hotel and clubhouse, and Tom quickly grasped the overall picture. He was able to get a mental picture of where each block was to be built, as well as being able to visualise where each apartment type would be located and the aspect that would be enjoyed by each property. He was mentally drawing up his sales pitch, working out a strategy for selling every apartment no matter which way it faced or on which floor it was located. His selling experience in the timeshare development would stand him in good stead; he had developed an ability to carry a mental three dimensional picture of each apartment building in his head, so that he could make a sales pitch for almost any apartment and sound like he knew it intimately.

Alan had been good enough about his leaving under the circumstances, and paid him most of what was coming to him. 'We're nearly out of this one anyway, Tom, and I think I'll give it a rest for a while. It's getting harder and harder to stay ahead of the newspapers and the television stations and their investigative journalists; everybody wants to throw mud on our profession nowadays.'

The taxi man was foreign, hadn't much to say except to ask for directions several times. Tom wondered at the rapid changes taking place in his native city; it was a first to meet a taxi driver who seemed to have no idea of where he was going.

Harry was at work before him the following morning; this guy wasn't afraid to get stuck in. His desk was piled high with brochures, enlarged photos and all kinds of publicity material. He pulled out two photocopies of advertisements from the pile and handed them to Tom.

'Welcome to Sunspots, Tom, sorry I haven't time to roll out the red carpet. These two ads are going into two of the Sunday papers this week; I need you to write the editorial to go in with them.

Tom was surprised. 'Do the newspapers allow you to write the editorial? I thought that that was their job.'

'If you saw what I'm paying for the bloody ads to those gangsters... There's no bloody way that I'm giving them that amount of money and not be allowed to write my own editorial.' Harry was under pressure.

'Ok. Give me a general idea of what you want; do I just praise the development up to the skies, no hint of objectivity or anything?'

'That's the idea. The last thing I want is objectivity, just make it half and half, deal with the development itself and then the prospects for investing in Spain. Make it look like Connor Morris wrote it, his name will go on it. There's a copy of the paper there from last week, give you an idea of his style, stick to that more or less.'

'And the same with the other one, the one for the Globe?'

'Yes, but don't make it the same article obviously, just the same message. Do it in the style of Murtagh, make it look like he wrote it. Shouldn't be too hard, the fucker is nearly illiterate by the look of a lot of what he writes. I think he just copies out brochures and puts his name to them, nice handy way to make a living.'

Tom cleared a space on the desk in the corner and got stuck in. It was good to be back in a normal work environment, even if the sky outside was grey and the rain wasn't far away. If truth be told, he had been getting tired of selling to the losers who trudged in to Pueblo Alto Blanco; the only good thing about that place was the money. Still, it should be even better here if Harry had his sums done.

By ten o'clock the two articles were ready for the Sunday papers. Harry looked them over and nodded his approval. 'There's a great property journalist lost in you, Tom, these are better than the junk that those two peddle every week. They'll have an easy ride this week, all their work done for them. Pull out the best pictures you can get from the developer's stuff and let them off. That's that job done at least.'

They retired to the meeting room with two cups of coffee to discuss strategy. Harry seemed to have most of the problems figured out; he had obviously been thinking about this operation for several months. He outlined the way that they would approach the selling process; they would need to sell substantial numbers of apartments if this was to work.

'I'll have to spend a lot of money on advertising, but that's not your problem. I'll also do a lot of public relations work, but the idea of hundreds of Irish people owning homes abroad is one that will tickle the fancies of the media people and it should be easy enough.'

'So do you want me to have an input into that side of things?' Tom didn't want to take on anything that he wasn't paid to do, but he also wanted this business to work and was prepared to give it his best efforts.

'You know the Costa del Sol like nobody else in this business around here, so it would be useful if you did some bumph on that side of the business. I'll need you to write the website material as well, background stuff on Marbella and the Costa generally. I can do bits on the golf; I didn't waste all my time down there.' Harry smiled.

'I don't know much about websites, I never really did anything in that area.'

'Don't worry about the mechanics of it, just write the stuff and I have a technical guy that will shove it into the right place on the website. Keep it like the stuff you wrote this morning, half on the location and the development, and half on the potential for investment down there.'

'So what about the exhibitions? Where will we do them?'

'I have the ballroom of the Old Masters Hotel booked every second weekend for the rest of the year, and hopefully we can fill it every time. We start on Fridays at lunchtime, about twelve o'clock so we can catch the office crowd, and we work late Friday nights. Then we do two full days on Saturday and Sunday, start about ten and finish whenever the last person has left more or less.'

Tom liked the sound of it all, it seemed like there was a chance to make an awful lot of sales if Harry's PR could talk up the idea of investing in Spain. Sunspots seemed to be a very focussed company, and it enjoyed the backroom backup of Harry's existing estate agency business, so it carried very little in the way of overheads. There was one thing worrying him though.

'Will you and I be enough to deal with a stampede of sales if the crowds are big? Do we need some extra salesmen?'

Harry pondered the question. 'I don't want to hire anyone else, I think you and I can do most of it, what do you think yourself?'

Tom paused, if they took on another salesman it would dilute both their returns, but on the other hand what if they lost sales because people got tired waiting to see someone? 'I have an idea that might be worth considering. I have a friend in the business here, and he doesn't work weekends, maybe he could do the Sundays if they prove to be busy.'

'Is that Walter, the guy you're staying with?'

'Yes, top class salesman, old enough to give an air of respectability as well when he teams up with yourself.'

'Might be a good idea, do you think he would like to work a few weekends? Maybe his boss wouldn't be too happy to see him working for the opposition.'

'I don't really see a problem; I mean they aren't in the foreign property business, and Sunspots is completely separate from your own home-based operation. Anyway, if you're happy to go with it, I'll ask him tonight.'

They went through a list of items that Harry had made on his notepad, and Tom was surprised at how much of the detail the older man had thought of. He had obviously been working on this project for months, and his grasp of the small issues was impressive. In particular, his idea about the lawyer was very good.

'There's this guy Miguel, he's a young lawyer from De Silva's law office in Marbella. He'll fly in every Friday of an exhibition weekend and set up his stall in the hotel. Ostensibly he'll be there to give Spanish legal advice, but in reality he will be there to make sure that as many sales as possible are tied up on the day. He can take deposits as well as tying down the buyers, and that will mean that we have already moved on that buyer to the legal process in Spain, so we can more or less forget about them. We can then spend the early part of the week chasing up the ones that have paid deposits but haven't talked to the lawyer.'

'I think that an essential part of the selling process will be to persuade buyers that they should deal with the lawyer, save themselves a trip to Spain and all that.'

'Yes, but not at the expense of dropping a sale, some people will think that we are out to do them anyway, and they'll be paranoid about dealing with a Spanish lawyer. In fact, De Silva's are one of the best firms in that area; they won't do any better if they go out to Spain and look for their own lawyers.'

Harry pushed back his chair; they seemed to have covered most of the issues and everything looked to be well on track for the first exhibition. 'How about yourself, Tom; any questions, or do you see any problems?'

'No, I'm happy enough with the way it's going, just raring to go really.'

'Just one thing.' Harry looked straight at Tom. 'I know you're a great salesman, and I also know that you are ruthless, that's why you're here to some extent. We may differ on how far each of us would be prepared to go to get a sale; I'd ask you to keep this operation clean, don't sell to anyone who doesn't know what they are getting into, don't promise them too much regarding rental income from these properties for instance, keep it the upper side of realistic but no more than that.'

'You don't believe in 'buyer beware'?' Tom was smiling. 'I don't see it as our role to give advice on property, or investment either. Surely we are just there to sell the stuff and it's up to them to check out the background to what's on offer.'

'Look, I know we have a different view on this, and in many ways I have no problem with that, but all I'm saying is that I'd rather lose a few sales than to walk someone into something that they can't afford.'

'But surely if they are coming in to us to buy an apartment, then it presupposes that they can afford it?'

Harry pondered Tom's response for a moment. 'There can always be the odd exception to the rule, the person who gets carried away with it all. Somebody like that really throws themselves at our mercy; all it takes to ruin their lives is for an unscrupulous salesman to tell them for instance that they can get fifty two weeks rent a year at so much a week, and that maybe they can borrow the money for the property and it will pay for itself. I just don't want Sunspots to go down that road.'

'But don't you accept that it might be a valid sales pitch to suggest that you might get a hundred percent rental? I mean, it does happen sometimes, so why not mention it?'

'Tom, we could argue the toss about this all day, but I'm just saying, let's not screw anyone, ok?'

'You're the boss, but maybe we should concentrate on the rule rather than the exceptions; I want to sell as many of these apartments as possible, and maybe the other issue won't arise. Anyway, I take your point.'

***

The ballroom looked great. The video presentation that the developer had produced was running constantly in a loop, projected on to the big screen on the wall opposite the entrance. The large display posters were stretched on their aluminium frames, showing off the development at its best. Three desks were set along the entrance wall, one each for Tom and Harry; Walter would be joining them on Saturday and Sunday. Miguel, the young Spanish lawyer, had a desk on the side wall, along with a huge display stand manned by the Spanish tourist board. This had been Tom's idea, although late in the week, but the Spaniards were delighted at the opportunity to show their wares and had even been persuaded to pay for the stand.

The Flamenco guitarist had been Tom's idea as well, and his lively strumming in the lobby area helped give a festive atmosphere to the place. A long table by the other side wall had rows of coffee and tea cups lined up on it, and the hotel staff had been instructed to keep the tea and coffee pots replenished every half hour.

Harry looked around at the layout; he was pleased, it had been a hard morning's work setting up all the displays. 'Now that it's done, I'm suddenly nervous. If nobody turns up, we're both fucked.'

'They'll turn up all right.' Tom was more optimistic. 'If we only go by the media interest all week, we seem to have struck a chord with the public. I think that we are on the cusp of something very big.'

'That will bring its own problems.' Harry was in a pessimistic mood. 'If we start a big ball rolling, every other company will jump on the bandwagon and we might get lost in the rush. We spend the money to create the market, and everybody else benefits.'

Tom was less worried. 'We have a six month start on them, and we have a great product. It'll take anyone else several months to get off the start line; we're ahead and we just need to stay ahead.'

'True enough, but that reminds me, we need to be aware that some of the customers here over the weekend will be spies from other companies, picking our brains. If we spot that line of questioning, make sure we give nothing away.'

'Good thinking. Once we're aware of the possibility, we may be able to spot them. Feed them a line of bullshit maybe; send them off on a wild goose chase.'

Harry laughed. 'Just be careful that you're not feeding the bullshit to a genuine customer, someone who just asks a lot of questions. I know what you mean though; we should be able to spot some of them at least.'

Tom looked at his watch. 'Ten minutes to lift-off, time for a quick cup of coffee before my public arrives.'

Harry nodded towards the door. 'Too late, here they come.'

A couple of people wandered in through the doorway, looking around hesitantly as though they might run out again at the slightest excuse.

'Don't make any loud noises, you might frighten them away.' Harry spoke quietly as he watched the tentative progress of the first customers towards the display stands.

'I'll cut them off at the pass.' Tom strolled towards the door and came up behind the first customer, a middle aged man in a business suit who was studying the displays intently. 'Good afternoon, sir, welcome to the show. Can I be of assistance?'

'No thanks, just having a look.'

Tom wasn't to be deterred. 'Let me tell you what's on offer. We are here today to give investors a chance to buy one of the best developments in Spain at pre-launch prices, a chance to buy a home in a dream location at a better price than you will be able it get it for when it comes on the market in Spain.'

'So they're not built yet?' At least he was starting to bite.

'No, this is an off-plan opportunity, but the development is covered by a bank guarantee; your funds will never be at risk and we expect strong capital appreciation on this one.'

'How much do you think it will come up by?'

Tom paused, conscious of Harry's instruction not to oversell the project. 'It's hard to predict exactly, but I'd personally be expecting at least fifteen percent annual growth between now and the completion date. This is the first phase; the later phases will be on offer at higher prices, that's for sure.'

The man was suddenly interested. 'So are you buying it yourself?'

Tom swallowed. 'Of course, I've taken two so far; probably take more if I can get hold of the money.' A little lie never hurt. 'So, are you interested in a few?'

The man was doing a mental calculation. 'Yes, ok, can I book them here?'

'Yes of course, come with me and I'll pick out the best ones. You're our first customer, so you get the pick of them.

Tom picked up the sheet that listed each apartment along with its size and price. He turned his back and made ticks opposite two apartments; these would be the two that he was supposed to have bought for himself.

'These are my own two, that's one of the best locations, view over the golf course, hard to go wrong with those.'

He was surprised how easy it was; the man was seated at Miguel's desk in minutes and was writing a cheque for the deposits. Compared to selling timeshare to tourists, this was a pushover. At this rate, he would be hitting the weekend target before tonight.

The woman who had arrived at the same time was hovering around, eavesdropping on his conversation with the first customer; he caught her eye and smiled at her. 'Do you want to beat the rush, madam; get the pick of the best apartments?'

'I'm just looking thanks, getting information; it's a big step you know, buying a place in Spain.'

'It is and it isn't, this is a no-brainer in many ways. These are on sale at a pre-launch price, they can only go up. It's a matter of whether you want to buy at today's price or wait until they get dearer, that's all that's at issue really.'

She looked nervous. 'But is my money safe? I was left some money by my grandmother, and she loved Spain, so I would really like to own a place there. I'm just afraid of what might happen; you hear so many stories…'

Tom sensed an opening. 'That's why you should buy from a reputable Irish company, you know who you are dealing with and your money is safe.'

She was wavering, coming around; he could almost see the cogs meshing in her brain. 'Did I hear you say that you bought some of them yourself?'

'Of course, too good to pass up. I'm not going to keep them, just wait until they are completed and flip them.'

'What do you mean, flip?'

'I'll just pay the deposit and wait until they are almost completed, that's in about two years time, then I'll sell them on at a profit. All I'll have invested will be the deposits, and I'll double what I invested at least.'

'Can you do that?'

'Of course, that's what all the big players do, just roll them over and move on to the next off-plan project and do it all again.'

'That's a comfort to know that they are set to go up, but really I just want to have a place there for holidays and maybe for longer times later on.'

'You could always buy two, one for yourself and one to flip; it would leave the one you keep very cheap.' Tom was conscious of Harry's warning, but a sale was a sale.

'Do you think that would work?' She was getting greedy now, the ball was on the penalty spot; just a good kick into the top corner should do it.

'Let's go over to the desk and pick out the two best ones before the crowds get here.' It was proving to be easy, like taking candy from babies, and the show hadn't even started yet.

Chapter Six

The weekend passed in what could only be described as a blur. There was no doubt that Sunspots had hit a winning streak; the market was ready for Spanish property and was reacting accordingly. Long the preserve of the rich elite, anyone could now afford a home in the sun and it was just a matter of getting this message out, and the advertising and publicity were paying dividends. The show was attracting the interested as well as the curious; selling to the first was easy but the second only presented a small challenge for the Sunspots team.

Walter called Tom over to his desk. He was trying to sell an apartment to a middle aged couple who were full of suspicion and sure that they were going to be conned out of their money. They had already taken up half an hour of his time and other buyers were hovering around; it was time to push them hard and make them jump either way, time for the double act that worked so well when a washing machine had to be sold to a reluctant customer.

'Mr and Mrs Elliot, this is my colleague Tom Murphy; he's an expert on Spain and all things Spanish, and especially on this development. He can advise you on your best options.'

Giggs to Rooney.

Tom gave them his best smile. 'Which apartments are you looking at? I know every apartment in this development, there isn't a bad one in it but there are always a few that are extra special.'

Rooney passes to Giggs.

'They are trying to get the best value for money.' This was another way of saying that they didn't want to spend too much. *Giggs back to Rooney.*

'I bought one here myself.' Tom pointed to one of the cheapest north facing apartments. 'I always buy north facing, its cooler in the hot sun in Spain, and the Spanish won't buy anything else. It's much easier to resell a north-facing apartment on the local market, and of course you're paying less for it in the first place.' *Rooney boots it up the wing.*

Walter caught the pass and ran with it. 'That's what I was saying, these four here are underpriced for the local market, you should grab one while you can. *The ball was coming across the middle, time to put it away.*

Tom looked at Walter, time to go for it even if it scared them off; there were too many buyers still floating around, no sense in wasting time on these two. 'There aren't four left any more, I just sold two of them and I know that the other two will go today. You should grab one of those now while they're available; you'll have to pay a lot more after today for something that good. Will I put you name on this one; it's the better of the two?' He raised the pen and made to write their names on the sheet.

'Ok, I suppose so, yes, why not?'

Goal!

***

The team retired to the bar at nine o'clock and Harry ordered the drinks. Miguel was on his way to the airport with a bulging brief-case; he would be very busy for the next few days. The stands were taken down and packed away, and all the material was stored in one of the hotel's store rooms for use at the next show. It had been a gruelling weekend, but the results had been spectacular.

'Seventy four I make it, give or take; an amazing run of sales for one weekend.' Harry raised his pint in a toast. 'Here's to the best sales team ever assembled; I never in my wildest dreams thought we could do that level of business, I would have been happy with thirty, ten a day.'

Tom was very content with what he had achieved over the weekend. He had sold more than thirty five himself, and he was being paid for every one sold by Walter as well. He had agreed to give Walter five hundred for every sale, so between his take from these and his own sales he had earned nearly fifty thousand for the weekend, not a bad haul by any means.

'Of course not all of them will stick; we may have some dropouts when they go home and realise what they have done, but I don't think we'll lose many.' Harry was cautious as usual.

'Don't forget that we have a lot of enquiries as well, ones that didn't buy today. If I'm worth my salt I should be able to squeeze a

good few sales from that list over the next few days.' Tom knew that
he could push a lot of these less decisive buyers over the line in the
course of a half hour phone call. 'As well as that, most of the ones we
sold here have already signed contracts with Miguel, so I don't think
we'll see too much slippage.'

Walter was tired; he was slumped back in his seat. 'I never saw
such a feeding frenzy, never saw so much money cross the table. This
caper is a salesman's dream.'

'I could sleep right here.' Tom was putting into words how the
others felt; the excitement that had kept them going at full tilt all
weekend had drained away and left them all exhausted.

'So, do you guys want to go and eat something, or take a rain
check on it?' Harry looked shattered too; the few days had worn
him out.

'I think we should call it a day, all I want to do is go to bed, and
I'm only the boy around here. I can only imagine how you old guys
must be feeling.' Tom was past being interested in food, and he knew
that if he had another drink he would stay at the bar for too long
and wouldn't be able to move in the morning. 'I'm heading home
anyway.'

Harry finished his drink and pushed the glass across the bar.
'I think we should all get out of here, maybe meet up tomorrow
evening for a bit of grub, talk over the few days and see how we can
do things better for the next show.'

Walter stood up and drank the dregs of his pint. 'See you tomorrow so, and thanks guys. I haven't enjoyed myself so much since I
worked in Milton's. Great to have the old double act back together.'

'It works well.' Harry liked Walter and he had observed how the
two salesmen could manage to close a reluctant sale with ease. 'The
whole is greater than the sum of the parts and all that.'

Tom pulled on his coat. 'Ok, amigos, until tomorrow, hasta man-
ana.'

* * *

Harry stopped at Tom's desk, he was carrying two coffees. 'Have
you got ten minutes, in the boardroom?'

The smell of fresh coffee was enticing; the deli hadn't been open earlier when Tom was coming in to work, and he missed his caffeine fix. He followed Harry into the big meeting room.

'How are we doing, Tom, are we all set for Friday?'

'We're not, but we will be; it's still only Wednesday. Have I ever let you down?'

Harry smiled. 'No, but there's always a first time.'

'Not when it's my money too, I want this thing to keep working for us the way it has been. Seems to be rolling along well, how are we doing overall?'

Harry turned on the laptop and peeled the lid from his coffee as he waited for the machine to start. 'I'll give you the exact numbers in a second, I was working on them last night, but it's about five hundred and thirty units so far, still well ahead of target.'

Tom tore off the ends of two sugar packets and sprinkled them into his coffee. 'That's about where I figured we were at, not bad for less than six months work.' He was very satisfied with his move back from Spain, nearly half a million in the bank so far and no sign of a slowdown.

Harry scrolled through a spreadsheet. 'It's actually five hundred and thirty three confirmed sales, and another fifteen that still have to have contracts signed, so best case scenario is five forty eight assuming we don't lose a few.'

He opened the morning paper. 'Have you seen this?' He pointed to a colour advertisement that covered half a page.

'Tom looked at the paper in amazement. 'Who the hell are Sunny Climes? Never heard of them. Cheap stuff too, but its all up in Alicante, scrag end of the market.'

'It's a new player, just started up. The guy that's running it is Sean Simpson, he owns a couple of bicycle shops, Simpson's Cycles. You know their advertising jingle from the radio, 'Simpsons, Simpsons, Simpsons, big wheels in bicycle sales'. Annoying bloody tune.'

Tom had heard it a few times. 'Hang on; let me check my folder for a minute.'

He returned to the room with his file of contact sheets from the shows. 'There it is, he was at one of our shows just six weeks ago, I have his details here. I never copped him as being in the business.'

'That's the problem; he wasn't in the business up to now. We don't have any way of defending ourselves against that kind of competition. We spotted the two others easily enough, but God knows how many spies we have had, pretending to be customers.'

Tom was annoyed. 'I remember the bastard, wasted half an hour of my time and then bought nothing. Just picking up sales technique for this stuff. Bastard!'

Harry was none too happy either. 'You remember we thought that we were six months ahead of any competition? Well this guy didn't exist in this business six weeks ago. They're snapping at our heels, Tom.'

Tom was concerned as well, but less worried. 'Look, we are leading the market, let's stay there. It would be naïve to expect that we would have it to ourselves without competition, but I'm not worried about Simpson or anyone else. As long as we have good product and it's well priced, we can stay ahead.'

'We can do without this kind of thing all the same.' Harry was a worrier, never stopped thinking the worst.

***

'Tom, have you a minute?' Harry was dealing with a well-dressed blonde woman at his desk.

'Just a second, this couple are about to buy the best apartment in the project and I want to be there to share the moment.'

His customers smiled and relaxed a bit. They had been dithering around for ten minutes, but Tom hadn't pushed them; it was Sunday lunchtime and the big rush was still to come. The man was on board but the woman seemed less convinced. 'Do you really think that this is the best one?'

'Absolutely. Always buy a west-facing apartment, you get the evening sun, and that's the time you need your terrace to be in the sun. It's too hot to be out there at midday, but the evenings are when we do most of our outdoor living.'

The man pulled the cheque book from his pocket. 'This is exciting; who do we make it out to?'

'Playa Verde Developments, thanks. Yes, I love uniting nice people with good properties; I still find it very satisfying every time. I know you will get great pleasure out of this property. Now can I introduce you to Miguel?'

Tom left the couple with the lawyer and walked over to Harry and the blonde woman. She had appeared younger from across the room, now he could see that she was older, maybe in her late forties. She was dressed in a smart business suit, and was heavily made up. Harry appeared to be nervous around the woman; he was standing up awkwardly with his hands on the back of his chair, and he seemed ill at ease in her company.

'This is my colleague Tom Murphy, he knows this project very well and he has lived in that area for the last year and a half. Between us we can answer any questions you might have. Tom, this is Tania Sherry, she is interested in making a large investment in this project.'

The woman stood up and shook hands with Tom; she exuded confidence and appeared to be used to being in charge of any situation. 'Hello, nice to meet you. Yes, I am interested in the possibility of making a major investment in Playa Verde.'

'Well, you've come to the right place.' Tom immediately regretted his attempt at levity; the woman wasn't smiling. He recovered ground as quickly as he could. 'What scale of investment had you in mind, Ms. Sherry?'

'I would like to look at the possibility of buying an entire block and then engaging your firm to sell it on for me in about a year's time. I believe that the Spanish market is showing signs of a re-awakening and that there may be profits to be taken.'

Harry had used Tom's arrival to give himself a chance to gather his thoughts. 'We would of course be interested in such a deal, but the only complete block left is block five, and that hasn't been released yet, so we don't have prices on it. I am assuming that that phase will command a higher price than the previous phases.'

The woman turned to Harry and responded sharply. 'No question of higher prices if I buy an entire block; in fact I expect a discount on the total if I buy such volume. I also want to look at the project and I expect you to take me there and show it to me, at your expense.'

Tom moved to reassure the client. 'We would certainly look at escorting you to Spain to view the project. We don't of course go down the route of paying for inspection visits, that is a ploy used by less reputable companies to sell poor quality investments, but one of us would be pleased to escort you there of course.'

Tania Sherry gave Tom a withering look. 'We will go on Wednesday, back Thursday, buy the bloody tickets and arrange accommodation and stop pontificating about what lesser firms do. If you want my business, I will see you at the airport on Wednesday morning.'

Harry looked at Tom. 'Arrange for two tickets, Tom, yourself and Ms Sherry. We can make an exception in this case I think.'

'Thank you.' The woman turned quickly and left the room, her heels beating out a rapid staccato as she crossed the hard floor and headed down the corridor to the outside.

Harry ventured a slight smile. 'Jesus, that one knows what she wants; I wouldn't like to be married to her. Still, it would pay us well to give her a small discount and to get shut of a big chunk of the project in one swoop with no advertising or exhibition costs. And the beauty of it all would be that we would get a commission again for the sale of the block in a year's time.'

'That's if she's on the level and not a dreamer.' Tom was being cautious.

'There's always that, but it's worth a chance. At the worst it will only cost us the flights, and you have to go over anyway. Maybe you could put her up in your place, keep her away from the sales offices around the port and keep an eye on her twenty four seven so she doesn't get in with any other agencies out there.'

'Ok, I can do that, good idea.'

'And keep your hands off her; she's a fine looking woman.'

'Don't worry; she's old enough to be my mother. As for fine looking, I reckon they're not real.'

Harry laughed. 'She looked a bit top-heavy surely, but maybe she's just well made. I don't want you finding out anyway, just get the sale and get her back here in one piece.'

'Believe me; I have no interest in older women.'

Harry poked him in the ribs. 'Of course, if you think it might make the difference...'

'Tom.'

'Yes Walter.'

'Don't fall off, we're not insured for that kind of thing.'

***

'Another bottle of the Rioja please.' Tania Sherry was hard work; Tom felt like a sheriff taking a prisoner back to jail. He had stuck like glue to his client all day, showing her around the project in Playa Verde and pointing out all the features of the scheme. He was tired now and not in the mood for entertaining this pushy middle aged woman; he would have preferred to have gone back to his apartment and have an early night, but he had his orders.

The apartment; that was another thing. Why had he agreed so readily to put the bitch up in his apartment? Apart from the headache of having her in his face every waking hour, his reputation had now firmly disappeared down the drain with everyone he knew in Puerto Banus. Carmen had been working in the office when he had dropped by to collect his keys; she had practically thrown the bunch at him and turned sharply on her heel. 'Stupid Irish bastard, now you sleeping with your grandmother. I am glad I dump you.'

The only way to pass this evening was to get enough of the wine inside him to numb the tedium, but at least Miz bloody Sherry seemed to have the same idea and they were now on their third bottle. Pepe invited him to try the wine but he waved him on. 'Just fill her up, Pepe, don't interrupt the flow.'

The food had as usual been superb; Tom felt comfortably full from the grilled sole that had barely fitted on to the large oval plate. He passed on desert but Tania had ordered the lemon tart, although she had barely touched it when it arrived and seemed to be concentrating on drinking as much as possible of the vintage Rioja. Mesa Bella never failed to please and was ideal for entertaining a major client, but at this stage Tom was of the opinion that maybe it might have been easier to sell the fifth block off one apartment at a time. At least there would be less questions; this woman wanted to know everything.

'Are you married, Tom?'

'No, never got round to it. Not yet anyway.'

'Stay away from it as long as you can. I tried it twice; neither of them were any use. I was a good housekeeper though; I kept the fucking houses!' She screeched with laughter as she poured more wine into Tom's glass.

'You're a good looking young fellow, that combination of sandy hair and an olive skin is very attractive to women you know, do you get that from your mother or your father?'

'My father was red haired in his younger days; my mother was the daughter of an Italian family that came to Ireland years back.'

'That explains your skin colouring. Is she beautiful?'

'She was, she died when I was quite young.'

'I'm sorry. Have you a partner or do you still live at home?'

'No, I live alone. There isn't much time for a social life in this job. Anyway, I never met the right woman.'

'Would you like to settle down? Most men have a vague ambition of life with a nice wife and kids.'

'I suppose I would, but there's plenty of time for all that.'

'Time passes a lot faster than you think. Before you know it, you'll be thirty, and it's a slippery slope from there on. Did you never meet anyone that you thought might be the one?'

'One or two, I met a nice girl before I went to Spain, but I lost touch with her.'

'What was her name?'

'Amanda. She was cute. I tried to find her one evening recently but I couldn't remember where her flat was. It's a long story.'

'Nice name, Amanda. So, how much commission do you get from the developers to sell this project?'

Despite the wine, Tom was alert enough not to disclose the commission level. Irish buyers were happiest if they thought that you were getting nothing for selling property, or cars or washing machines for that matter. It was important never to disclose that bit of information. If this lady knew that they were on a massive eight percent of the total she would want that amount of a discount, or she might go directly to the developer and offer him a better price than he was getting. No, important to keep shtum on the old commission.

He fielded the question. 'I'm afraid that that is commercially sensitive information, between us and the developer. If other companies knew how little we were getting for this marketing work they would have an advantage on us, I'm sure you understand.'

She smiled across the table at Tom and raised a glass. 'Of course, just wondering, just a friendly interest, but of course I understand. Here's to a successful outcome to our discussions this week.'

Tom felt the wine beginning to go to his head. His eyes wandered to the deep cleavage that Tania Sherry was displaying, wondering if the enormous globes protruding from this woman's chest could possibly be the real thing. Surely not?

'They're real all right.'

Tom was embarrassed, had his gazing at her breasts been that obvious? 'Real, what do you mean, what are real?'

She hefted her boobs in both hands. 'These puppies, they're real right enough. Real fucking expensive.' She cackled with laughter.

Tom laughed nervously. 'I wasn't wondering, honestly, they look fine to me and all that.'

'Best that money can buy. Cost me nearly ten grand each, but worth every penny, don't you think? I know you were looking at them, men always look at them.'

Tom was uncomfortable at the way the conversation was going, he wasn't used to middle aged women going on about their boob jobs. 'They look great, not that I noticed, but now that you mention it...'

'Senor, Senor, more wine.' She was getting louder.

Pepe was smiling politely, but the smile was strained. 'Of course, madam, another bottle of the Rioja?'

'Bring it on, my toy boy and I are having a night out and Sunspots is paying, no expense spared. Open it up there, Senor.'

Tom caught Pepe's eye and tried to convey his apologies for the behaviour of his guest; he liked this restaurant and he didn't want to offend the friendly owner or his staff. The old man tapped the side of his nose with his index finger; the matter would never be mentioned. He poured the wine into the two glasses and she swallowed half of hers in one gulp.

'Drink up, Tommy, the night is young and so are you.' She cackled manically again, laughing at her own jokes.

Tom was a little worried now, wondering what was coming next.

She leaned forward and spoke conspiratorially, her voice slurred. 'My mother had a black sense of humour, calling me Tania Imelda

Teresa Sherry. Can you imagine; how a girl had to live with that all through her teenage years? Can you?'

Tom couldn't see any problem with any of the names, maybe Imelda was a bit old fashioned, but the bitch must be nearly fifty, and maybe it wasn't such a bad name fifty years ago. He was feeling the effects of the wine and she was looking a bit blurred; he tried to focus on her face but his eyes kept being drawn back to those enormous breasts.

'I don't see any problem with those names, very o.k. names most of them actually, no problem.'

'Are you thick? Can you even begin to imagine how a girl felt when her initials were T.I.T.S? Tits, that's what they called me in school, fucking Tits. And me as flat as a fucking wardrobe door. But not any more, no sir, I have tits now, oh yes I have, best ones in the shop. Haven't I, Tommy baby?'

Tom started to laugh, he couldn't help himself. Tits, what a set of fucking initials. And what a set of bloody tits, they were like two footballs stuck to her chest. He almost choked at the good of it; Jesus, wait until I tell Harry and Walter he thought to himself.

He focussed on the mad woman across the table; she was laughing as well, juggling her two huge breasts in her hands and shouting 'Tits, Tits!'

The other diners were laughing too, politely behind their hands, but all conversation had stopped and she was now the centre of attention. The waiters were hovering nearby, smiling as she roared again.

'Tits, Tits, now I have tits, haven't I, Tommy baby? You'd like to see my tits, Tommy baby, wouldn't you?'

A woman at the next table was able to contain herself no longer. She almost choked on her food, and burst out laughing as her embarrassed husband tried to pretend that everything was normal.

Tania grabbed the bottle and sloshed wine into the two glasses, downing hers in a couple of swallows and rapidly filling it up again. 'You're not drinking, Tommy baby. Eat drink and be merry; Sunspots is paying.'

Tom resignedly swallowed most of glass and refilled it again. If she was going to get plastered, then he might as well get some more inside him. It would cover his embarrassment if nothing else.

'The doctor asked me if I wanted peaches or melons.' Her voice was slurred now, and getting even louder. Every diner in the restaurant was silent, waiting for the next outburst.

'What do you mean, he told you to eat fruit?' In his drunken state Tom was lost at this turn of conversation.

'No, he wanted to know how big I wanted them.' She hefted her breasts in both hands. 'I went for the melons Tommy. A peach is only a mouthful, but a melon can feed a whole fucking crowd.'

The woman at the next table was now laughing out of control, her shoulders shaking and tears running down her face. Tania turned her attention to the woman's hapless husband, who had been trying in vain to hold the laughter in.

'What are you looking at, you pervert? Did you never see a pair of tits before?' She peered at the woman and looked her up and down. 'Not at home you didn't anyway.'

Drunk as he was, Tom knew that this had gone too far. He took his companion by the arm and attempted to lead her to the door. Pepe and two of the waiters were hovering nearby, doing their best to keep straight faces, but not always succeeding.

'Pepe, I'll drop by tomorrow and pay you, ok?' Tom didn't want to let go of her arm, he just wanted to get her out of the restaurant.

The owner waved him away. 'No problem, Tom, whenever you are passing, it's ok. I have called you a taxi; he is here in two minutes.'

Tom led his staggering client through the crowded restaurant between the tables of laughing diners; all of them were trying to avoid catching the gaze of this crazy woman in case she turned her attention on them. She stumbled and almost fell as she came down the steps, grabbing at a large statuette of a naked woman whose raised arm held an unlit candle. The nearest waiter made a dash and caught the statuette before it could be smashed to pieces on the marble floor, and a bizarre tug of war ensued until she finally relinquished control of the candle-holding figure. She gave one last look at the small breasts on the statuette. 'Peaches, only peaches. Not a real woman. Take me home, Tommy baby.'

* * *

Tom felt ill; he had drunk far too much and his head swam as soon as he tried to close his eyes. He could hear her blundering around

100

between the spare bedroom and the bathroom; with any luck she would soon go to bed and stay there and he could stop worrying about her. This was the last time he would ever put up a client in his own apartment; it was just too complicated.

It had been hard enough getting her to go to bed. She sang all the way home in the taxi and made several suggestive comments about his youth and lack of experience with women, but he managed to get her inside the apartment without any major incident. She wasn't finished yet though.

'Look what I found!' The bitch had gone to his sideboard and pulled out the brandy bottle. 'Bring glasses, Tommy baby, brandy makes me randy, never know your luck.'

In the hope that she might get so drunk that she would fall asleep and stop giving him a headache, Tom got two brandy glasses from the kitchen and poured a decent measure for her and a smaller one for himself. 'Here's to a successful trip, Tania, and I hope that you liked what you saw.'

'Oh I liked what I saw, Tommy. Question is, did you like what you saw?' She hefted her expensive breasts and jiggled them at him, leering at him drunkenly.

'Very nice, I'm tired though, see you in the morning.'

'Well if you're not too tired, I won't lock my door.'

Tom was drifting off to sleep when he heard the door handle. Shit, he thought, she's in the wrong room. Too late, he realised that she knew what she was doing; the mad bitch was in the bed and grappling with him.

'I know you like them, Tommy. You can play with my melons, I know you want to.' She grabbed his hand and placed it firmly on one of the enormous breasts. She was naked and she stank of wine and brandy fumes.

He wanted to throw her out, but in his drunken state he vaguely knew that he needed to keep her on side. After all, if she bought the full block he stood to pocket more than a hundred grand for his efforts. Worth putting up with the bitch for a couple of hours for that kind of money.

He was shocked at how hard the breast was; it was nothing like a real one, felt more like a football that had been over inflated. The football comparison was all the more apt by the thick scar that ran all the way around the lower surface, like the stitching on a soccer ball.

'Yes, Tommy baby.' She grabbed his right hand and slapped it on the other giant protuberance. He felt the other scar and the laughter started low down in his body, rising to the top in spite of itself. It was football time. He squeezed the left breast.

Rooney has the ball.

He squeezed with his right hand.

Rooney to Giggs.

'Oh yes, Tommy.'

Giggs back to Rooney.

Yes, Tommy, don't stop, don't stop.

He plays it down the field.

Oh yes, Tommy.

Here comes the cross, there's nobody in the goal.

'Tom darling?'

'Yes, Tania.'

'How much will you charge me to sell the block if I buy it?'

What a question at a time like this. 'Eight percent, eight percent.'

Goal!

***

The alarm on his mobile phone seemed to be coming from somewhere far away. His head throbbed and his throat was raw, he was never going to drink wine again. He looked at his watch on the bedside table; it was eight o'clock and he had to get the client to the airport by half past nine. First problem would be to get her up; he turned over in the bed but she wasn't there. He hadn't heard her get up; he must have been out for the count.

Tom crawled out of bed and headed for the shower; she wasn't in the other room either, where the hell had that woman got to?

Five minutes under the hot shower and he felt a bit better; he switched on the coffee machine and got shaved and dressed; the face looking back at him from the mirror was haggard and his eyes were bloodshot. It was true what Walter always said, stay away from the wine and stick to the few pints; it pays on the morning after.

The coffee pot was almost full when the doorbell rang. Tom tapped the intercom button and saw Tania Sherry's face looking back at him on the small monitor screen; he pressed the key button and let her in.

'It's a lovely morning out there; I had a great walk around the area. You live in a classy part of town, Tom.'

'It's not bad.' He wondered at her cheerfulness, she had drunk a lot more than he had, and she was as fresh as a daisy. He wondered whether to mention the fact that they had ended up in the same bed; he was embarrassed and he hoped that nobody ever got to hear of it. Harry and Walter would never let him live it down.

'Are you ready to drop me to the airport?' She was all business again; it seemed that she wasn't going to mention last night.

'As soon as I finish this coffee.' And not a minute too soon; it would be a relief to get rid of her and have the day to himself to finish his business in Spain before the evening flight. Just get her to the airport and see the back of her; her and her bloody artificial tits.

The journey to the airport was strained. Tom was studiously avoiding any mention of last night's transgression, and Tania was talking business as if nothing had happened. He dropped her outside the departures door and took her bag from the back of the car.

They shook hands. 'Thank you, Tom. I'll be in touch in a week or so, as soon as I have digested all the information.'

'Ok, I'll call you on Monday week.'

He drove back towards Marbella and onwards to Playa Verde, making a mental note as he passed the restaurant to drop in on the way back and pay the bill. It was going to be embarrassing meeting Pepe after the display by that crazy woman last night, but he would have to bite the bullet and do it. He knew that Pepe and his staff were far too polite to even mention the antics of the night before, but he was still cringing at the thought of having to meet them. At least there had been nobody in the restaurant who knew him; that would have been the pits. It was bad enough that Carmen had probably already told everybody in the saxophone bar that he was now sleeping with old women; he knew that the story would have improved with the telling. Carmen would get her own back for being dumped.

Marco was in the site office when he arrived at the site. The developer was happy to see him; Tom and Harry were selling more apartments than he had ever thought possible, and they were already talking of future plans when Playa Verde project ended. He stood up to greet Tom and called an assistant to bring coffees.

'Tom, I want you to meet somebody. This is Juan Carlos, he is developing a small project just down the road and he would like to speak with you about marketing.'

The older man stood up and extended a hand in greeting. 'Hola, Senor Tom. It is good to meet with you; Marco tells me many good things about your company.'

Hello, Juan Carlos, I'd be interested to see what you have on offer. We are doing very well with Playa Verde, but it's always useful to have another string to our bow. What are you building?'

'Just down the road, Playa Hedor, we make a small project with just twenty apartments, maybe twelve not sold and it is almost completed. Maybe it will suit somebody who wants an apartment immediately, and it is not so expensive also.'

Tom liked the look of the developer, he seemed to be an honest and open kind of guy, and he was obviously a friend of Marco's. 'Give me an hour here with Marco and I'll drop by your site and have a talk, say twelve thirty?'

'Ok, Ha' Luego.'

Marco gestured in the direction of his friend's departure. 'Nice guy, normally I would say that his problem is his problem, but maybe it's no harm to help him a little. I think we sell the full project easily anyway, especially if the Irish woman buys the full block. You think she will buy it?'

'I'm not sure, I'd be hopeful though. I mean, she would hardly have come out here for two days unless she was serious.'

'Yes, when she is spending her own money to view the project, is not for fun, no?'

'It wasn't her own money, it was ours.'

'Oh, that is not so good, but we live in hope, yes?'

***

Tom almost drove past Playa Hedor, but spotted the half-hidden sign at the last minute and turned down the gravel drive to the small site office. This was no Playa Verde, no fancy marketing suite and tarmac site roads, but the apartment block was well designed and looked to be well built, low rise and in a horseshoe shape around a small garden with a pool. The landscapers were hard at work, using a mobile crane to hoist large palm trees into position; this would look like a mature site in a matter of weeks.

Juan Carlos led him through the apartment block and pointed out the features of the units. All were well finished, and all had a southerly aspect with views towards the sea in the distance. The place lacked the scale of Playa Verde, and didn't have the golf course and hotel, but it wasn't bad at all.

'This is very good, compares well with Marco's place, and all south facing. Everyone wants south facing, should be easy to sell these, I reckon. Nice job.'

The Spaniard beamed with pride. 'I am a small operator, not like Marco, but I am a builder all my life and I like to build good projects.'

'So, how much do you want for these, and how much commission are you paying?'

'I think maybe ten percent less per square meter than Playa Verde, and I pay of course the normal two percent.'

Tom smiled. 'There's no way we could do it for that kind of money, but maybe we can come up with a plan to get you your money and give us our ten percent.'

'Ten percent! No, no, Senor Tom, never could I pay this kind of commission; it is most of my profit you understand. No. I am sorry, I can get local agent to sell for me at two percent.'

'Yes, but they haven't sold it for you, have they? I think we can solve your problem and also ours.'

The older man shook his head. 'Ten percent, not possible.'

'Let me explain my idea.' Tom was beginning to form a strategy that would give the developer a better price and at the same time provide Sunspots with a decent commission on any sales that might arise. 'We can market Playa Hedor as an exclusive development, at say twenty percent more than Playa Verde, and we take ten percent of the selling price. You make a lot more money as well.'

The Spaniard rubbed his head in amazement. 'You really think people will pay so much, this is just a normal project, not exclusive at all; why would people pay more?'

'People always think that more expensive is better. When I used to sell cars, and we had maybe three cars the same, we always marked one of them more expensive and it always was the one that people wanted. Do you want to try my idea? After all, you are selling these too slowly and you need to clear them out and get on to your next job.'

'Ok, I try your way. What do I have to do?'

'Nothing, we will do it all. I'll take some pictures and you need to give me any artist's drawings of the project and any other publicity material you have. Also, you must immediately remove the project from the local agent and get him to delete it from his website; we have to have exclusivity and we can't have it on sale at two prices.'

Juan Carlos smiled broadly. 'Ok, Senor Tom. We try it your way for three months, but we need sales badly, so do your best please.'

Tom shook hands with the Spaniard. 'Six months or nothing, but we will sell it, don't worry.'

The big billboards along the motorway were more frequent than he had remembered from the last time; they advertised new developments all along the coast. There was definitely a surge of new projects coming on stream in the Costa del Sol. A lot of them were now being built out close to the motorway, away from the beach but surrounded by new golf courses. There would be no shortage of product if the demand for Spanish property kept growing.

He braked and turned off at the Calahonda exit; there was plenty of time to spare before the flight and he wanted to check out the timeshare project at Pueblo Alto Blanco, to see if it was nearly finished and whether Alan and his sales team were still working there. A couple of minutes brought him to the narrow road leading up the hill, and he swung the rental car off the road and into the car park of the Pueblo.

The sales office was closed, no sign of Alan, and all the signs had been removed from the windows. The second and third blocks looked to be more or less complete, and the site fence had been moved back to the front of the fourth building. The builders were busy on the site, and Tom was glad to see that all the apartments looked like they would be delivered, and quite soon at that. He peered in through the window of the sales office to see if there might be anyone around.

'That's him, that's one of them.'

Tom didn't realise at first that the woman was referring to him; he was stepping back from the office when he saw her reflection in the glass. She was rushing towards him, an elderly grey-haired woman in pink shorts and a yellow tee shirt, followed by a woman of similar years in a floral print summer dress who was waddling from side to side as she struggled to keep up with her.

He turned away from the building and looked in astonishment at the woman who was hurrying in his direction. She looked to be in her late sixties, at least, and from her accent it was clear that she was English. She didn't look too happy.

'You, you're the one, bloody crook. I'm getting the police for you, you thief.'

'Are you talking to me? What are you talking about?'

The woman was breathless from running, and she found it hard to get the words out.

'You stole. Our money. Thief!'

'I stole nothing. What are you talking about?'

By this time the other woman had arrived to join them. She was calmer, and she spoke quietly.

'You sold a timeshare to my sister and her husband, and now he has passed on and she needs to sell it back. She really needs the money.'

'So, what's stopping her? I'm not a thief; she got what she paid for didn't she?' I don't like being called a thief. I'm sorry about your husband madam by the way.'

'Thank you. But what about my money? Will you give it back to me?'

'I only worked for the company, I don't know anything about re-sales, you'll have to talk to them. I don't work for them any more.'

'Stop pretending that you don't know about it, it was a deliberate crime, the police know about it. You're all going to jail.'

'I'm not aware of any crime, we sold fractional ownerships of apartments here, that's all I know.'

'You did, and you sold a lot of them twice too. That's how you swindled us.'

'Twice? That's the first I heard of anything like that. Are you serious?'

'Bloody right I'm serious, sorry for the swearing, but we've lost our life savings and I'm going to lose my house in England because I can't pay the mortgage on my pension. I doubt very much if you don't know about it.'

'I don't, really. I only worked here; I'm as shocked as you are. What happened?'

'You must know. All the apartments in the first block were sold twice. They had been sold originally to various people and then the developer went bankrupt, but the people that bought them still owned them because they had paid for them and the ownership was registered. You and your friends sold timeshares in them, but you had no right to sell them, and we lost our money. I can't believe you didn't know.'

The woman sat down heavily on the steps and started to cry. Her shoulders slumped and she looked old and beaten. Her sister put her arms around her shoulders and looked up at Tom.

'May the good Lord forgive you all, you greedy people. Do you not care about ruining people's lives?'

Tom was shocked at what Alan had done, but he knew that he needed to talk his way out of this situation as quickly as possible. He was going to take the rap for Alan Merchant's shady dealings if he didn't think fast.

'I really knew nothing about all of this, I just worked here and I was laid off a few months ago. I came back today to see if I could get my wages. I wasn't paid for my last two months. I thought that there would be someone here today, they're usually here about six o'clock every evening.'

They were wavering; he could see that they wanted to believe him. A little more of the sales pitch and he would be able to get out if here before the police were called and he found himself in a Spanish jail.

'It's nearly five o'clock now; I'm hoping they'll be here in an hour. I have a dentist's appointment in ten minutes, but it would be great if you could hang on here until I get back, delay them for a few minutes so that I can tackle them about my wages. And your money too of course.'

They cheered a little at his words; the woman looked up at him gratefully.

'I'm sorry for attacking you; you're as much a victim as we are. Will you really help us to get our money?'

'Of course, just delay them for me in case I'm not back at six. I'd better rush off or I'll be late back.'

'You do that, get moving and hurry back. You're a good lad.'

Tom's legs were shaking as he ran to the car and headed off down the hill. He looked in the mirror to see if they had taken his number, but there was no sign of them looking in his direction. The two elderly women sat forlornly on the steps of the apartment block, looking lost and bewildered. It was impossible not to feel sorry for them, but he needed to get out of there and catch his flight. He felt his stomach heaving; just before he joined the motorway he pulled over to the side and got out of the car, and vomited on the verge. He didn't know if it was the shock of the meeting with the two women, or the amount of drink he had consumed the night before, but he didn't feel good at all. He got back in the car and headed for the airport.

CHAPTER SEVEN

Harry was sceptical. 'Playa Hedor? Why did you take on such a small project? It's hardly worth our while and it only diverts buyers from Playa Verde.'

'We had no choice. If someone like Sean Simpson got hold of it and started selling it at the price that Juan Carlos wanted for it, we'd look bad.'

'You're right, never thought of it like that, it's too close to Playa Verde and people would make comparisons all right.'

'Apart from that, we needed a project on our books that would make Playa Verde look cheap, and by persuading him to raise his prices to twenty percent above ours we make our stuff look like it's great value.'

Harry raised his hands. 'I should have known better than to question your call on it, it makes sense to me when you put it like that. Do you think we'll sell any of it though? You only have six months exclusivity on it and he'll start to sweat even earlier than that if we don't deliver a few sales.'

'I reckon we can sell a few no problem, people always want the more expensive option. Anyway we can always invent a few sales to keep him happy; we'll be out of Playa Verde in well less than six months, especially if Miz Sherry comes across. Once we're out of the big project, Juan Carlos' problems won't be my problems.'

'What about the client, do you think she'll deliver, did she like the project?'

'She liked it all right, but she was bloody hard work. Next time you can do it, or send Walter, I'm knackered keeping her entertained for the last couple of days.'

'Do you think she is serious though?'

'I did, but Marco put a doubt into my mind when he asked if she paid her own way to Spain. He was a bit dubious when he heard that we picked up the tab. We'll have to wait and see; if she hasn't got back to me by the weekend I'll call her Monday morning.'

'That's all we can do, in the meantime let's try to clear out block four this weekend. Life goes on.'

***

The client sitting across the desk was new, but the type was familiar enough. Tom and Walter had started compiling a list of buyer types to pass the quiet periods that seemed to hit the shows from time to time. It was usually 'a feast or a famine' as Harry described it; they were either overrun with buyers or the ballroom was quiet. It did give them a chance to grab a sandwich and a coffee before the crowds descended on them again, and it allowed them to share a joke or two, usually at the expense of the buyers.

Walter had started it; he had devised a categorisation system that could be used to describe every client that came into the room by putting them into half a dozen different categories. Everything from 'The Quiet Man' who was reluctant to part with any personal details to 'Johnny Cash,' who wanted to use his Spanish property purchase to launder a large wad of cash.

This one was definitely a 'Dirty Sanchez.' He sat in front of Tom but seemed to be focussing his gaze at a spot on the wall some distance behind the salesman; he didn't want to look anyone in the eye.

'What's the story in this place, is it worth buying there for the, you know yourself?'

Tom wasn't going to humour him, but a sale was a sale. 'I'm not with you, worth it for what exactly?'

'Ah you know, is there good pickings around there?

'Pickings?'

'For birds like?'

Tom looked him over. The buyer was a florid faced man, probably in his mid fifties, and with black hair slicked down with oil and combed over to cover a bald patch. Tom decided to humour him; he leaned forward conspiratorially. 'Oh yes, best part of Spain for women, the place is full of them.'

'And is there a good few birdhouses around there?'

'Birdhouses?' Tom was not too sure what he meant.

'Ah you know, birdhouses.' He dropped his voice even lower. 'Jiggy jig houses, you know yourself.'

The penny dropped with Tom, he had never heard either term before, but it was clear enough what the man wanted, a home in the sun with a few brothels nearby. If that's what he wants, that's what he'll get, he mused. 'Of course sir, the place around there is wall to wall em, birdhouses. Yes, lots of birdhouses in that area, you wouldn't have to go too far for some jiggy jig.'

The man relaxed a bit. 'I have a few quid, want to buy something out foreign, and I heard the birds in Spain were, you know yourself.' He sniggered knowingly.

Tom wondered if this old fool had any idea of what a ridiculous figure he presented. Overweight and middle aged, his comb-over hairstyle crowning a bright red face, he was hardly some woman's ideal man. Still, he had 'a few quid,' and Tom would now separate him from it as quickly as possible.

'These properties will be ready in less than two years, but you might like to make a few visits between now and then to check on progress. I'm sure Mrs...' he looked at the sheet where he had written the details ...'Mrs. O'Reilly will understand that you will need to make a few business trips to the area.'

The old fool was on the hook, he figured that Tom was a man who understood. 'Inspect a few birdhouses as well, hehe.'

'Yes indeed, you could do that for sure. The Spanish girls like Irish businessmen.'

'Do they, is that a fact? I heard that all right. You're a man of the world, I can see that. Can you advise me maybe what's the best value in this place?'

Tom flipped through the floor plans, looking for the special unit. Every development had what they called a 'special' apartment, one that would never sell once the place was built but which might just possibly be shifted off plan. He found it on the ground floor, the apartment that bridged the underground ramp to the parking garage; anyone living in that place would have to put up with the constant noise of the automatic gate opening and closing.

'Look at this one.' Tom put on his most friendly tone. 'Great apartment, ground floor and east facing, gets the morning sun. Always buy east facing if you can, easier to resell. Great place to bring an auld bird as well, you know yourself.'

'Is that the best one in it?'

'There are others, but none of them as good as this one; there's no point in me offering anything less to a businessman like yourself. It's definitely the best one that's left; will I put your name on it?'

'I like your style, I'll take that one so. Let the good times roll, what?'

* * *

The woman was reluctant, he knew that he almost had her but she was holding back. You got customers like this some days; they wanted a property in Spain, and they had the money, but there was never a good time for them to make a final decision and they would happily go from agency to agency for years without committing. They had to be given a huge push to dislodge them from their positions, and Tom had a few weapons in his armoury that usually could be counted on to shift them. This one though would need a fairly hefty prod.

'The next phase will cost fifteen percent more, so in other words you can save money now and the property will be worth at least fifteen percent more when it is complete.' That often worked.

'I'm just not sure, I mean they seem like good value, but how do I know that they are worth what you are asking? They might seem cheap by our standards, but they might be very expensive over there.'

It was the opening he had been waiting for. 'We know that they are very reasonable by Spanish standards, there is a development down the road, not half a kilometre away, exact same apartments more or less and twenty percent dearer.' He pulled out the brochure for Playa Hedor.

The woman was suddenly very interested. 'Why is this one more expensive? It looks like the same size apartment, and as you say it's on the same road.'

'No reason, the Playa Verde project is very keenly priced of course, maybe the other one is smaller and has that bit of exclusivity about it, but hardly makes it worth over twenty thousand euros more. No, Playa Verde is just amazingly good value.'

'I'm curious about the smaller development, where can I buy it, do you sell it?'

'Yes of course we do, we are agents for it but to be honest we don't bother much with selling it because it is expensive compared to Playa Verde. It sells itself anyway; it's a great place and closer to the beach as well.' Tom sensed an opening for the smaller project;

this woman fell into Walter's 'superior intellect' category, someone who knew that she was a cut above the herd and didn't mind paying to prove it.

'I'm definitely interested in this Playa Hedor place; can you show me the layout of those ones?'

Tom opened the file and took out the drawings. All the apartments were south facing, no 'special' units anywhere in the building. 'These are all excellent, all looking over the gardens and the pool, sun for most of the day on the terraces. It's a great project, even if it's a little bit more expensive.'

'Do you think that they will appreciate?'

She was on the hook. Time to land a killer punch.

'I just bought one myself, this one here.' He pointed out one of the apartments that had already been sold by Juan Carlos.

'You must have a lot of faith in the development so.'

'I have, I mean I bought in Playa Verde too, but I bought one here for investment, I think that they will do very well.'

'I would like to buy two of these please; can you pick out the best two, maybe the two next door to your one?'

'Those are still free, won't be there for long, wise choice madam. Can you come over here and meet Miguel, he is an independent Spanish lawyer and he can advise you on how to proceed.'

***

Tom joined Harry in the boardroom and pulled the weekend's sales sheets from his briefcase. Harry was already working, the laptop was open and he was inputting details from the master sheet. He motioned to Tom that he wanted to finish the spreadsheet.

'Well?' Tom sorted the customer sheets in alphabetical order. 'How did we do?'

'Exceptional weekend, I'm not sure where this is going to end but we are making serious money, Tom. Seventy two sales in Playa Verde and six in the small project; that's the one that surprised me, I never thought that people would actually pay more for the same apartment.'

'I always thought that we could sell a few of the dearer one, but I didn't think it would be more than the odd one. One woman bought two of them, can you believe it?'

'To be precise, she didn't so much buy them, more a case that she was sold them.' Harry laughed at the thought of the snobbish lady being convinced that dearer was better. By the way, any contact with Tania Sherry?'

Tom grimaced. 'Don't remind me of that bitch, I called her a dozen times but I keep getting either her voicemail or 'may have their unit powered off' message. My feeling is that she's gone, she just wanted a free trip to Spain.'

'But surely she didn't go to all that trouble just for two days away? I mean, she didn't get a few days on the beach or anything. Fair enough, she got well looked after, but nothing out of the ordinary.'

Tom put his head in his hands. The memory of the night in Mesa Bella and in his apartment was embarrassing in the extreme. It might have been worth it if she had bought the block, but now...

Harry looked at him in amazement. 'You didn't, did you?'

'I don't want to discuss it.'

'You mad bastard, you did, it's written all over your face. I don't believe the things you will do for a sale, you worry me sometimes. Fine looking woman though, don't blame you in one way.'

'Drop it Harry, I'm not in the humour for talking about it.'

'Ok, ok, I won't mention it again. What about block five, we're going to have to start selling it next week, there's only about twenty left in block four.'

'I'll leave a message on her phone that we can't hold it beyond the middle of the week, but my gut feeling is that she has done a runner on us.'

'Ok, in any case we need product, and if we haven't that we'll have to start selling some of the new project that Henry has, plus whatever's left in Playa Hedor.'

'Only a handful there, can you believe that people paid so much over the odds for a few apartments?'

'I can't help thinking sometimes, are we selling stuff that is a bad investment? The Playa Verde project will make money for buyers for sure, but will that little block down the road ever be any use as a resale punt?'

'You worry too much Harry, that's the buyers' problem. It's our job to sell it, but it's their job to buy it if you know what I mean.'

'Maybe so, but I don't want a pile of manure hanging over my head. Keep it clean, Tom; don't get too carried away and get us get a bad name over a few extra sales.'

'You're the boss, Harry.'

'I wonder sometimes.'

***

Tom poured a cup of coffee and popped another slice of bread in the toaster. It had been a busy weekend and he wasn't going to rush into the office; time to have a leisurely breakfast for once. They had done well again over the few days of the exhibition; they had cleared the fourth block and moved on to the fifth, the project would be sold out in a couple of months by the look of it. Harry seemed to be still anxious to carry on with the business, even thought his original idea had been to make a quick killing on the Playa Verde job and to retire with a nice nest egg. Marco had bought another project that was ready to go, and they could start selling it almost straight away if they sold out Playa Verde. It was time to take stock.

Things had worked out well since he had moved back from Spain; Harry's promise that he would make a lot of money had proved right, and to be fair Harry had always paid him as soon as the contracts were signed. The new apartment was great too, Walter had found it for him and made all the arrangements, and he had moved in a couple of weeks ago. The old apartment was rented through Walter too, as were the other two that he had bought for investment. The rising property market meant that he looked set to double his money in a couple of years if the upward trend continued, and the apartment in Spain was now rented full time to somebody who wanted a Spanish base until the Playa Verde project was complete. Everything was moving along nicely, no problems on the horizon and all well with the world. Tom was still the right side of thirty and he was already a millionaire, not bad for a fellow who couldn't pass an exam and whose teacher always said that he would amount to nothing. She used to joke that he would make a great artist, 'drawing the dole' was her punch line. Who had the last laugh now?

The only cloud on the horizon was the problem in Pueblo Alto Blanco; meeting up with the two elderly women had upset him more than he had thought possible. It was easy to sell things to people when you didn't have to deal with the consequences, but when it came back to haunt you like this, it was hard to handle. He felt really sorry for the two women, but what could anyone do? He understood why Harry was so insistent about not over selling, but then again you could be too careful and you would never sell anything.

He didn't think he would get arrested or anything, he had always been paid in cash by Alan and his name wasn't on any records that he knew of. As long as he kept away from the Pueblo site he would be fine; it had been a mistake going there but he had managed to talk his way out of it ok. The image of the two old women sitting on the step was still fixed in his mind though, and it would be hard to forget it. Every time he made a sale to an older person from now on, he would remember those two. He hoped it wouldn't put him off his game too much.

It was ten o'clock when he picked up the coffees from the deli and sat in the chair opposite Harry's desk. He tore the ends from the sachets and stirred the sugar into his cup, but it was clear that Harry was in a very bad mood. He was reading the morning paper and swearing, and it wasn't like Harry to swear, at least not like this.

'The fucking bitch, I'll kill that bitch if I ever set eyes on her. I'm sick to my stomach; can you believe what she has done?'

'Calm down Harry, can't be that bad. Who did what to you?' Tom was still in a good mood after the successful weekend. 'Drink your coffee and calm down, maybe I should have brought you a de-caf, relax you a bit.'

'I'm as sick as the plane to Medjugorje; I never thought a woman could be that devious. She wasted our time and money, and now she wants to take the bread out of our mouths.' He threw the paper across the desk to Tom.

Tom turned the broadsheet around and looked at the half page advertisement that glared back at him. A photo of white houses and blue skies, overlooked by a smiling picture of Tania Sherry, promised buyers the best value ever in Spain. 'Why buy overpriced apartments when you can own your own villa on its own grounds for less? Trust

Scorpio Properties to find you the best value overseas properties in the best locations. Trust Scorpio, your partner in Spain.'

Tom was stunned into silence. He felt used, like someone who has been conned out of his money by a three card trick merchant. He read the piece over an over. 'Make the move now to a better value investment in Spain, forget the rest, buy from the best. Scorpio works for you.'

'I'll kill the bitch.' Harry was very upset; Tom had never seen him so angry about anything. 'Can you imagine? The cheek of the bitch, going to buy a block no less, and too fucking tight to pay for her own ticket even.'

Tom put his head in his hands and thought of his trip to Spain. He was mad with himself for falling for the lies from that mad bitch, he had even given away the commission levels that they had managed to get from Marco; no doubt she had squeezed the same deal out of the developer in wherever she was selling these bloody villas. To think that he had ended up in bed with the sly old bitch, and even worse that a lot of people knew about it. He looked at the paper again, no mention of where the properties were located, just a freephone number. He angrily punched the number into his phone and got up from the desk.

'Are you going to ring her? I wouldn't give her the satisfaction of knowing that we were mad with her. Don't ring her, Tom, forget about the bitch and let's get on with selling apartments. The last thing we want is for her to put us off our stride. Let it go.'

'I just want to find out where they're selling, I won't talk to her.'

Tom retreated to the quiet of the boardroom with his coffee and closed the door. He was very annoyed with Tania Sherry, and even more annoyed with himself for not spotting that she was a phoney. Marco had spotted it straight away; anyone who was going to buy an apartment block would have no problem paying for their own ticket. The fact that she was a woman made it worse if anything, if a man had tried that stunt they would have spotted it. This devious bitch had pulled a fast one on them and it was a bitter pill to swallow.

He called the number and a female voice answered. 'Hello, Scorpio properties, how can I help you?'

'I'd like to have some more information about the Spanish villas that you have in the paper today.'

'Certainly sir, if I can take your name and details please.' The bitch had her contact staff well trained; get all details at the first call.

'Before we go there, I just need to know where you are selling. I might not be interested in the area you are dealing with.'

'Of course, I'm Catherine, we are selling in the South of Spain but we will be expanding to cover most of the Spanish coast. What do I call you? Just your first name, it's hard to talk to someone unless you know their first name.'

'Ok, Catherine, I'm Tom.' They were well trained right enough, very persistent.

'Ok, Tom, we are initially selling a development of villas near Alicante, about an hour from the airport. Private villas on their own grounds with pools if required, for less than anything you have seen on sale before now.'

'Where exactly, and how much?'

'Tom, I'm just the receptionist, I don't have all the details, would you like to speak with an investment advisor? I just need your second name please and I will put you through to someone.'

'Tom Jones.'

'And may I have a contact number for you, Mr Jones?'

Tom thought for a second and gave her his personal mobile number, no point in giving her his company number, it was too well known.

'I'll have someone call you back in a few minutes, Mr Jones, would you like me to have some information emailed to you? If you would like to give me your email address I can have you added to our mailing list and you will get automatic updates of all our properties.'

There was no doubt that they were well prepared, trained to get as much information from callers as possible. Scorpio was going to be a hard sell operation.

Tom had barely finished his coffee when the phone rang. 'Tania Sherry here from Scorpio, Mr. Jones, I understand that you have an interest in some of our Spanish offerings?'

He was shocked to hear her voice, he had expected a salesman. Maybe she was still recruiting and didn't have her full sales team in place. For a moment he was unsure as to how to proceed.

'Mr Jones, I see from the note that you want to know where we have properties for sale.'

'Yes.'

'We have a fabulous development at a place called Montana Fea, about an hour from Alicante airport. Villas in their own grounds; two, three, and four bedroom houses with sun terraces and optional pools, fabulous properties.'

'Well, Tania, congratulations on your new venture.' Tom tried to hide the irony in his voice.

'Tom Murphy, is that you? The call note says Tom Jones, that's naughty, pretending to be something you're not.'

'That's good, coming from you.'

She laughed loudly. 'Can you not take a joke, lover boy, it was all in good fun, and didn't we have a great few days?'

'I'm not impressed at the way you did things, Tania; a bit more openness would have left me with a bit of respect for you maybe.'

'Grow up, Tom, the world is a tough place and I'm a tough wom-an. Get over it, kid.'

'Just keep off my pitch, Tania; stay up in Alicante with the junk merchants and leave the Costa del Sol to us.'

Her voice hardened. 'Don't tell me what I can and can't do, Tom Murphy, it's a free market and anyone can compete, but I'm not out to go head to head with Sunspots anyway. I can deal with much softer opposition elsewhere, without fighting with you guys.'

'As long as we understand each other.'

'Look, Tom, I'm not out to fight with you, after all we have a bit of a history.' She was laughing again.

'Don't remind me.'

'Come on, don't tell me it was a chore.'

'No, hardly that.'

'Then how about we bury the hatchet, there's plenty in this for both of us, what do you say to dinner next week, on me?'

'I'm not going there again.'

'I'm not suggesting anything of the sort, just a civilised bite of food in a decent restaurant, make up for pulling the wool over your eyes last month.'

'No thanks, I'd rather pass on that one, Tania.'

'Come on; is a big lad like you afraid of a little girl like me? I'm not going to jump you. How about next Monday night?'

Tom thought about it for a minute, it would be better to have this discussion face to face, give her a piece of his mind. 'Ok, Monday night it is, but bring your credit card, you owe me, big time.'

'Ok, it's a date.'

'It's not a date, it's a meeting, get anything else out of your head.'

'Whatever you wish, I guess you don't fancy me any more.'

'I never fancied you, you just happened to be in the right place at the wrong time.'

'See you Monday, lover.'

***

Tom thought about his coming meeting with Tania several times during the week, he wondered what she was playing at. No doubt she was looking for more information, but this time she wouldn't be getting anything from him. If anything, he might give her a few bum steers, send her off on a few wild-goose chases and waste her time like she had wasted his.

He didn't tell Harry about his phone call; something held him back from keeping his boss fully in the picture. It was quite possible that Tania Sherry had a business proposition for him; why else would she be so anxious to meet him again? He wasn't kidding himself to think that she had any feelings for him; her willingness to climb into his bed was just a mixture of too much drink and her need to find out more about the Sunspots operation in Spain. Bloody whore really, but then what did that make him? He didn't want to think too much about that.

The sales material for Marco's new project, Playa Marron, had arrived and Harry wanted to make inroads into it as a matter of urgency. 'The tide is lapping at our ankles, Tom, the place will be full of foreign property agencies in another few months and we will get lost in the rush if we're not careful. I want to try to hang on to our lead for as long as possible but I can see a time coming when this becomes a free for all and descends into chaos.'

They had an exhibition arranged for the weekend, but it was one of four Spanish property exhibitions scheduled for the city that week. The bicycle man, as Harry called him, was selling his villas, as was Tania Sherry, and an English company was trying to cash in on the boom and had sent a sales team over for two days. They were unlikely to pose much of a threat; they had booked an obscure location that was off the beaten path, and anyway people preferred to deal with local companies. Sunspots was still the big player, and they had three projects on sale, the original two and the new one at Playa Marron.

Far from suffering from the extra competition, the show proved to be a big hit. The increased awareness brought about by the extra advertising in the broadsheets, and the feeling that bargains were still to be had but not for long, was driving people to the shows in ever increasing numbers. Tom had worked late on writing the editorial pieces for the newspaper property sections, and his glowing reviews of Playa Verde and Playa Marron were driving the punters into the Old Masters Hotel in their droves. The pressure was on the sales team, but they were well used to stress and they kept ticking off the sales. Miguel had brought an assistant with him from Spain and the queues had been shortened at his desk, and Harry's niece was marshalling buyers from the salesmen to the lawyers and weeding out the tyre kickers and timewasters.

This one was definitely a 'Care in the Community,' according to Walter's categorisation system. The man was anxious to talk, and had obviously found that a salesman at a property show was a perfect captive audience for his ramblings. He had to be got rid of as soon as possible, the floor was full of buyers and valuable time was being wasted.

'I want to buy a place in Spain, I'm going to sell my flat and move to Spain.' He was about thirty five, give or take a few years, and had a slightly haunted look.

'How much do you have to spend?' Tom was humouring him, looking for a chance to ditch him and get on with business.

'The lads said I'd get a lot of money for my place, it's worth a packet they said.'

'The lads?'

'Down in Fortune's bar, I go there on Fridays.'

'After work?'

'No, I don't actually work, I was on a few training schemes though.'

'And the lads, your friends are they?'

'Oh yes, I have lots of friends actually, seven actually, they tell me that I'd get a woman no bother in Spain, she'd wash and cook for me and all.'

'I think that the best person to help you would be Walter, the man over there, he's the man for relocations to Spain, I just do holiday homes.'

'He sent me over to you, do you have any brochures?'

Tom gathered a copy of each of the brochures and handed them across the table. The client opened a pull-along suitcase and added the brochures to a substantial amount of similar paperwork in the case, including as far as Tom could see another set of the same brochures. However there was still no sign of him moving.

'Do you think I'd get a woman in Spain? Have you a woman yourself?'

Tom ignored the second question, it was none of this idiot's business, and anyway he didn't have time for a woman in his life, not just yet while this crazy rollercoaster of work was still running.

'I reckon you'd get a woman no bother, they love Irish men, but we don't really do properties that are suitable for relocating, more rental properties or holiday homes, that sort of thing.'

'And who would sell me a place that I could live in?'

Tom wrote a telephone number on a piece of paper. Try this fellow, Sean Simpson, he's an expert in that field, relocates lots of people every year, he's your man. I wouldn't want to take your money and sell you the wrong thing, talk to Sean. Or better still, go and see him.'

'Ok, I'll do that, where would I find him?'

'He has a bicycle shop as well, down the quays, Simpson's Cycles. You'll get him there any morning.'

'Oh I know that place, 'Simpsons, Simpsons, Simpsons, big wheels in bicycle sales.' He sang the advertising jingle in a tuneless monotone.

'Ok, thanks for dropping in; good luck with Sean Simpson.'

'Big wheels in bicycle sales, big wheels in bicycle sales.' The man was slow to move; he just sat there, tunelessly repeating the jingle.

Tom drummed his fingers on the desk. 'Could you make room for the next customer please? Thank you.'

'Why would you need a sail on a bicycle? It wouldn't be much use to you would it? Not unless your chain was broken maybe.'

Tom tried to keep his temper. 'Not that kind of sail, can you move along now please?'

'But then again, unless the wind was blowing the direction you were going in, then it would be useful maybe. So you think I should go and see this Simpson man?'

'That's it exactly; he'll be glad to help. Now I'll have to move you along, that lady wants to talk to me.

As soon as there was a lull Tom grabbed a coffee and sat down at Walter's desk. 'Thanks for sending me a 'Care in the Community,' just what I needed at the busiest time of the day.'

Walter laughed. 'I had him at the last show as well, he was hovering around your desk then too but he didn't get near you, I thought it was only fair that you got to meet him as well.'

'Next time, send him to Simpson's, that's what I did.'

'Sean Simpson will love you for that, on top of all the calls you make to his secretary asking her for brochures.'

'She's Spanish, doesn't get the nuances, the Zoo must have a pile of Simpson brochures for Tom Lyons and Paddy Lyons at this stage. 'As well as Mr T. Iger and Mr. Leo Pard. Simpson's client database must read like the jungle book.'

'Anyway Walter my old buddy, don't send me any more like him, deal with them yourself. I reckon he's a few cans short of a booze up.'

Walter smiled. 'It's not right to mock the afflicted as they say, but he's delusional. His flat probably belongs to the Council and the local wags have persuaded him that it's worth a fortune and that he could sell it and move to Spain. He drags around a wheelie suitcase full of property brochures and holiday brochures, probably living on a few bob welfare. Anyway, Sean Simpson will have something for him, might sell him a bicycle.'

'Tell him to get on his bike, more like. You'd wonder sometimes though, wouldn't you?'

'Wonder about what?'

'Is it him that's mad, or is it the people buying all this stuff?'

***

Tom wasn't in the humour for dining out; the weekend had been tough and he really felt like spending a night in front of the TV and getting to bed early, but he was a little curious as to why Tania Sherry was so anxious to buy him dinner.

He hadn't been to the restaurant before, although he had heard of its reputation as one of the best places in town. He got out of the taxi and almost fell through the front door as the uniformed doorman jumped to attention and opened it suddenly. The place certainly looked expensive, with valet parking and the tables crowded with gleaming silverware on thick white linen. She was waiting for him in the small bar area, and within a few minutes they were being shown to their table.

'Would you like something to drink, madam, sir?' The waiter was hovering.

'I'll just wait for the wine, do you want something, Tom?' Different when she was paying herself maybe, in Mesa Bella she had demolished several gins and tonic before the food arrived.

'Nothing for me either, just the menu please.' Two could play at that game.

They ordered the food and kept the conversation light, Tom was still very annoyed with this woman and it was showing. Tania tasted the wine and indicated to the wine waiter that he should pour it. She raised a glass.

'Here's to future success, Scorpio and Sunspots, may we conquer the world.'

'I'm not sure I should be toasting your new company, seeing as how you picked our brains for your start-up.'

'Oh come on, Tom; all's fair in love and war. Don't hold grudges; let's get on with making some money. Plenty of room for us all.'

Tom reluctantly raised his glass. 'Good luck with your scheme, but try to stay on your own side of the road, ok.'

'Whatever you say.'

Tom had ordered a steak, and it arrived perfectly done, just as he liked it. Tania attacked the lobster slowly and methodically, like a scientist dissecting a specimen, but she just picked at the meat as she freed it from the shell and didn't seem to be eating much. Tom kept the conversation to a fairly good humoured banter and avoided issues of contention, no point in spoiling a good meal with uncivil conversation. By the second bottle of wine he was feeling a little more mellow; Tania Sherry was actually quite good company if you ignored the fact that she was a bit mad.

'What did you do before you got into the property business?' Tom knew nothing of her background, but she appeared to be successful at whatever it was that she did.

'I'm actually a doctor', she said, 'Doctor Sherry at your service.'

'That's interesting.' He couldn't resist a dig. 'But if you're a doctor, why didn't you do your own tits then?'

She took it well and laughed uproariously.

'Not a medical doctor, although sometimes I let people make that mistake if it suits me. I actually have a doctorate in Spanish, from Barcelona University; I spent two years there on post-graduate study.'

'So you speak Spanish fluently.'

'Of course, and before you ask, I did understand everything that your developer friend said to you that day on the site.'

Tom thought for a minute, was there something he had said to Marco that she wasn't meant to hear?

She laughed at his discomfort.

'Stop worrying; you didn't say anything out of order. Just teasing you.'

'So, what business were you in?'

'I run a very successful translations company, we provide translators for everything from the courts to the customs, and we translate technical manuals for some of the big electronic companies. I do ok.'

'So why do you want to go into the property business?'

'Lots of easy money to be made, I mean, eight percent?'

Tom reddened at the memory. Harry had negotiated an amazing deal with Marco, and now this woman was going to quote it all over Spain and try to make it an industry norm. Why did he have to blurt out the figure that night in Marbella?

'That's an extreme situation, you won't get that everywhere.'

'That's what you think. How much do you think I'm getting in Montana Fea?'

'Don't tell me, you're getting eight?'

'No, I'm not. I'm getting more.'

Tom was surprised; this woman must be quite a negotiator. 'How much more?'

'Twelve and a half, but it's almost all added on top, I agreed to sell at their asking price plus ten percent. Twelve and a half in total.'

'But what if someone goes out to Spain and sees them on sale at the lower price?'

'Can't happen, I have guaranteed to sell them all for them, sole agency, all local arrangements cancelled.'

Tom swirled the wine around in his glass. 'That's quite a margin, but then you are selling a cheaper product than we are, so it balances out I suppose. If you sell a lot of them you'll certainly make a lot of money.'

'That's why I'm in the business, Tom, to make a lot of money. Why are you in the business, Tom?'

'Same reason, I don't know anyone who works for any other reason.'

'Then how would you like to make a lot more money than you're making now?'

'I wondered when that was coming, Tania.'

'Well, are you interested? How much would you want to work for me? I need a good sales manager to run the show; you are the most experienced around, and you have the track record.'

She waved the empty bottle at the waiter. 'More wine please, another bottle of the same.'

Tom sat back and looked at his host across the table. Under the outward shell of a somewhat ditzy woman was a core of toughness, this was somebody who tended to get what she wanted. It was a difficult call, Harry was a decent guy to work for but he had a conscience and was fussy not only about what he sold but how he sold it. Harry didn't have the killer instinct that was now facing him across the table. His boss had gone nearly as far as he wanted to go in any case, he had made the one big killing that would ensure a comfortable retirement, and from now on he would be getting more and more careful, and Tom's earnings would be getting less and less.

'I'm pretty comfortable where I am at the moment, Tania; why would I want to move to a start-up company?'

'For money, Tom. How much would you want to move?'

'Like I said, I'm happy working for Harry, but I'm curious as to how much you were thinking of offering.'

'It's up to you to know how much you're worth, Tom, and then I'll see if I can rise to that.'

'Look, Tania, cut the games. I know that this is a head-hunt, how much are you putting on the table?'

She leaned forward and looked him straight in the eye. 'Tom, I intend to make Scorpio the biggest overseas property agency in the country in a matter of months, and I intend to have a bottom line of between five and ten million in year one. I'm not offering you a salary; I'll give you twenty percent of net profits, but there will be conditions.'

'What kind of conditions?'

'Mostly to do with work rate, I'll expect you to work seven days a week and not bitch about it. You'll have to train salesmen, I'll recruit young guys with ambition and pay them commission only and you will show them how to close sales quickly and in a way that won't come unstuck. And of course you'll only get paid when I get paid, I'm not carrying anyone.'

The deal was marginally better than what Harry was paying, but the question on Tom's mind was whether Tania Sherry would shift more volume than Harry and become the market leader; he had a feeling that she might just do that. There was also the issue of her complete lack of scruples. Harry was always holding back from making a real killing because he wanted every customer to get a good property and make some money from it; Tom was more inclined towards maximising the take from the business.

'Make it thirty percent and you have a deal.'

'No chance, Tom; I have the start-up costs, and the risk is all mine too. No, twenty or nothing.'

'Nothing it is so.' Tom decided to play hardball; twenty wasn't too bad, but twenty five would be a good deal. He raised his glass in salute. 'Thanks for considering me anyway.'

She poured wine in the two glasses. 'Don't play hard to get, I can give you twenty five percent, but that's it, there's no more there. Deal?'

'Deal.' He took her outstretched hand and they shook on it.

'Welcome aboard, Tom, now let's celebrate.' She took a long swallow from her wine and refilled the glasses again.

The wine flowed and they discussed the future. Despite his outward calm, Tom was excited at the prospect of having a free hand with selling. Without Harry's moderating influence he could sell a lot more property, he knew that. Harry had always warned him not to promise the possibility of big rental returns on holiday property, mainly because these returns were largely mythical. Now however he could attract a lot more business from investors who believed that their home in Spain could generate an income. This was going to be good; he had a good feeling about it.

The only problem was his new boss; he would have to find some way to keep her away from the drink. Tania was now well lubricated and was slurring her words. She had ordered more wine, and when the waiter showed her the label she began to get abusive.

'Up here, my face is up here.' She jabbed a finger in the general direction of her forehead.

'Yes, of course it is, madam.'

'Then stop staring at my fucking tits.'

The headwaiter rushed over, alarmed by the raised voices. 'What seems to be the matter, madam?'

'Your man here, he's staring at my tits.'

'I'm sure that's not the case, madam.'

'Can't take his eyes off my tits. Jesus, now you're staring at them as well, are you all fucking perverts in this place?' Her voice was now quite loud and conversation had stopped at the other tables.

'Madam, Sir, maybe you would like to settle the bill now, perhaps more wine might not be a good idea.' The headwaiter was being a diplomatic as possible.

She threw a gold credit card at the hapless waiter. 'Take your fucking money, you fucking pervert.'

'Let's get out if here when he comes back with the card.' Tom didn't want to get in the middle of a row.

'I'll go when I'm fucking ready.' She turned around to look at the people at the next table. The man seated opposite was unlucky enough to catch her eye. 'What are you all looking at; did you never see a woman with a proper body?' The woman nearest to her giggled nervously; Tom knew what was coming next but he could do nothing about it.

'You never saw anyone with a decent figure, not at that table anyway. Bunch of titless fucking wonders.'

Tom grabbed her arm and led her towards the door, where the waiters were holding their coats. The headwaiter never lost his polite smile. 'Thank you for coming tonight, I hope we'll see you again.'

'Up here, up here, my fucking face is up here.'

Tom managed to drag her out the door and into a taxi at the rank outside. This was going to be a tough job in more ways than one, he wondered if it was going to be worth it.

CHAPTER EIGHT

Harry sat and shook his head over and over. 'Whatever about leaving me, going to work for that double-crossing bitch, are you mad?'

'I'm sorry, Harry; I just got an offer that was too good to pass up.'

'But you'll be working for someone that can't be trusted; you know that already, how do you know that she'll even pay you?'

'I'll take my chances on that.'

'And what about Sunspots, how are we going to manage the sales with our key salesman missing? You're dropping me in the shit here, Tom, I expected better after all we've been through together.'

'I'm sorry about the short notice, Harry, but part of the deal was that I come on board immediately. I'm not leaving you stuck though.'

'Looks like it to me.'

'No, I spoke to Walter last night, he is willing to come to work full time with you; he enjoys this game a lot more than the local stuff that he does during the week anyway, and he's well able to fit into my shoes here.'

'I appreciate that; Walter is a great guy, reliable too.' Harry couldn't resist the barb. 'Ok, Tom, I'll make up what's owed and pay you at the end of the month. I don't want us to fall out over this, mad and all as I am with you.'

'Thanks, Harry, and I'm sorry about the way this has ended, but I really got a big opportunity with Tania Sherry and I'd be foolish to pass it over.'

'Ok, don't worry about it; I suppose that if I was your age I'd want to make a killing. Can you do me a favour though; can you do the editorials to go with the ads in the Sunday papers?'

'Did them last night, oh ye of little faith.'

Harry laughed as he took the pages from Tom. 'That illiterate jackass Murtagh will have to start earning his wages from now on; he'll have to go back to school and learn to write his own column.'

Tom sipped from his coffee. 'I'm sorry to be leaving, Harry; it was great working here but I need to go with this one, like you say yourself this business won't last for ever and I need to make hay while the sun shines.'

'You're right, Tom, I'm in retirement mode I suppose and you're looking to expand and go big time. I hope you made the right choice with that crazy bitch though.'

'I'm twenty seven years old, Harry; I can handle her, I'm a big boy now.'

***

'Now pay some serious attention, guys.' Tom looked at the two fresh-faced salesmen who sat across from him in his office. 'You think you can sell property just because you sold a couple of houses a week in your last jobs. This is a whole new ball game, you'll be expected to close up to twenty sales a day each at busy times, a whole new way of working that you have no concept of at this point.'

'Twenty? In one day?' The young man sounded incredulous. 'How could a person do that, I mean you usually have to put half a day into any customer to sell them a house.'

'This is different, its high volume, high pressure stuff, and you can make a lot of money if you work your asses off. If you don't per-form, not only will you be earning small money but you'll be earning it somewhere else.'

'So how do we do it, I mean what are the logistics of it?' The other man seemed eager.

'Simple process, I'll do a presentation every hour, ten to fifteen minutes of hard sell on the project, dressed up as an information ex-ercise on Spanish property. Then you get behind your desks and sell like crazy. No more than fifteen minutes per customer from pitch to close; any more and they are timewasters, tyre kickers, lose them.'

'And will you be selling too?'

'Damn right I will, probably selling two to every one of yours, but once you get the feel of it you'll start to put lots of sales on the meter. Now, are we ready to make some money, guys?'

The two were excited now; Tom was talking about the kind of money that they had only dreamed of up to this.

'Ok, you've studied the project, but study it again. Learn every house type and learn the site layout, no point in looking up stuff when the customer is sitting across from you. Have it all in your heads, ok?'

They nodded.

'I've put your names on a couple of houses on the master sheet; if anyone needs a push, tell them that you've bought those ones. That's what closes sales, if they think that the salesman has faith in his product they are a lot happier. My own name is on the one just inside the gate; better not tell them that one isn't for sale, its going to be the security office.'

They laughed at Tom's little joke.

If they're flagging, remind them that they can earn a lot of money from renting the house out when they aren't using it themselves. You have the spreadsheets showing the different rates for the different times of the year?'

'We have, but what's the real deal on rentals?'

'You won't be telling them any lies in one way. I mean if they work on it and advertise, they could conceivably get rentals all year round for a house in Spain. Of course it won't drop out of the sky, and it would be a best case scenario, but no point in giving a negative view of things.'

The quiet one interrupted. 'What happens when they don't find tenants? Are they going to come back at us?'

'That's down the line.' Tom reassured his team. 'The place won't be finished for nearly three years realistically, although you need to tell then two years so as to encourage them, and who knows what will happen by then? Anyway, we'll be sitting on a pile of money, lads, and we won't be worried about a few punters and their lack of tenants. They'll have a house in Spain, that'll make them happy enough, and who knows where we'll be? So, let's get to work, there's a lot of stuff to do before the weekend; I want you guys to make more money this week than you ever made in your lives.'

***

The room was packed. Tania Sherry did things in style, renting the biggest function room in town and packing it with display material provided by the developer. Two saleswomen from Spain, also provided by the Spanish company, were working at two desks along the side wall. The receptionist from Tania's translation company and one of her Spanish translators were meeting and greeting people as they came through the door and capturing their details on pads of contact forms. Three lawyers from Alicante had their own stands on the other side, each displaying large nameplates. This had been Tom's idea; give the clients the idea that they were being offered a choice of law firms, although all three were under instruction to help close the sales in the case of any customer who might be wavering.

Tom and his two salesmen had their desks along the back wall, opposite the dais from which he made his presentation every hour; it was an unashamed selling exercise although the screen described it as an information presentation. This was Tom's chance to make the sales pitch to a large group of buyers, saving time at the tables when they went to talk to the sales team individually.

The coverage in the papers had been good too, helped along by Tom's emails that just needed to be cut and pasted into the editorial. Murtagh had waxed eloquent in his front page piece on the Globe; He readily switched allegiance from Sunspots, helped along by a voucher for an expensive meal for two. One of the more respectable Sunday papers had at first declined any offer of assistance with the editorial, until Tom had called the advertising manager and asked him whether or not he was interested in Scorpio's advertising business.

Tania was floating around, charming customers and keeping control of the master sales sheet. There was no point in delivering sales at this kind of volume only to lose one because the same villa was sold twice. He joined her for a coffee on Sunday afternoon, in the first lull that had occurred in two days.

'Well, Tania, looks like we're mining a thick seam.'

'True in more ways than one, Tom, some of the clients for this stuff aren't the brightest.'

'Any idea of the score so far? I've a feeling that we're close to the ton.'

'Hundred and six as of a minute ago, we're well in the black, Tommy baby.' She was in high good humour; it was all working out very well.

'With any luck we should put another fifteen across the line between now and close, that would be the best anyone has ever done in an exhibition. I can't believe how well it's working.'

'Wait until your two protégées get up to speed, although whatever pep talk you gave them seems to have worked.'

'Just a matter of focussing their minds, teaching them to lie creatively, that kind of thing.'

'Time to move, Tommy, here comes the next wave.' She moved towards the door to greet the fresh crop of buyers.

Tom stepped on to the podium and lined up the slideshow on his laptop. He tapped the mike and spoke confidently.

'Ladies and gentlemen; welcome to Scorpio Properties information presentation. Please take your seats and we will shortly commence a short presentation on investment opportunities in Sunny Spain.'

***

'Ten weeks at this rate and we'll have sold out the entire project. That's quite an achievement, Tom; we're going to make ourselves a shed load of money.'

'We're not there yet, there are a thousand villas left on the plans.'

'Don't be so negative, Tommy, this is all going very well and there seems to be no bottom to this particular well. I reckon that we should be looking around for another project, maybe sell it alongside this one.'

Tom nodded.

'That worked well for us in Sunspots, we bumped up the price of a small project and offered it as a choice, mostly to show how cheap our main offering was.'

'Did you sell any of it?'

'That was the funny thing, it sold out with no effort in a couple of weeks; people reckoned that because it was more expensive, it must be better.'

'Then maybe we need to do that, get a similar project and bump it up a bit, make ourselves some extra margin.'

'Let me think about that. Maybe we should split this project, give the far side of it a different name and sell it at say twenty percent more than we are selling for now. If it doesn't sell at the higher price, we can shrink it back into the main project.'

'Or if it takes off, we could enlarge it, eat into the cheaper part? I like it, Tom, milk it for every possible euro.'

Tom pondered the possibilities. 'I'd say we need to talk to the developer, get him to offer a different finish to the exteriors on the more expensive one, not necessarily better quality, just different. We'd need to change the literature as well, but they would do that in a couple of hours in Spain.'

'If you go to Alicante this afternoon you could get all that done and be back tomorrow night. Do you want me to come with you?'

Tom laughed at the memory of their previous trip.

'No thanks, Tania, once was enough.'

'Don't be such a baby, Tom, but I won't go where I'm not wanted. By the way, I have a CV here from a guy looking for the front of house job, he says he knows you.'

'We badly need someone at the shows to oversee the marshalling of the people, ideally someone with a sales background. Who's the guy you're looking at?'

'Andrew Milton; works as a salesman in a men's fashion shop. Is he ok?'

'Good old Andrew! I wondered where he had got to. He'd be ideal, great personality and he was a good salesman as well. Yes, grab him.'

'Is he good looking? Should I grab him in the other sense?'

Tom laughed. 'Good luck on that one; that would be a first anyway. I'd better get a move on if I'm going to Spain, see you on Wednesday morning.'

***

The evening sun was still warm as Tom came down the steps, it had obviously been a very hot day and the heat still glowed back from the tarmac and the airport buildings. He flashed his passport at the nonchalant policeman at the desk and strode past the customs area and through the sliding door to arrivals. Juan was waiting at the doorway and he turned and led the way to the car.

'Good trip?' Juan was a man of few words.

'Yes thanks, on time, no problems.'

'Enrico already has made the changes to the brochures; we can send them back with you. I collect you in the morning, eight o'clock, and we go to the site and decide on the finishes and the pricing structure.'

'Ok, but we have already calculated the new prices.' Tom didn't want the Spaniards to make the running on this.

Juan put the ticket into the slot and the barrier raised; he drove out on to the main road and headed for the hotel. 'We must decide how much we each get from the increase, not as simple as just raise the price, no?'

'Juan, we already have a contract with you to sell all the project at the price you wanted, anything on top is ours, that's already agreed.'

'No, only twelve and a half percent, not another twenty percent as well. Is no fair that we are building, doing all work, and you are making more than we are. Our profit is fifteen percent only, now you want to make twice that amount.'

'A deal is a deal surely?'

'A deal is a deal, no problem, but this is excess, we have to get half of the extra markup or we make other arrangements. Already Senor Simpson has been here and he ask us to give him some of this project, we say no, we have good partnership with Senora Sherry. Pero if you can not meet us half way, we must make other arrangements.'

Tom had expected this approach, and he had agreed with Tania that they would give as much as half the extra price back to the developer, but Juan had shown his hand and left room for a bigger slice. 'I can't possible do that, Juan, your costs are still the same but we have to spend a lot more on marketing now that this is essentially two projects. I propose giving you four percent extra, that's all we can do. And if you give the back end of the project to Simpson, we can always show that we're selling the same project for less money, he won't make a single sale.'

Juan hadn't thought of that angle, he was suddenly conciliatory. 'No need for this, Tom, we work well together. How about you give us seven and a half, leave twelve and a half for you?'

They were pulling up outside the hotel, time to bury this one. 'Six percent, my last call; you got me when I was tired after a long day, don't leave it until tomorrow or I'll be a lot harder to deal with.'

Juan sighed. 'Ok, is fair I think, from now on we both making a lot more money. See you in the morning.'

Tom pulled the curtains and lay back on the bed; time for an early night. He suddenly felt that he was getting old; there was a time when he would have headed straight out on the town, but tomorrow was going to be a busy day and he needed his sleep. He picked up the phone and called Tania.

'Struck a deal, six for him and fourteen for us.'

'Well done, lover, better than we could have hoped for. Now if you can squeeze good quality finishes out of him, you'll be worth what I'm paying you.'

'That's the easy part; I could nearly go home now and be happy with the trip. I thought he'd put up a bigger fight. By the way, Simpson was sniffing around the project, wanted a slice of it.'

'Simpson? That little jerk! The cheek of him, I hope that he was sent packing.'

'He was, they just wanted to use him as a lever to put pressure on us, but I blew that argument away. I don't think he'll be a threat, he's too small time and he thinks too small. If he was any use he'd be finding his own stuff and not following us around. Don't worry about him.'

'I won't, but it's time his wings were clipped a bit. Talk tomorrow, and behave yourself in Alicante.'

***

Hiring Andrew proved to be an inspiration. The organised chaos of the exhibition room was suddenly transformed into a well-oiled machine. Nobody got past Andrew's charming approach; every visitor was recorded and assessed and their details were inputted into the laptop by the receptionist from the translations company. By the time they got to a salesman their information was on screen, along with any extra snippets that Andrew had gleaned from his short conversation with them.

'Oh it's great to be back among friends.' Andrew raised his gin and tonic and Tom and Walter lifted their pints in salute. The Willows was quiet, it was still early on Sunday evening and they had all had a tough weekend.

'Pity we're not all on the same team.' Walter was feeling the heat, managing shows on his own, but he looked happy enough.

'How did you do this week?' Tom wasn't prying, just curious to know how his old firm was doing.

'Fifty seven closed, probably another ten will close on Monday or Tuesday.' Walter had been busy. 'How about you?'

'Just short of the hundred, but Andy will move another ten on the phone during the week if the last few weeks are anything to go by.'

'That's me, Andrew the mover. And shaker of course.' Andrew was happy, earning decent money again after his sojourn in the clothing business.

Walter was in one of his philosophical moods. 'Isn't it an amazing phenomenon when you think about it? I mean, if you tried to sell a house here without letting buyers see it, you'd be laughed out of the shop, but the punters for the Spanish stuff have no interest in looking at the location, although I suppose there's nothing to see yet anyway. Still, you'd think that they'd want to view the site or something, but very few are bothered.'

'Same with us, out of seven hundred sales on Montana Fea, only three went out to see it.'

'How do you deal with that, do you go with them?'

Tom shook his head. 'Not worth the effort, would cost too much of my time, I'd rather lose the sales. No, Juan looks after them on that side, part of the deal, and we only lost one out of the three, went to another agent when they were out there.'

'That happens, hard to keep them herded, you need to sit on them twenty four seven or they stray. Still, one dropped sale is nothing with the numbers you're doing.'

Tom agreed. 'If you start that inspections trip racket, you need to do big groups and keep them away from any temptation to go elsewhere. I heard that up in Mojacar the agents are so pushy that if you go up to the bar to buy a drink, another agent will be sitting at the table with your client when you come back.'

Andrew laughed. 'The cheek of them, maybe we should brand the customers with a hot iron, make them keep their sticky fingers off them.'

'We'll leave that kind of thing to you Andy.'

'Now now, Tom, I don't do the pain thing.'

Tom called for three more drinks. 'Seriously though, what next? I mean, there must be a finite number of customers for a property in Spain, so how do we move this on to the next level?'

'We could always move into the furnishing business, fit out the houses for them when they're finished.'

'That's an idea, Andy, but everything we sold so far has a completion date at least two and a half years down the road, so what do we do in the meantime if this river dries up?'

Walter took a long draught from his pint. 'Anyway, the margin on the furniture wouldn't give us the kind of returns we are getting from the property sales. I mean seriously, lads; we're getting money for old rope here.'

'Speak for yourself, Walter, I'm just barely getting by.'

'Yes ,Tom, we'll have a collection for your rent next week. Anyway, Harry and myself have opened another furrow, or we're about to.'

Tom was suddenly interested. 'Have you moved in to the French market then?'

'No, that's too specialised, we're looking at opportunities further east.'

Andrew was curious too. 'Where, in China?'

'No, not that far away, we have signed up a deal in Hungary, in Budapest.'

'Oh lovely.' Andrew was excited. 'I'd love to go to Budapest. It's supposed to be a lovely city; they have those great thermal baths and all that kind of thing.'

Tom was interested. 'What's the score in Budapest? I was looking at those cities, you know, Budapest and Prague, didn't know where to start. Budapest looks promising right enough, good quality location, nice city.'

'This is between us of course.' Walter didn't want to give away too much. 'We got two projects from an Israeli developer in the city centre, on the border between Districts six and seven, best part of town and at a good price. He was in a bit of financial difficulty so he let us in as the sole agent. We promised to clear at least fifty percent of the projects or we suffer penalties, but if we go over the target we make a killing.'

Tom was surprised at how far ahead Harry and Walter had moved in such a short space of time. 'You guys are really going international, fair play to you.'

'We're just trying to stay ahead of the game, Tom, trying to avoid a slump if Spain peters out.'

'Anything over there that might suit us? If two companies go in there it might start a stampede. If you are trying it on your own you might have an uphill battle, but if Scorpio goes in as well it could create a stir. What do you think?'

'You're probably right, Tom, there might be strength in numbers, but I don't want you trampling all over our patch. We have big projects to sell in a good area; there mightn't be room for competition. I'm thinking of our penalty clause.'

'How about a secondary area? I don't particularly want to go head to head with yourself and Harry either. We've managed to avoid getting in each other's way in Spain so far; I'd like to keep it that way.'

Walter pondered Tom's suggestion. It might be a good idea to have two players in Budapest; the papers would be carrying twice as much advertising and it would put the city on the map with Irish buyers. 'You have a good point, Tom, we need a lot of publicity to make this work, most buyers don't even know where Budapest is, there'll need to be a big information campaign to kickstart it.'

'So, have you a contact for me over there?'

'You could try Amir Mamzer, but count your fingers after you shake hands with him.'

'Is he that bad?'

'I wouldn't like to do business with him, but he seems to know his stuff; it's just that he's a bit shifty. You could handle him all right though.'

'So why didn't you do business with him yourselves?'

'He works in areas where sites are cheap, and he sells cheap apartments to Israeli investors who buy in the expectation that these areas will come up in value at some stage. Only thing is, I think that he works in places that will be slow to improve, so maybe even Scorpio wouldn't like to market his stuff.'

Andrew had been listening with interest. 'We sell in Montana Fea don't we? I'm sure that this chap can't be any worse.'

CHAPTER NINE

The plane lost height slowly and the details of the countryside below came gradually into focus. The Danube looped around and almost back on itself as it wended its way through flat land ruled by straight lines into a patchwork of huge fields. A small partly-wooded hill loomed ahead and the plane banked around it; the city opened up beyond the hill, clustered around a large island in the huge river that was spanned by several long bridges. The part of the city close to the Danube seemed old and sedate; Tom could make out a large castle on high ground overlooking the river. Further out, neighbourhoods appeared to alternate between red-roofed suburban housing and large tower blocks of apartments. He could see what looked like the Grand Prix circuit, and a football stadium, and then the plane banked steeply and turned and descended towards the airport.

It was pleasantly warm and sunny, and the bus brought the passengers quickly to the terminal building. He had expected more formalities, but the policeman barely glanced at his passport before stamping it with a red stamp and waving him on. The sliding door opened and he walked through. Look out for the airport minibus desk, Walter had told him, and there it was; you couldn't miss it.

'Which hotel?' The woman was curt but not unfriendly.

'The Central.'

'Single or return?'

'Return please.'

'Wait over there, the driver will call you.' She indicated a row of seats close by the desk.

Tom was impressed, it seemed like a good system, and not too expensive as far as he could judge. Hard to figure out this money, a thousand forint was about four euro, more or less, so the return ticket was about ten euro, or was it twelve? Walter had warned him about the taxis, how they were known to fleece foreigners; the airport minibus was safe and reliable.

He didn't have to wait very long; the driver collected some papers from the desk and called out the names of several hotels, including the Central. A few other passengers trooped out behind the driver and boarded the bus; Tom sat in the back seat and called Amir Mamzer.

'Good evening, Mr. Mamzer, Tom Murphy here, just confirming our meeting tomorrow morning. Where do you want to meet?'

'Welcome to Hungary, Mr. Murphy.' He pronounced is as 'Ungaria' in a heavy Israeli accent. 'Where are you staying, which hotel?'

'The Central, do you know it?'

'Of course, very good hotel. I can meet you near there, in Gerbeaud's coffee house, nine o'clock in the morning, ok?'

'Sounds good, how do I get there?'

'Is no problem from your hotel, just come out front door and turn towards the river, walk five minutes to Vorosmarty Ter, very near.'

The hotel was comfortable, and he was tempted to lie back and watch TV, but he dragged himself out and went to find some food. He followed the Israeli's directions to Gerbeaud's coffee house; it was only a few minutes away, facing on to a pleasant square that was surrounded by old buildings for the most part and which was only spoiled by one modern office building that seemed entirely out of touch with its neighbours.

Looks like the planners here are no better than anywhere, he mused. Maybe this city is an easy place to do business.

Gerbeaud's didn't have much in the way of food, it was mostly a coffee house that sold a mouth-watering selection of cakes and desserts, but the friendly waitress in her traditional garb of long skirt and puff-sleeved blouse brought him a pot of tea and a perfectly presented sandwich on a small silver tray. He ate slowly, taking in his surroundings. The coffee shop dated from the eighteen hundreds; it hadn't suffered much from modernisation in the meantime, resulting in a pleasing place to while away some time and watch the world go by. Dark mahogany cabinets with brass edging and crystal chandeliers gave the place an authentic period feel.

There was nothing period about the bill though. Even allowing for some continuing confusion with the currency values, Tom reckoned that this coffee house was as expensive as anything he had seen anywhere. Still, the square was obviously a tourist area, and you would expect to find tourist prices in such a place.

He finished his tea and walked outside; the café was closing and the waitresses were hovering around, anxious for him to be out of their way. He walked across the square and down towards the river; it was a balmy night and a lot of people were out strolling and taking in the ambience of this pleasant city. He stood for a while along the promenade above the riverbank, leaning on the heavy cast-iron railing and looking across the river at the floodlit castle on the hill on the far bank, and at the huge suspension bridge that was lit up by thousands of bulbs along its span and cables. An old yellow tram rumbled past close beside him on the track by the riverbank, its iron wheels squealing as it negotiated the bends close to the big bridge.

It was time to head back; Tom turned and retraced his steps, crossing Vorosmarty Square and passing the darkened façade of the coffee shop. The numbers of strollers had diminished and his footsteps echoed as he entered the narrow street leading up towards his hotel.

'Do you speak English? Can you help us please?'

The two girls looked like tourists, poring over a street map by the light from a shop window.

'I'm afraid I can't be of much help, I'm a stranger here myself, but I do at least know where we are.'

Tom took the map from the dark haired girl and refolded it to show the area around Vorosmarty Square.

'We're here, just beside the square and on the street leading to Deak Ter.'

'Then can you help us to find this pub?'

The blonde girl unfolded a piece of paper with the name of a bar and a street address written on it in block letters.

Tom looked at the address, and then back to the map. He spotted the street name in an instant; it was very near to where they were standing. 'That's it, just there.'

The girls seemed puzzled. 'So it is that direction.' The brunette pointed towards the river; Tom shook his head.

'No, the other way, over there, just two streets away.'

'Can you show us? The blonde had a lost look about her, seemed anxious to find the bar.

'Are you meeting friends there?'

Tom thought she was attractive; maybe a drink in this company might be a nice way to spend an hour. She pointed to her dark haired friend.

'She is meeting her boyfriend there, we said we would be there half an hour ago but we could not find the place.'

'Let me show you the way.' Tom took the map and headed off in the direction of the street. The blonde girl walked alongside him, her friend following behind.

'So, where are you from?' Tom wondered at her accent.

'I am from Hungary, but not from Budapest. We are from a small town in the East of the country. I think maybe you never heard of it.'

'You have very good English.'

'Yes, is not too bad I think; we studied English in school.'

They turned into the street that Tom had spotted on the map; it was narrow and not as brightly lit as the main street, and the lights from a small bar glowed brightly about half way along it. A thick-set man stood at the doorway, arms folded, but on seeing Tom and the girls approach he spoke into a small radio that crackled back at him. Tom immediately slowed, he didn't like the look of this; it smelled of a setup.

'Come, that is the place, let us have a drink.' The brunette now had hold of one of his arms and the blonde was clinging to the other.

'Just a minute.' Tom was buying time, the street was quiet and he felt that he was being led into a trap.

'Why are you stopping? Let us all have a drink together.' The blonde was pleading, almost whining. He was sure now that he was being set up; maybe going to be mugged as soon as he entered the bar. They were pulling at his elbows now but Tom had seen enough; he broke free and retreated back down the street, the swearing of the two women echoed after him as he sprinted around the corner on to Vaci ut and back to his hotel.

He was panting as he entered the lobby.

'Are you all right, sir?' the concierge was concerned about his guest.

Tom told the man of his experience; the older man smiled sadly.

'Every night they do this, always to men on their own. The police move them along but it not illegal, they are breaking no law.'

'But surely if they rob you, then that is against the law.'

'No they do not rob you exactly, just you buy them a drink maybe and one for yourself, then they bring the bill, maybe five hundred euros each drink, fifteen hundred euros for the bill.'

'And this is legal?' Tom was incredulous.

'Yes, is on the menu, very small print on the wall, anyway most foreigners do not easily convert the prices from forint, they think they are making mistake themselves, until bill comes.'

'And what if I didn't pay?'

'Always they pay; the barmen are big and strong. Yes, always they pay.'

Tom shuddered at the thought; the doorman had indeed been a huge man, broad shoulders and no neck, thick muscular arms straining the material of his suit. Yes, he could imagine it; you would probably have to pay right enough.

He headed for the lifts. 'Thanks for the information; I should have talked to you before I went out.'

The elderly concierge smiled. 'You are welcome, sir, and I hope that you have a good stay in Budapest. Please do not judge us all by the behaviour of these mafia types.'

'Of course not, and thank you.'

'Good night, sir.'

***

The morning was bright and sunny and the stroll to the coffee house was agreeable; the events of the previous evening were just an unpleasant memory. He pushed open the door of Gerbeaud's and looked for Amir Mamzer.

He wasn't hard to find. At first it looked as if a small fire had broken out in the bay window in the smoking section. The small fat man had spread himself out around a table with his coat and briefcase occupying several chairs; a cigarette smouldered in the ashtray and another burned smokily between his lips. His eyes squinted from the column of smoke that rose in front of his face. 'Mr. Murphy?'

Tom extended his hand. 'Mr. Mamzer? Yes, I'm Tom Murphy, nice to meet you.'

'Sit down, sit down. You like maybe some coffee?'

'Thanks, I'll have a coffee please.'

The fat man dropped heavily to his chair and lit another cigarette from the last one. 'Welcome, welcome. I hope we can do much business together.'

A smiling waitress placed two coffees on the table; he pushed one cup over to Tom. 'You like some cakes maybe? Good cakes here, but damn fucking expensive, is better in my local coffee house but it is hard to find and I don't want that you get lost.'

The hotel breakfast had been good, but the cakes behind the glass looked appetizing. 'Have they got apple pie? I fancy an apple pie.'

Mamzer waved back the waitress. 'Bring one angle amlet.' He turned to Tom, 'that's English apple pie, that's what they call it, no idea why, stupid fuck Ungarians.'

'You don't like Hungarians?'

'Stupid lazy fuck bastards. Can't do nothing for themselves, first the Russians have to do everything for them, now the Israelis.' He pronounced it 'Es-roy-elish'

'So are there many Israeli developers in Budapest?'

The little man lit another cigarette and looked at Tom in amazement. 'All Es-roy-elish, no Ungarian developers, stupid lazy fuck bastards.'

'So what kind of project have you got to show to me? Is it near here?' Tom wondered if this guy was for real.

Amir lit another cigarette, ignoring the one that smouldered in the ashtray. 'No, not near here, is in eight district; I make a nice small development, maybe one hundred apartments, but I make you very good price.'

'What's a good price?' Tom peered at the man through the smoke cloud.

'How much you want to pay, we can make any price, make smaller or bigger, depend on what your buyers want to pay.'

'But does the planning permission not stipulate the size of apartments in the development?'

The small man laughed loudly, coughing with the cigarette smoke. He tapped ash into the ashtray and sucked in smoke from the cigarette. 'Stupid fuck bastards do what I tell them, I bring jobs and work to their district; no, don't worry about small details, I sort out small details. How much your buyers want to pay?'

Tom pondered for a moment. Walter had said that they were going to sell high end apartments in the city centre for about a hundred thousand, so probably a cheaper area might be sold at sixty or seventy thousand. He decided to pitch low.

'Maybe forty thousand? Depends on the project.'

The match flared and he took another deep drag. 'Ok, we can make a project for forty thousand euros, no problem.'

Tom was surprised. If that was the case, and if Irish buyers were going to behave as they did in Spain, it might be possible to sell these apartments for twice as much, or at least for sixty or seventy thousand. The possibilities were limitless.

'So what commission would you pay us?'

'Commission? You want commission? Make your own commission, put up the price of the apartments to make your commission.'

Tom was surprised at the way business was done in Budapest; Walter hadn't mentioned such a system. Still, this way might be better, a chance to make some serious money.

'So, can we go to the project? I'd like to see it.'

The Israeli laughed again. 'There is not already any project, only some land where they park cars, but I have the project design in my office, not far to walk, Falk Miksa Street.'

He threw some notes and coins on the table and gathered up his coat and briefcase, moving with surprising agility for a fat man with such a smoking habit. He propelled his stout frame along the sidewalk with enough speed to cause Tom to walk briskly to keep up, although the flow of his forward progress was interrupted by occasional pauses to light another cigarette.

He stopped at a corner and pointed out a magnificent gothic style building that filled the view on the left across an open area. It reminded Tom of the English houses of parliament; a huge dome topped off the impressive structure.

'Is the parliament palace, where stupid fuck Ungarian government works. Bastards!'

'Beautiful building.' Tom was impressed.

"You know why is on top a, how you say, cupola?'

'A dome?'

'Yes, a dome. You know why is on top a dome?'

Tom smiled; this was obviously a local joke. 'No, why is there a dome up there?'

'Because every circus must have big top.' The little man laughed loudly at his own joke.

Tom laughed along with him. 'Yes, every country has its clowns in power; we certainly have enough of them in government in Ireland. I suppose you have the same problem in Israel, in the Knesset?'

The Israeli's demeanour changed immediately; his face darkened with anger. 'No, in my country the parliament is serious business, no clowns; we live in a tough neighbourhood, mister.'

They waited in silence for the lights to change; Tom resolved not to make any more jokes about Israeli politicians, it was obviously a sore point.

Across the street Tom did his best to keep up with his guide as he scampered along. The little man pointed to the building on their right. "Here is fuck museum, appear many times in movies, very famous.'

'Fuck museum?' Tom was astounded; maybe this meant something else in Hungary. That's what they call it?'

'Yes, fuck museum, in very many films it appears.'

The building was an impressive structure, tall stone columns adorned the façade and the huge ornate entrance doors were approached by wide and elegant stone steps.

'What kind of films? Porno films?' Tom was having difficulty getting his head around the concept of a 'fuck museum.'

'No, no porno films, don't be stupid, you young guys have sex in the brains. Hollywood movies mostly, of course also films about fuck lure.'

'Fuck lure?'

'Exact. Fuck lure, from the villages of Ungaria.'

Tom suddenly realised what the fat man was talking about. 'Folk-lore museum, of course.'

'Yes, how many times I have to tell you, fuck lure museum, is no charge to enter also, some day you have time you enter, but not today, we have work to do.'

They crossed another busy junction and entered a quieter street. 'This is Falk Miksa, not far now.' He stopped and lit a cigarette.

'Safest street in Ungaria, my office is across road from ministry of spies.' He pointed to a large concrete office block.

'They still have spies in Hungary? I thought that was all in the past.'

'Maybe not spies any more, but the building is still here and many many people work there, maybe they spy on each other.' He laughed and clapped Tom on the shoulder. 'Anyway, always plenty policemen taking care of the building, safest street in Ungaria.'

A large door was set back slightly from the pavement, beside a sign that read 'ANTIK.' The half-basements of these buildings seemed to be made up almost entirely of antique shops, their low ground-level windows packed with small items of glass and brass-ware. Amir opened the door and Tom followed him into the tiled hallway, past a bank of mailboxes on the left hand wall. A few steps led up to an old fashioned lift that ran in an open cage. The fat man punched the button impatiently several times and the lift dropped to the ground floor.

'We go up, to the top.' He slid the gate aside and motioned Tom to enter the lift cage. The lift was small, and Tom felt overpowered by the closeness of the fat man and the reek of cigarette smoke from him. Mamzer pressed the top button and the lift creaked upwards.

Through the mesh cage Tom could see the layout of the build-ing clearly. The lift rose at the end of an internal courtyard, with iron-railed open-air balconies running right around each floor. The floors of the balconies and the ground floor of the building were tiled with small black and white tiles in a chequerboard pattern, and the balcony railings were ornate and capped with hardwood handrails from which a lot of colourful flower baskets were suspended. The occasional sound of a radio came through an open window, but this inner core of the building was quiet and peaceful in comparison with the noise and bustle of the street outside.

The lift came to a sudden stop and Amir slid the gate back, hold-ing it against its return spring to allow Tom to exit. They walked through the doors on to the balcony and Tom looked down; it was quite a dizzying drop into the courtyard below.

'Not a place to bring up kids. Hard to watch them on the balconies.'

The small man nodded. 'Not exactly balconies, corridors, the corridors are outside in Ungaria. Is the same all over Budapest, all buildings the same as this one.'

'Even the new ones?' Tom liked the layout, but couldn't see it working with a new building.

'Sometimes with new buildings also, but usually now we make with internal corridors. Es-roy-elish show stupid fuck Ungarians how to build good buildings, good as Tel Aviv.'

Tom could see no sign of an office, but the Israeli motioned him to an almost hidden staircase in the corner. 'Up, up one more floor, to the attika.'

He followed the man up the narrow flight of stairs to a cramped landing and through a door with a small sign for Kover Ember Developments. If this was the nerve centre for the developer's operations in Hungary, Tom wasn't too impressed; he had expected a more high-profile place.

The office was surprisingly spacious and bright; it was obviously an apartment that had been converted for office use, and the interior was clean and well fitted out. The parquet floor shone and two desks faced each other across the room. The larger desk was piled with papers and architectural drawings; a pretty dark haired girl was working at a computer at the desk near the window.

'Monika, this is Mr. Murphy, Mr. Tom Murphy, he is our partner from Ireland.'

The girl stood up in welcome and shook his hand.

'You like some coffee?'

'That would be good, yes please.' Tom didn't see any coffee machine, but maybe it was in the next room.

'The older man pulled some notes from his wallet and thrust them at Monika. 'Go, bring us coffees, and some cakes also, nice ones from The Europa, not from the jerk at the corner.' He motioned to the couch. 'Sit down, Tom, sit down.'

'Great office, nice and quiet.'

'Yes, it is good for me, near everything, but the rent cost me very little. You like my secretary?'

'Pretty girl, yes. Is she Hungarian?'

'Yes, they are stupid girls, but ok for just do what they are told. Make nice decoration for the office also.' He leered at Tom. 'You like Ungarian girls?'

'Yes, very nice, very pretty.' Tom wished that he would get down to business.

'Very good for the bed, Ungarian girls, always say please and thank you, never complain about the curtains, you should try one while you are here.'

'Maybe.'

'You are not an Arab? You like girls?'

'An Arab?'

'You know, a how you say, a homokos, a faggot?'

'No, of course not, of course I like girls.'

'Good, good. You are married?'

'No, you?'

'Yes, I have wife in Tel Aviv, three daughter, no son unfortunately, I was very unlucky. You have no wife, why? You sure you are not an Arab?'

'No, I'm not gay, just never got round to getting married, maybe soon. So your wife and family live in Israel, but you live here, isn't that difficult?'

'No, I don't live here, just work here, I live in Tel Aviv.'

'So how much time do you spend here?'

'Most of the time, but I go back five, six times a year for long weekend and for a two week vacation in summer. Is good to go home, I have nice home in Tel Aviv.'

'Sounds tough.'

'Is ok, I am used to it. And Irish girls, they are good for the bed?'

'Of course.'

'That is what I hear, Irish and English girls, they like very much the bed.'

'What about Israeli girls? Are they good in bed?' Tom wanted to turn the conversation around.

The fat man's face darkened with anger. 'Es-roy-elish girls not like that, they are good for wife, for family.'

Tom was beginning to get the measure of this guy; all discussion or criticism of Israel and the Israelis was off limits; all other races were lower down on the respect ladder. The conversation was mercifully terminated by the return of Monika with the coffees and the cakes. Tom reckoned that it was no surprise that Mamzer was so fat if he had such an appetite for sweet things, but it had to be said that making cakes was one thing that the Hungarians seemed to do very well; it would be hard to pass up on the pastries that Monika was now putting on to plates.

The developer spread the plans on the low table in front of the couch. The apartment house looked good, at least on paper, much better than Tom had expected; maybe this crazy Israeli was actually very good at his job.

He seemed to read Tom's mind. 'In Israel I make many big projects, much bigger than this one. This one is easy, small apartment house, any fool can make this project, is easy.'

'So who will build it, have you an Israeli builder, or is it someone local?'

'No, Es-roy-elish constructor too expensive, Ungarian constructor too stupid, I use constructor from Austria, but of course he use Ungarian labour. They ok if they have someone in charge.'

'And this builder, this constructor, have you used him before?'

'Yes, I build two apartment houses before now in Budapest, I can show you today if you want.'

'And are these sold or do you need to sell them?'

'No, they are sold, all sold to Es-roy-elish investors. They buy all together and then sell apartments afterwards at higher price, but not my problem. I build; make quick sell, and then move on to next project. Can you sell this one quick?'

Tom looked at the plans, the project seemed to be well designed and looked like it might be easy to sell at an exhibition. 'Yes, I reckon we might be able to sell it, it's just a hundred apartments; we often sell this much in one weekend.'

'In one weekend? That would be good, make quick sale and then quick build. We both make some money, yes?'

'When do you expect to start building?'

'When everything is sold, not before. Maybe when ninety percent sold, but at least this. I keep the commercial also, that is my bonus.'

He stabbed a finger at the two shop units on the ground floor at the front.

'If we sold all this in a month say, could you start building straight away?'

'Yes, we don't have building permit yet, but all is agreed so is simple to get. Constructor is ready, finished last job and waiting for this one, I have agreed price with him.'

'What about the area, is the eighth district a good place to live?'

'Oh yes, good place, the project is close to a metro station so good location. Not Falk Miksa, but ok for investors.'

'Will it rent well?'

'No problem, you can find tenant. Good apartment, no problem to find tenant.'

Tom decided to get down to business.' If we sell at a higher price, is that a problem for you?'

'No, no problem, you put commission on top, as much as you want, not my business.'

'No limits?'

'Only what market will stand, there is of course limit, buyers will not pay more than is worth, maybe a little more, but not much.'

Tom said nothing; this guy hadn't seen the scramble to buy Montana Fea. There was a chance here to get maybe an extra twenty or maybe thirty thousand on top for each apartment; they seemed cheap by Irish standards, even at twice the price that Amir wanted for them. Best to nail him down to a contract for the prices before showing him what they would actually be sold for in Ireland. If he knew what Tom had in mind he would put up his prices for sure.

'These are for you.' The Israeli gathered two sets of drawings and some sales literature and pricelists and handed them to Tom. Monika took the papers and put them in a large envelope for him.

Tom sensed that the meeting was over. 'Can you show me the project location, maybe the projects you have built before?'

'Sure, we go now, we take the metro, is better than my car.' He grabbed his coat and briefcase and led the way back to the lift. 'Maybe we get some lunch first, some sandwich?'

'I don't mind either way, it's early for me but if you're hungry I'll join you in a sandwich.'

They turned left outside the front door and Tom followed him to a busy street that crossed at the end of Falk Miksa. It was a wide and bustling, lined with impressive buildings and with two tram lines running down the middle of the thoroughfare. Yellow trams rumbled up and down, and traffic flowed past in an endless stream in both directions. The fat man led him to a coffee house a short walk from the corner.

'This is my local coffee house. You will see, is like Gerbeaud's but not the same prices, not a tourist place.'

The coffee house was good; display counters of cakes and pastries along the wall to the left and plenty of small marble-topped tables with bentwood chairs. They went through to the smoking section at the back and Amir sat heavily on a chair and lit another cigarette.

'My favourite place, this is the Europa, best coffee house in Budapest.'

'Looks good right enough.' Tom was scanning the menu; the prices were very reasonable indeed, this definitely was somewhere for the locals and not just for tourists. 'They seem to have a lot of good coffee shops in Budapest, not just chain store places like in other cities.'

'Is tradition in Ungaria, coffee house.' He sucked deeply on his cigarette. 'In old days, apartments were not big; the coffee house was the living room. If you had visitor, you bring him to coffee house, not to your apartment.'

Tom ordered a club sandwich, and Amir asked for a sandwich and some cakes. The waitresses here were dressed in long old fashioned skirts, it seemed to Tom that this was a tradition with waitresses in Budapest, but he didn't want to ask Amir any questions about girls, or politics for that matter. Probably religion was out of bounds as a conversation item as well, he reckoned. Best to stick to business from now on.

The club sandwich was generous, and Tom decided to skip dessert; Amir ate two large cakes and drank several coffees, punctuated with endless cigarettes. Tom called for the bill and fumbled with the Hungarian money. He handed the waitress a large note, but she pointed to the smaller note in his hand; this place was not expensive by any standards.

They retraced their steps down Falk Miksa and past the rear of the parliament building. The metro station was close to the parliament, just across the road; Amir bought a bundle of orange coloured tickets and they descended the long escalator to the platform deep underground.

'Very deep metro, long way down.' Tom was impressed.

'Yes, must go very deep to go under river, under the Duna, the Danube.'

'Of course.' Tom agreed; it made sense, the river was close by; the parliament building sat on the river bank.

The train arrived quickly; it was just one stop to Deak Ter, the main station that was close by Tom's hotel. Amir pushed his way off the train and scuttled along the crowded platform and on to the escalator to another line; the station seemed to Tom to be a hub for three different lines, a kind of central junction for the metro system. Here again a train arrived in less than a minute and they found seats readily; most of the people had disembarked at the central station.

Amir spread himself along the seat. 'We go not many stops, will not be long.'

Tom was impressed at the efficiency of the metro system. 'You don't have to wait long for a train, great system, wish we had something like this at home.'

'Built by the Russians. Never would the stupid fuck Ungarians build such a thing; is true, is very good system.'

Tom was going to ask whether Tel Aviv had a better system, but thought better of it. Talk of nothing except business from now on; that was the best idea.

Amir rose suddenly from his seat as the train slowed; Tom had forgotten to count the stops but it didn't seem that a lot of time had elapsed since they had left Deak Ter. He followed Amir out of the train and up the escalator into the sunshine.

It was clear that this area was not as fashionable as the city centre, the buildings were shabbier and the shops were basic and functional. There was a high incidence of graffiti on almost all the buildings, and many empty shop buildings had been turned into unofficial bill-posting sites with their windows covered by layers of pasted-on advertising material. The overall impression was one of shabbiness.

'Is not far, very near to metro, good investment for future.' Amir seemed to be trying to convince himself that the place had potential. It seemed clear to Tom though that the main attraction of this area had to be the low cost of building land.

To be fair, it was not far, especially if you covered the ground as fast as Amir Mamzer in full flight. Despite his guide's one pause to light another cigarette, Tom found himself having to almost trot to keep up, and in a short time they arrived at the spot that was destined to be Kover Ember Haz. It was just as he had promised, there was nothing there, just a vacant lot with a crumbling blue-painted plywood hoarding around it, and a dozen cars parked in a row by the rear wall. An elderly man emerged from a tiny hut by the gate when he saw them enter the site. He wore a flat cap and was dirty and unshaven, and his yellowed grin revealed several missing teeth.

'This is my security man, is Ungarian Gypsy, stupid fuck lazy bastard.'

'Security? What is there to steal?' Tom wondered at the need for security on a vacant site.

'Steal? Is not the problem. Problem is Gypsies, they move things on to my land if I no have security.'

'Things? What kind of things?'

'Rubbish, old cars, broken cars, Gypsy stuff.'

Tom hadn't been aware of many Gypsies in the city, although he had a faint recollection of having heard something about Gypsy musicians in Hungary, part of the folklore. Or maybe 'fuck lure.' he laughed to himself at the memory of the earlier misunderstanding.

'So, are there Gypsies around here?' He didn't know whether the question might be politically correct or not.

Amir laughed heartily. 'Not many, but one is enough to make problem, is best to be careful.'

Tom pulled the plans from the envelope and mentally began to arrange the building on the site. There would be two basement levels below ground, mostly car parking but also storage and plant rooms. The building itself would have a small courtyard to the rear, allowing windows to the rooms on that side of the development. It wasn't award winning architecture, but it was a very good use of the site. He was beginning to develop some respect for this crazy Israeli; this guy knew his stuff. He had managed to squeeze the maximum number of apartments on to the site, but without making it look that way; this was a skill that developers often lacked.

'So, you want to see some of my other projects?' Amir was anxious to be off.

'Yes, are any of them near here?' Tom was now more confident that this guy could deliver, but it would be good to see a finished job.

'One is very near, just two blocks, come.'

The small man set off again at a quick trot, trailing a cloud of smoke from the ever present cigarette. By now Tom had found a way of matching the developer's peculiar stride; he kept back a short distance behind him and walked briskly. They turned a corner and crossed two narrow streets, and then turned another corner.

'There, there it is, Kover Ember Palota.' He gestured at a new brightly-painted apartment block that stood out in an otherwise shabby street.

Tom was pleasantly surprised; apart from the slightly down at heel surroundings, the building was well finished and seemed to be well built.

'Nice job, you do good work.'

'No problem, I told you, I build many many apartment building in Tel Aviv. I was projects manager for some big developers, serious peoples, and I build also some small projects for myself. Here is not difficult, good ground, no difficult to construct a building in this city.'

They made their way back to the metro station and Amir peeled two more tickets from the bundle and cancelled them in the machine. 'On metro you must always use tickets, Tom. Never think maybe you can take some small chance, stupid Ungarian bastard train persons stop you, cost you many thousand forints. You can make some gamble on trams ok, mostly in the evening, but never on metro.'

They got out at Deak Ter, the central station; the Israeli shook his hand. Your hotel is just here, I go to next station to my office, we can talk on phone, on emails during next few days, ok? Maybe you want to go to Gerbeaud's, take some coffee, some small cake?'

'Not me, I couldn't look at another cake today, but thank you.'

'Ok, call me tomorrow morning, have good trip home. I look forward to we do much business.'

The little fat man headed for the escalators, and Tom made his way up to the street. He was faced with a multitude of exits from the station, and he took the nearest stairs and emerged into the bright sunshine. He looked around to get his bearings; he could see familiar buildings across the other side of the square but the streets were busy and there were no crossings for pedestrians, nothing for it but to go back down and take another exit. This time he was successful and he headed back to the hotel.

He sat in the lobby and pored over the drawings and price lists; this project was going to be simple enough to sell; it was straightforward and easy for punters to understand, and the fact that it was near a metro station would be a plus for buyers back home that had no idea of local nuances around property values. It would be easy to pitch the area as 'up and coming.' Maybe he could give the area a new name for marketing purposes; the 'revival quarter' sounded about right, maybe they would try that.

The prices were great though; a real surprise. Quite a lot of the apartments were priced at forty thousand euros; he reckoned that they could add thirty thousand on top of that and sell them at seventy, maybe slightly less, maybe sixty eight or nine. A brand new apartment beside a metro stop, in the Revival Quarter, for sixty nine thousand euros; who could resist that? Not the buyers who were spending twenty grand over the odds for the back section of an already overpriced Montana Fea.

The waitress brought him his drink and he left it on the table while he went over to the Concierge to check on the airport minibus. The older man who had spoken to him the night before was on duty.

'Good afternoon, sir. I hope that your day went well.'

'Yes indeed, thank you. Can you ask the airport minibus company to collect me?'

'You are supposed to call them the day before you need them, to reserve, but don't worry, I will call them and arrange, it is not a problem.'

The man made a phone call and spoke in Hungarian; it seemed as if he was arguing politely, and eventually he put down the phone and smiled.

'That is fine, sir; they will be here at four o'clock. Is there anything else we can help you with?'

'No thanks, that's all. No, wait a minute, can I ask you a general question?'

'Of course, sir.'

'Are you from Budapest, from the city?'

'Yes, sir. I have spent all my life here, and my family before me.'

'Which part of the city do you live in?'

'In the fourteenth, sir, at the end of the metro line, do you know it?'

'Yes, I have an idea where you mean. Do you know the eighth district at all?'

'Yes, of course.' He leaned closer to Tom and dropped his voice. 'Not so nice, sir, many cigány, gypsy people, they live there.'

'Just a minute.' Tom went back to the table and picked up the drawings that Amir had given him. He pointed to the street name on the bottom of the drawing; 'do you know this street?'

'Yes, sir. I know of it, it is close to the metro stop.'

'Yes, that's it. Are there many gypsies in that area?'

'Yes, sir. That area is where all the cigány live.'

'So, would you buy an apartment there?'

The old man smiled. 'I am not a rich man, sir; I could not buy an apartment anywhere. But if I understand your question correctly, in theory, no, I would not buy an apartment in this place. I believe that most Hungarian persons would avoid this area, sir, that is my opinion only, you understand.'

'Thank you very much for letting me have your views on it, I appreciate that very much.'

'Not at all, sir. I am glad to be of help.'

CHAPTER TEN

The minibus got him to the airport in plenty of time and the check-in formalities were smooth and efficient; he had an hour and a half to wait for the flight so he went to the business lounge and poured himself a drink, retiring to a quiet table with his papers and a calculator. A germ of an idea was beginning to form in his mind; it was a very exciting thought, but he would have to turn it over a bit in his head, to think it through some more and test it against a lot of counter arguments before he would mention it to Tania.

The more he thought abut it, the more he was convinced that it would work. He wrote lines of figures on the pages of the pad, and made the calculations over and over. He poured another drink from the cabinet and called Tania.

'Well? How did you get on with the Israeli?'

'He's a bit crazy, but he knows what he's doing as far as I can tell. Good project, a bit basic but ok. It's in a crappy area though.'

'So what's new?' She laughed loudly. 'I'm sure you can write a few newspaper articles that will move it up the social scale.'

'Just thinking about that.' Tom looked at the pad where he had crossed out 'Revival Quarter' and written 'Renaissance District.' 'The possibilities are there, I'm happy enough with the overall project and I think we can go with it.'

'How many apartments? Enough to give it a big marketing push?'

Tom looked at the sheets again. 'A hundred and four apartments and two commercial units, but he's keeping the commercial and the front penthouses himself, so a hundred and two for us. I've agreed a fully exclusive deal with him, nobody else will have it, here or anywhere else.'

'What kind of commission is he offering, three percent?'

'No, we make our own, base price plus whatever we put on top. Good possibility for margin I would say, better than you mentioned.' He was conscious of other people in the lounge; a couple had sat down close to him and you never knew who was listening. 'I have an idea to really make it fly, can't discuss it now but I'll talk to you in the morning.'

'You have my interest, Tom, I can't wait. I gather that there are people there, call me tonight if you like, or call round to the house, I'll have the bed warm.'

'Talk to you tomorrow, Tania. Goodbye.'

The receptionist in the lounge touched him on the arm. 'Sir, your flight is closing, gate twenty seven please; it is just beside us here.'

Tom hadn't noticed the time passing; he gathered his stuff and headed for the gate. He was excited at his plan; he had a feeling that he had just come up with a scheme to make him very rich indeed. It would make crazy Tania even richer, but that didn't matter; a rising tide would lift all boats.

***

'Sit down, lover, tell me your news.' As usual, Tania looked very chirpy for this early in the morning. She sat behind her desk with a paper cup of coffee in her hand; she was wearing a white linen suit that looked on the one hand very businesslike but which showed off her attributes to the full. 'You didn't call around last night; I was waiting for your ring.'

'Slipped into something comfortable, had you? Damn, I missed out on that.' Tom was in a good humour himself; he had worked on his figures on the plane and again when he got home, and he knew that he had a winner, something to blow away the opposition and make Scorpio the biggest player in the overseas market. He took a sheaf of papers from his briefcase and put them on the desk.

'First of all, let me tell you about Amir Mamzer.' He went on to tell her all about the eccentric Israeli and his penchant for cakes and cigarettes.

She laughed at the story of the fuck museum. 'Must have been an interesting trip, there seems to be a lot of crazy people in this business. So what about the project, does it look anyway ok?'

'Yes, the project is fine; it's a plain apartment building, but fine for our purposes.' Tom unfolded the plans for each floor and the elevation drawings; Tania took a quick look and moved on to the crucial issue.

'What about our margin, how much will we make on it?'

Tom selected one sheet of figures and turned it to face Tania. 'The column on the left is the apartment number, then the size, and the third one is the price; I converted it to euro for simplicity.'

'Forty grand? That's bloody cheap. How much can we sell them for?'

'See the fourth column; I added thirty grand more or less, to everything, pro rata with the more expensive ones.'

Tania gave a low whistle. 'Can we push it that far? Bloody hell, we'll make a killing on this if it sells anyway quickly.'

'Sunspots are selling nothing under a hundred grand in the city centre, so why wouldn't people think that this is good value? I mean, most people couldn't even find Budapest on a map, let alone differentiate between the districts. This street is almost on a metro line, only about ten minutes from the city centre, and it's in the Renaissance Quarter as well.'

'She laughed at Tom's marketing language. 'Renaissance Quarter, it has a nice ring to it, so is this the idea you couldn't talk to me about on the phone?'

Tom shook his head. 'Look at the last column; it's the full price plus ten percent. That's what we'll be selling them for. A forty grand unit will be marked up to seventy grand, and then pushed up another ten percent to seventy seven thousand, but we'll only be getting the seventy grand.'

Tania looked puzzled. 'You've lost me at this stage, what's the extra ten percent for?'

Tom sat back in his chair and smiled' 'It's the guaranteed rent, five percent a year for the first two years, we'll give them back their own money for two years, minus a letting fee of course.'

'So we will guarantee the rent, in the case that tenants don't pay, is that it?'

'No, there won't be any tenants; that's the whole point. We just add the rent to the price, makes the whole project a real winner in the eyes of the punters. Nobody can compete with a project with guaranteed returns, we'll sell it in a weekend, I'm sure of it.'

Tania sat back and smiled. 'It took a devious bastard to come up with that one, why didn't I think of it before you? Tom, you're a genius, I don't mind admitting it. I wonder can we do this anywhere else? Maybe in Spain?'

'No, I don't think we need to do it in Spain, most buyers are buying there either for their own use or to flip when the places are built; according to Walter, the people enquiring about Budapest are looking for investment for the future, buy to let and that kind of thing. Most of them are small time, amateurs just re-mortgaging their homes here and ploughing the surplus into something in a foreign city.'

'Maybe we can do it again in Budapest when we sell this one.'

'It's possible, but I reckon that Amir Mamzer won't be too excited at us doubling the price of his project, and I can't see him coming in that cheap next time around. I won't tell him anything until I have a contract signed, but that should be today, I'm emailing him our standard contract with a few additions this morning and I'll get it back by courier tomorrow.'

'He'll hit the roof, will he?'

'Probably, but I'd drop him a sweetener in the form of the administration on the guaranteed rents, let him keep the handling fee in return for running the 'rental office.' Maybe we could let him keep any rent he manages to collect as well during the two years.'

'So we'll hold on to the 'rent' and pay it back to the buyers in a couple of years when the job is built?'

'Yes, but I think maybe we could vest the rental guarantee in another company, one with no assets preferably. Maybe we could set one up in Hungary or something, in case we decide to default on the rental part of the deal when the time comes. I haven't thought that end of it through fully yet.'

'But you will, no doubt. Well done on all that, Tom, I suppose you have the articles written for the Sunday papers as well.'

'Yes, wrote them on the plane last night, just have to finish them off. Thinking of sending Murtagh to Budapest for a couple of days, get a front page spread from him.'

'Send him somewhere else, maybe Paris or somewhere, we don't want him sniffing around Budapest's Renaissance Quarter, he might get a shock.' She laughed loudly at the idea.

'Good idea, boss, you're not just a pretty face.'

'And a stunning figure; don't forget that bit.'

'Hard to forget something so obvious.'

She was smiling smugly. 'I did something about Simpson while you were away.'

'I hope you didn't do anything silly, he's just an irritant really; he's no real threat to us. What did you do?'

'I heard that a lot of his customers were taxi drivers so I decided to take a small initiative.'

'Do I really want to hear this?'

'I sent Andrew off for a few hours to take taxis in and out to the airport, he must have been out there three or four times.'

'What on earth for?' Tom was puzzled at her strategy.

'You know how gossipy taxi drivers are. He pretended to be going and coming to a flight to Spain, told all the drivers that he used to work for Simpson and that he left because the stuff he was selling was rubbish.'

'Nice one.'

'The taxi men are always gossiping at the ranks and over the radios, so I reckon that the story will spread like wildfire.'

'But apart from hurting Simpson, how does that help us?'

'I'm holding a special evening next Monday that will be confined to taxi drivers. The taxi firms are going to put it out on their radios, and we will sell a section of Montana Fea that will be reduced in price especially for them.'

'After you've put the price up beforehand?'

She laughed. No, I've just asked Juan to leave out the kitchen units; we can do them as an extra later. Now, am I not a clever girl?'

Tom couldn't help but laugh. 'I wouldn't like to get on the wrong side of you, Tania Sherry.'

She was serious for a moment. 'I just had an idea about the Budapest project.'

'Careful, don't stress that blonde brain.'

She threw a pencil at him. 'Stop messing, I really have an idea about this. If we're selling places with a rental guarantee, we should insist on a good standard of furnishing.'

It was Tom's turn to look puzzled. 'The whole point is that there won't be any tenants, so it doesn't matter about the furniture.'

'It does if we're supplying it. I'm sure we could easily pull an extra five grand profit off each apartment on a furniture package. I have a friend in Barcelona in the furniture business, he imports into Spain from Eastern Europe all the time, I'll find out who makes his stuff. I reckon that there's another half million there for the taking.'

Tom wondered at his boss; every time he thought he had her figured, she came up with another surprise. It took a very clever head to think that far ahead and see the possibilities in a proposal that he had pitched to her just twenty minutes earlier. He resolved never to underestimate her; she might have a mad streak, but this was a very shrewd woman indeed.

***

The exhibition was billed as an international property show, and Andrew had excelled himself with the displays and the layout. The papers had reacted well to the guaranteed rentals on offer in Budapest, and coverage had extended well beyond the usual stuff that Tom wrote for them every Monday morning. Boosted by his promised weekend in Paris, Murtagh had devoted the entire front page to Kover Ember Haz and the Renaissance Quarter of Budapest. Tom had written a feature on his newly invented Renaissance Quarter, including some inside information from the local town hall about future spending on the public spaces in the area. Apart from some small detail that he had got from Amir Mamzer, the entire piece was a work of fiction, but who was going to check? Already other newspapers were talking about the Renaissance Quarter as a matter of fact, and nobody was querying the story.

Amir Mamzer wasn't too happy when he saw the prices that Scorpio intended to charge for the project. He ranted at Tom and Tania in a half hour conference call, alternately demanding and pleading for a bigger slice of the pie, but they stood firm.

'Look, you were happy enough to sign up for the prices we suggested, and we're giving you the administration of the rental scheme as well as any rents you can get from the apartments. How much better does it get?' Tom wasn't going to give an inch; he had a watertight contract.

Tania wasn't for turning either. 'We are spending a fortune on advertising, and taking huge risks, but we fully expect to sell this project in less than a month. That's better than anything you ever did with your Israeli clients, and you have no marketing or agency costs. I'm sorry, Mr. Mamzer, a deal is a deal, but maybe we can make a concession on the next project if this one works well for us all.'

Reluctantly the Israeli agreed to the package. 'Ok, let's all get to work and move this project off the desk, we all got to make a living.'

The publicity was working; suddenly everyone was talking about Budapest. Tom had done several radio interviews in the past few days; this was a new approach by Scorpio. He explained the rental guarantee by claiming that they had done advanced deals with a number of multinational firms that were planning to open in Hungary, and if anyone questioned him further he invoked a confidentiality clause; nobody pushed it, and it quickly became accepted lore.

Amir Mamzer arrived for the weekend, curious to see how his project would be received; it was clear that he was impressed.

'My project, is all over your newspapers, everybody talks about this Renaissance Quarter. Do you think we will sell many apartment this weekend?'

Tom was confident; the publicity had been incredible and he already had telephone reservations on nearly twenty apartments ahead of the show. Small investors were excited at the possibility of getting a guaranteed return on their purchase, and there was something of a stampede to grab the best apartments. He didn't want to appear too confident to the Israeli, but he wasn't going to downplay things either.

'I think we'll easily sell half the project, maybe more. We've invested a lot of time and money in the marketing side, so hopefully it will all come together this afternoon.'

Tom called his salesmen to a final meeting before the doors opened. He wanted the Hungarian project to move well, but he didn't want them to lose focus on the core business, the project in Spain. Hungary was a gamble that might pay off hugely, but Spain was where the steady income was coming from and he didn't want them to forget that.

'Andrew, your role is key today. Try to separate the buyers at first point of contact and push most of the Hungarian ones to me; I know the project better than the lads and I'll be able to sell it faster. We're going to be stretched with doing two countries, but we'll get used to it after a couple of hours and it'll all go smoothly. Lads, don't get carried away with the excitement of a new destination; keep selling Spain the way you have been, don't lose your focus. Now, let's go earn some serious money.'

Amir Mamzer called Tom aside. 'Is looking good, Tom, I think you guys will do the business.'

'Don't worry, Amir, we'll give it our best shot.'

'Something else, Tom, your friend Andrew, is he Arab?'

'Arab?'

'You know, Homokos?'

'Oh Andy's gay, sure, but he's still very good at his job, Amir.'

The Israeli shook his head. 'I am not used to work with Arab, Homokos. In my country we do not have such persons.'

'You have a problem with Andrew?'

'No, no problem, he seems nice guy, but I just not used to being near to Homokos. I don't know how to talk to him, what do I say to him?'

'Say nothing, I don't know, if you get into conversation, I don't know, tell him a joke maybe. Just act normal, no big deal.'

'Ok, thank you, Tom, I am just not comfortable, you understand?'

Andrew came back into the room. 'Showtime guys, they're lining up outside, we better open the doors.'

'Ok, Andy, let them in, let's put some money on the meter.'

***

Nobody had ever seen a property show like it. At one point they had to close the doors for half an hour to allow the crowd get small enough to make it manageable. Andrew was playing a blinder, but even he was under serious pressure. By Sunday morning every apartment in Amir Mamzer's building was sold, and they had started taking names for future projects with rental guarantees.

Tania was beside herself. 'Tom, we're making a fucking fortune, this is going like a dream. I need to send you away more often, that rental thing was a stroke of genius.'

Tom was exhausted; he just wanted to get home to bed. They had sold over a hundred apartments in Hungary and almost ninety villas in Spain. He had no idea exactly how much money he had made, but it was an awful lot, probably well over three quarters of a million euro in just three days. He felt a sudden surge of pride at what had been done; so much for his smartass bloody teacher who had joked that he would end up drawing the dole. So much for Mister Maurice Milton who had duped him out of his money back in the electrical store. He was making a lot more than his father with his lousy building business. Thomas Murphy had arrived, with no help from anyone, just using his wits and nothing more.

Amir Mamzer was as excited as a small boy in a toyshop. 'We did it, we did it, we make one hundred percent selling; you guys are the best, the best.'

Tom smiled at the Israeli's exuberance, and at the way he was hugging all the sales team, including Andrew. 'Just doing what we do best, Amir; you build them, we sell them.'

'Is amazing, never did I see such a thing, is amazing. I buy you all dinner, is on me, I insist.'

Tom was too tired to think of eating, and he knew that the rest of the lads must feel the same, but maybe it would be good for all the team to sit down together for a meal and a few drinks.

'That's kind of you, Amir, maybe we'll do that, it would be good after such a weekend.'

The mood was muted in the restaurant at the beginning but the team soon got their second wind as the wine flowed. Tom was sitting beside Tania; he tried for a while to limit her intake of wine but it was a lost cause, his boss was determined to celebrate in style. Despite having made millions from the business over the weekend, she was delighted that Amir Mamzer was paying for the meal and the drinks, and she was doing her best to get her money's worth. Tom would never understand her mentality; this woman would never be happy with having enough.

He thought about his own situation; he was now a rich man, and the business was showing no signs of slowing, although he knew that it would have a finite life as buyers became more discerning and as more and more players entered the field. He just needed to make hay while the sun shone so that he could withdraw quietly whenever the inevitable downturn arrived.

The wine was taking effect; Amir and Andrew were telling jokes and keeping everyone amused. Andrew's voice tended to become shrill when he had a few drinks on board, and the Israeli's strong accent and loud voice meant that he also could be heard above the din. Andrew had the floor; he was trying to explain the nuances of a joke to his new friend.

'It's a nursery rhyme, Amir, like they tell to children.'

'Ok, say again slowly, I understand, child verses.'

'Little boy kneels at the foot of the stairs,
Clutched in his hand are a bunch of white hairs,
Oh dear, fancy that,
Christopher Robin castrated the cat.'

The others howled with laughter, as much at Andrew's very camp delivery of the verse as at the vulgarisation of the old nursery rhyme. Amir laughed along, but he looked puzzled.

''Who this Christopher Robin?'

'He's a character in Children's stories.'

'Ok, I see, but what is castrated?'

Andrew leaned close to Amir and whispered in his ear. The Israeli spluttered with laughter.

'Yes, yes, now I understand. The little boy remove the testikal from the cat, yes? Very good, I learn that one, very good.'

Andrew turned to his new friend. 'Your turn now, Amir, you must have plenty of jokes, tell us one of yours.'

'Ok, there is man, goes to doctor, tells him, doctor, I have problem, every night I peepee in the bed.'

Everyone at the table was now all ears.

'So the doctor examine him and say, all is ok, all is working good, no reason why you peepee in the bed. Then the man say, no, doctor, problem is that when I go to sleep a doo-off come to me in the dream and say, Did you peepee? and I say, no, not yet, so the doo-off say, is ok, you can peepee now. You understand doo-off?'

Andrew nodded, 'yes, a dwarf, a small man.'

Amir took a long swallow of his wine and continued. 'The doctor say to the man, is no problem, when the doo-off come to you tonight and ask you if you peepee, you just say, thank you, I peepee already.'

'So the man come back to the doctor and the doctor say, is ok, no? Did the doo-off come to you last night? And the man say, yes he come, but is not ok. Doctor say, but did he ask you if you peepee?'

'Yes.'

'And did you tell him, no, is ok, I peepee already.'

'Yes, I say to the doo-off, is ok thank you, I peepee already. But then the doo-off say, but did you make shit?'

The whole table erupted in laughter. Amir was in hysterics at his own punchline, he was bent over the table and pounding on his thigh with his fist. Andrew was repeating the last line over and over, and the other salesmen were choking on their food and heaving with laughter. Tania's laughter level had gone up a few decibels; Tom knew that it would be time to get her out of the place very soon.

Amir was still laughing, pounding his fist on the table and almost choking on his drink. He moved up the table to sit opposite Tom and Tania.

'I have another joke, very good joke. Is for you, Tom, you want to hear?'

Tom wondered at what was coming. 'If it's as good as the last one...'

'Is better, is better.' The Israeli was having trouble composing himself.

'Let's have it so.'

'You know when you make the name 'Renaissance Quarter' for the area where is my projects? I show the newspaper reports from internet to the guys at town hall.'

Tom swallowed, he hadn't thought of the fact that the story might get back so quickly to Budapest.

The Israeli was still laughing. 'They love it, now they are going to call this area the Renaissance Quarter, already they spending money, cleaning papers from shops, fixing sidewalk, and they make some small park where was the bad ground across the street from Kover Amber Haz.'

Tom relaxed; this wasn't bad news at all. He was amazed that his idea had been taken up so readily by the authorities; what could have been a problem had turned into a very good outcome. He raised his glass to Amir and toasted him. 'Here's to the Renaissance man, Amir Mamzer.'

They laughed at the story; it was funny, you had to admit it.

Mamzer was still laughing. 'There is another joke, very funny also. You want to hear, Tom?'

'Sure, Amir, we need a few laughs, it was a long weekend.'

'Ok, ok, you know the rentals, the guarantee? You know we agree that I keep any rent I can get for the two years?'

'Yes, that's what we agreed.' Tom was puzzled, what did the little man have up his sleeve?

'You remember Monika, the girl in my office? '

'Yes, I know Monika.' Tom remembered the pretty girl who had brought them the cakes and coffees.

'She is daughter to important man in Medical school. They are selling their old residence block; it will be redeveloped by private investors.'

'Israeli investors?' Tom was beginning to see a pattern.

'Of course. Stupid lazy fuck Ungarians never make such business. But while this redevelopment is happening, they need accommodation for students. I have contract, I sign on Thursday, just before I come here. I rent all block for two years after is complete.'

Tom was astounded, and it must have showed on his face. The Israeli looked at him across the table. 'Is good joke, Tom, no?'

Tom smiled; you just had to see the funny side. Fellows like Amir Mamzer had been around for a long time, living off their wits in a tough business, and you had to admire their initiative. He laughed along with the developer.

'It's a very funny joke, Amir, I have to hand it to you, you know your job.' He raised his glass to the Israeli. 'Here's to your continued success in Budapest.'

Mamzer raised his glass in return. 'And to your success also, we make good business together.'

The waiter brought more wine; he turned the bottle to show the label to Tom. Tania had been quiet; she was slightly drunk and still stunned by the revelations from Mamzer. When the waiter leaned in to show the bottle, she suddenly came to life. She jabbed her index finger in the direction of her own face.

'Up here, my face is up here, ok? You never see tits before? Stop staring at my tits.'

Tom waved away the wine. 'I think we're ok, I'm heading off; it's been a long day.' He wanted to break up the party, to get Tania out of there before she made a scene.

Somehow, he got his boss out the door and into a taxi, but not before she had insulted the waiter and a couple of people at a table near the door. He returned to collect his coat. Andrew was very drunk, as was Amir Mamzer. The salesmen were by now getting down to lines of shots, and the Israeli was enthusiastically joining in. It was time to be off; he called Andrew aside.

'I'm heading home, going to drop into the Willows for a quick pint with Walter and Harry, do you want to come along?'

Andrew smiled coyly. 'Not tonight, Amir has invited me back to his hotel; he has a big cake and some Hungarian wine to finish off. We're going to have a party.'

Tom raised his eyebrows. 'You know what you're doing?'

'Oh yes, he's a very nice man, he's invited me to come and stay for a few days in Budapest, say's he'll take me to visit the baths and all that.'

Tom slipped out quietly and took a taxi to the bar. Walter and Harry were sitting in the corner; they looked exhausted.

'Good weekend, lads?'

Walter nodded. 'The usual, seems to be no bloody end to it, not that I'm complaining.'

Harry put a pint in front of Tom. 'How was your show?' Did you do ok in Budapest?'

'We sold the lot, over a hundred units, and Spain did well for us too.'

Harry gave a low whistle. 'We did pretty well in Budapest, ourselves, better than I expected; we did over forty units downtown. Or maybe fifty, I'm not sure about the last ten. There's no doubt that your publicity drive helped us to put the place on the map, but you seem to have swept the board entirely, was it the rental thing?'

'No doubt about it, we even have a waiting list for the next one.' Walter was dubious. 'Don't tell me that it was genuine, Tom, I know you too well. You just added it on to the price, didn't you?'

'I have to admit, that was the original plan, but we managed to put a contract in place for two years; one of the medical colleges.'

Walter shook his head in disbelief. 'I always used to say that you'd sell shoes to the footless, Tom, and nothing changes. You have a lucky streak in you; I don't know how you do it, but try and keep it legal, or as near as possible anyway.'

Tom laughed. 'It's legal enough, they're promised rentals, they'll get them.'

'Even if they are renting from themselves?' Walter sounded a disapproving note.

Tom ignored the jibe. 'What did you mean about not being sure of the last ten in Budapest?'

Harry contemplated his pint. 'We sold ten in one lot this morning, but I'm not too happy about them, I just don't like that fellow. Mickey Macken, you know him?'

'The racing commentator? I just know him from the telly, never met him.'

Harry sighed. 'I never met him before this morning either. Heard a lot about him all right, small little fucker, used to be a jockey but he got too fat, there isn't a horse in the country could carry him. He's like something that came up in a trawl net.'

'If you knocked him over he'd be taller.' Walter didn't like the celebrity broadcaster much either. 'Women seem to like him though.'

Harry gave a chuckle. 'I had a nephew who was a stable lad when Macken was a jockey, they had a nickname for him in the weigh room; they called him tripod.'

Tom laughed at the descriptions. 'So is he buying property in a big way then?'

Walter shook his head. 'I reckon he's just a chancer; he called in before we opened and picked out the best ten apartments in the place, then told us he had buyers for them, playing on his name I think, cashing in the bit of fame and all that.'

'So what's the problem?' Tom was curious. 'Surely a buyer is a buyer, even that little jackass.'

'He wants a grand each from us for making the deal, no real problem with that, but I think he buys first and then tries to sell later, I'd say he'll break our hearts on this one. No deposits paid, nothing. Got stroppy when I asked him to write a cheque. Do you know what the little fucker said to me?' Harry was angry with the TV personality.

'What did he say?'

'He said 'Do you not know who I am?' He was pretty arrogant about it, not just asking me if I knew who he was if you know what I mean.'

Walter shrugged. 'Nothing lost anyway, just I wouldn't count them as sold until he pays up. It's not really a problem until we start to run out of stock, other than if people see ten cancelled units it will look bad, might start a run.'

'Thanks for the warning, Harry. If he comes to us I'll show him the door, we don't need that kind of crap. Why didn't you run him, tell him no deal?'

'Those media guys are dangerous, you can't afford to fall out with them and they know it. No, I'll string him along as long as I can.'

Tom held up his almost empty glass. Anyone for another?'

'Not me anyway.' Walter was exhausted.

'Me neither, but thanks, Tom. I could sleep right here, these shows take it out of you.' Harry was looking his age.

'Probably time for us all to call it a night so.' Tom got up and put on his coat. 'See you soon, lads, and good luck with the rest of the Budapest project.'

Walter finished his pint and pushed the glass away. 'You didn't bring Andrew with you, how is he doing?'

'Doing his bit for Arab Israeli relations.'

'I won't ask. Goodnight, Tom.'

CHAPTER ELEVEN

Tom switched on the computer and opened his emails. The office was quiet; the team always took a lie-in on Monday mornings to recover from the hectic pace of the shows, but he liked to use that time to look at new opportunities and to review the situation on current projects.

He opened the inbox and scrolled through the list of messages. The sales enquiries were forwarded to Andrew for dispersal among the sales team, and he quickly deleted the offers of cheap medicines and easy Nigerian money.

One particular email caught his eye; he had highlighted it and was about to click on the delete button when he paused and opened the message. It had initially looked like junk mail, but it was obviously from a developer who had found the Scorpio details on the web; the language was a stilted translation into English, but the content was interesting.

'We would like to introduce ourselves to you. Our company is Dengesiz Homes Ltd, has become one of the foremost builders and developers of luxury prestige homes in Kusadasi area of Turkey since many years. We are family owned business local to the area with 19 years in the constructor business with many previous project for our credit. Our company is also the owner of the well know Blue Apart Hotel in Kusadasi. The city of Kusadasi which lie near Izmir is most of the year round resort with flights in to Izmir airport which is just 45 minute transfer time. This area of Turkey is now becoming one of the most popular areas for foreign investor with increase uplifting in the demand for qualities property.'

The email had a link to a website, and the project looked good; white houses with a background of a deep blue sky. It reminded Tom of Marbella on a nice day, but with a more eastern look and feel to the architecture. The prices were the interesting part of the information; this was Spain but at a fraction of the cost. True, it was a long way away and hard to get to, and probably closed down in wintertime, but it just might have possibilities. He printed off a few of the website pages and put them aside.

Scorpio needed more properties urgently in the newer markets. The Spanish business was still steady and Juan was able to line up more and more villas as they sold the ones on offer; he seemed to have a direct line to the local town hall that allowed him to expand the boundaries of Montana Fea almost indefinitely. There was still strong demand for the Budapest market, but with Kover Amber Haz sold out and only Amir Mamzer's redevelopment project in the medical college on the books, Scorpio needed to expand if they were to sustain the current level of business. The overheads were rising, staff wages had to be met every week, and there was danger that Tom's share of the profits would be eroded if they didn't find some good new markets soon.

He didn't want Harry and Walter overtaking him either. It was a matter of pride to him that Scorpio was now the market leader in the overseas property field, and that the huge Scorpio weekend property shows were an essential port of call for anyone looking to invest abroad. Scorpio sales information, admittedly much of it made up by Tom himself, now formed the basis of a lot of widely held beliefs about various markets, and he was amused to see his own words being frequently plagiarised by other companies as they composed their sales literature.

Other companies; that was another thing. Harry had been right when he had predicted that the business would attract a lot of small players into the market. There were now almost twenty overseas property outfits up and running, many of them just one-man bands, but they were clouding the waters. Increasingly too, accountants and lawyers, many of them having inside information about their clients' funding strengths, were working with foreign agencies on a commission basis. There was even rumour of a psychiatrist having moved into the business in his spare time; it was reputed that he was making sales pitches to patients as they lay on his couch. Scorpio needed to widen the net, and soon.

Tania arrived at half past eight, looking fresh and rested as usual. She breezed in on a cloud of expensive perfume and put two coffees on Tom's desk.

'Morning, lover. Working hard for me I see, making me a rich woman. Keeping me supplied with shiny things.'

'Not just doing it for you; remember I have a slice of this business too. Not a big enough one for all the work I do, but I'll manage somehow. Thanks for the coffee, good timing.'

'So, Tommy baby, what's the story, where to from here?'

'We can't stand still anyway, Tania; we need to spread our wings a bit. As well as that we need to be seen to be the innovators, not to be following Harry into places but making the running ourselves.'

'I agree, but the way it worked out in Budapest it looked like we had made the running, not Harry. I mean, we stole the show completely with the rental trick, can we not repeat that again somewhere else, in Budapest even?'

Tom stirred two sachets of sugar into his coffee. 'Not in Budapest, the Israelis won't fall for that one again; they know the value of stuff on the foreign market now, no way will we ever get in with those kinds of margins again.'

She smiled broadly at the thought of the deal that they had made with Kover Amber Haz. 'It was good though, I still can't believe that we made so much bloody money in three days. Did you ever think, Tom, that all the ducks would have lined up like that? I still have to pinch myself to remind me that we did it.'

'The trick is to repeat that success somewhere else. But where?' Tom sipped at his coffee thoughtfully.

'What are our options? Let's deal with this in a systematic manner, list what's out there and decide whether to go for it or not.'

Tom flipped open a pad and picked up a pen. 'Ok, let's make a list. First we have Spain, that's going ok for now, we have three months stock left there with Juan at the current rate, and he seems to have more up his sleeve, so let's leave Spain for a moment.'

'Yes, Spain is the banker; we're ok there for now.'

'So, next problem is Budapest. Amir won't give us an inch on the next project; the college residence thing is ok but it won't be complete for more than three years and not everyone wants to go with something that far out. As well as that it's rented back to the college and the return is low, under four percent. Basically we're out of stock in Budapest.

Tania made a note on her pad. 'So, what else is on the horizon then?'

'Well, Amir has a cousin, Ehud Mamzer, he was working in Tel Aviv with Amir but he's moved to Bulgaria, reckons it's the next big thing. The Brits are already buying old houses in the villages and some of the older apartments along the coast at Varna. He has managed to tie down a big project up the coast, near the Romanian border, and he's very interested in talking to us.'

'But he knows the deal we pulled off in Budapest, he'll be watching for us if we pump the price up.'

'No, he's a middleman, he's not the developer. He's in for a slice of the action from the project owners and he also wants to get a percentage from us, but he has no hang-ups about what we charge for it, none at all.'

'When can you meet him?'

'I could go to Varna in the morning, back Wednesday or Thursday, depends on flights. I could have a look at what's on offer around that part of the world generally; maybe pick up a few projects at the right price.'

'Ok.' Tania scribbled on her pad and circled a few words. 'What else is out there?'

Tom passed the sheets that he had printed earlier across the desk. 'I got an approach by email this morning from these guys, Dengesiz Homes in Turkey, they're anxious to sell into Ireland. The project looks very good on paper anyway, and the price is right. There are about thirty houses left in it as far as I can see, and if we tie up an exclusive on it we could come close to doubling the price easily enough. Might pull the rental trick there again as well, just add on another ten percent and call it a five percent return for two years.'

'Tania flicked through the papers. 'Certainly looks good, and the price is amazing, could easily handle a double price or near enough to it. Do you think that there's any chance of rentals out there?'

Tom shook his head. 'Probably not a lot, although they have an apart-hotel themselves, but that might have been an apartment development that they built and couldn't sell, isn't that where apart-hotels come from?'

'We could always do what we did with Amir, let them manage it as part of their hotel and let them keep any rent that they get, or maybe half any rent that they get. I'm still mad that we let Amir away with that stroke in Budapest.'

'What's done is done, it was a miss but no real harm done, kept him on side after we pulled the fast one on him.' Tom was less concerned than his boss about letting the other guy have some of the action. 'What do you think, should we talk to this Turk?'

'I'll talk to him; you have your hands full this week in Bulgaria. My gut feeling though is that we'll run with it for next weekend.'

'But when are you going to get out to Kusadasi to see it?'

Tania smiled. 'You worry too much, Tommy baby, I'm going to take a chance on it; it looks ok to me.'

'But it might not even exist. All we have is an email and a website, might be nothing there except some sand dunes and a few camels, or whatever they have in Turkey.'

'You have to take risks in this life, Tom, but I'll tell this Turk to come over here tomorrow. If we at least know that he exists, then it's likely that the project exists as well.'

'But what about display stuff, will you ask him to bring it with him?'

'Yes, he can bring a suitcase full of brochures if he has them, and Andrew will make up display material from the website photos, it'll be fine.'

'But we might fall flat on our faces on this one, just for the sake of waiting a week; I could go there next Monday and check it out.'

'Tom, don't be such an old woman. I reckon that if we run with this project at the weekend, all our competitors will rush off to Turkey the following week and busy themselves over there while we are gaining a good head start in Bulgaria. I reckon that Turkey will never be any use long term, the country is backward and the government is nuts. Bulgaria might just be the place where you and I make our fortunes, Tommy baby.'

'I have to hand it to you, Miz Sherry, you have a devious head. I mean that as a compliment by the way.'

'Thank you, Mr. Murphy, I do my best. Now get us a sweet deal in Bulgaria and leave Turkey to me, and keep your travel plans between us, not a word even to Harry and company.'

* * *

The flight was late leaving Dublin, and they circled around London for half an hour waiting for permission to land. Tom worked his way to the front of the plane and was first on the airbridge when the door opened; it would be a close run thing if he was going to catch the flight to Varna.

It was a long sprint down the tubular corridors and through the flight connections area; he swore at the sight of the queue at the security screening area but there was little he could do but wait as one person after another fumbled with jewellery and belts. Breathless and panting, he made it to the gate as the airline staff were about to close the desk.

The plane was ancient; it looked like an old Russian model, a Tupolev or an Illyushin, not the kind of machine that inspired confidence. The crew was surly and unhelpful, and the breakfast was hot along one side and half frozen on the other. He pushed the uneaten food away and drank some of the gritty strong coffee. It had been an early start, and he was soon dozing, his head pressed against the side of the window.

The change in engine noise and the pressure in his ears woke him; they had started their descent to the airport at Varna. He was fascinated by the ice that was forming around the exit door just ahead of his seat; the door was leaking air with an audible hiss, and a frosty white bead was forming around the leak. This was one very old aeroplane.

The landing was surprisingly smooth, and he passed easily through the arrivals and customs area. He looked around for Amir's cousin; he expected someone of the same build, and he peered closely at every short fat man in the waiting area beyond the barrier.

'Mr. Tom Murphy?' The tall skinny man tapped him on the arm. 'I am Ehud Mamzer, cousin of Amir Mamzer. Welcome to Bulgaria.'

Tom looked at the stranger in surprise; the man was well over six feet tall and could best be described as gangly. His suit was a loose fit for his skinny frame, and his sleeves stopped short of his wrists. He moved awkwardly and slowly, bumping into people and trolleys as he led Tom through the arrivals area and outside into the sunshine.

The area outside the airport building was shabby and run-down; the communist administration had obviously been fond of poor quality concrete and their idea of tidying it up had consisted of the liberal application of blue paint. The area was drab, bordering on seedy, but somehow he was going to have to turn this place into the next El Dorado of the property business.

Mamzer led him to a car that was parked in a no-parking zone near the door; a policeman on a motorcycle was stopped beside the car.

'Looks like you got a ticket, sorry about that.' Tom wasn't happy that he might be the cause of putting his contact in a bad humour; it would be bad for business if nothing else.

The Israeli laughed. 'This is Bulgaria; that is Nikolai, he is one of ours, he come to bring us through traffic to our meeting. Is no problem.' He waved to the policeman who saluted and started his machine.

Tom got into the passenger seat of the Lada and threw his bag in the back; he fumbled for the seatbelt but Mamzer waved his hand.

'Is no need for seatbelts, police no bother us, is Bulgaria. Relax, all is ok.'

They followed the motorcycle out of the airport and through the city, the siren clearing their way through traffic; they were outside the built-up area in a very short time. Tom relaxed a little and took time to enjoy the sights as they raced north along the coast road.

'Over here is Sunny Beach, was favourite place for foreign tourist in old days, now not so good, quality of hotels not good but maybe it gets better soon.'

'What's the story with the policeman?' Tom was curious as to how a foreigner like Ehud could be entitled to a police escort as he went about his normal business.

'My partners here, they own the project; they are important people, they are mayor and deputy in their town. It make easy for me if they send policeman to lead the way, I do not want to waste time in traffic.'

Tom laughed at the idea. 'So they have a bit of inside track, you know, they have good information about property?'

'Of course, they make all decisions about permissions, also the zoning you understand. Is impossible to make business here without such connections.'

The Lada swayed and rocked along the narrow road; their escort forced his way past lines of slower traffic and kept them on the crown of the road for long periods. Tom gripped the seat tightly and held his breath; a person could die here, in this crazy country.

The little convoy swerved through a fairly large town and screeched to a halt outside a large old concrete and glass building festooned with flags. The Israeli unfolded himself from the car and waved Tom ahead of him through the main door.

'Is town hall, here I have my office for now, please come this way.' He stumbled up a flight of stairs to what looked like a public office, with a lot of people waiting around on long benches around the walls.

Ehud walked confidently past the waiting people and pushed open a door into a small room where a chubby woman sat before a computer screen. Two leather studded doors led off this ante-room, and the woman got up on seeing the visitors and opened the left hand door slightly to announce their arrival to the person inside. Tom caught a glimpse of a large desk and an array of flags, and a middle aged man in a white shirt and a leather jacket, before the door closed again. The woman showed them through the other door into a large room with a highly polished table surrounded by a dozen high-backed leather chairs. Ehud motioned him to sit in one of the chairs and he joined him across the table, deliberately leaving the chair free at the head of the table.

'Coffee, some drink?' The woman wrung her hands nervously.

'Some water would be good.' Tom was feeling dry and thirsty.

'With gas, no gas?'

'No gas' Tom turned to Ehud. 'Sorry, didn't mean to speak for you.'

The Israeli waved his hands, 'Is no problem, without gas is fine.'

'So, is that the Mayor in the other office?' Tom was intrigued by the setup; Ehud seemed to have installed himself at the heart of the administration in the town.

'No, is deputy mayor, he is boss of construction company. Mayor is coming, one minute please.'

'So what's the deal, are they building here in the town?'

'Yes, they have plans to build here some very big project, called Kukovo, but also more interesting project for start I think, near to Sunny Beach. Near enough to give it name Sunny Beach anyhow.' The Israeli laughed.' Irish buyers are not so exact about location, no?'

'They rely on us to tell them.' Tom smiled at the thought; lambs to the slaughter.

The secretary opened the door and ushered in a small man in a pinstripe suit; Ehud stood up and introduced the man. 'Tom, this is Andon, he is the Mayor of the town.'

Tom stood and offered his hand. The man looked nothing like the mayor of a small town; he was immaculately dressed in a very expensive suit and his hands were manicured. He turned to the door and called out something to the secretary.

The woman returned bringing a coffee for the Mayor, and she was followed by the deputy Mayor. The number two was a big man, dressed in jeans and a leather jacket, and his extended hand revealed the appearance of someone who was not unused to hard work. He welcomed Tom and Ehud warmly.

'I am Petar; I am deputy mayor of town. You will forgive my colleague, he speaks not English well, but I speak a little and Mr. Mamzer speak many language. We manage ok.'

'I'm afraid I only speak English, and a little Spanish.' Tom felt somewhat at a disadvantage in this linguistic tower of Babel.

The Mayor sat forward with his arms on the table and his fingertips together; he spoke for a few moments in Bulgarian, and Ehud translated.

'He say, you are welcome to Bulgaria. Also he say, we have opportunity to make good business here and maybe to bring employment and prosper to this region. He say he have many good connection with the party in all areas, not only here but also in Sunny Beach and Varna. His colleague is excellent constructor, has built many school, road, apartment for social housing, many things for government. They have land here and also near Sunny Beach, and they have projects designed and ready for construct. Licence for construct, no problem, can get in one, two days maximum. First only need selling so banks can finance projects. This is where you can make business.'

'So, are there any other foreign agencies operating in this area, apart from small players?'

The deputy Mayor interrupted. 'Yes, one big English company is starting to do business in Sunny Beach, they want to sell two thousand apartment. They expect commence this in one month, maybe little longer but not much. We want to get to market before them, maybe not many buyers, we need to get the buyers for our project first.'

Tom was beginning to get the picture; these guys had lost out to some other outfit when it came to marketing through a big English agency, and they wanted to steal a march on their rivals and get a project on the table first. 'So, what prices are they proposing for these apartments? Is there margin for us?'

Ehud translated for the Mayor; the deputy spoke directly to Tom. 'I understand how system work, Mr. Mamzer explain; you must make margin on top of our price, but we do not worry about this. We make exclusive deal with you, so no person can come to Bulgaria and buy at lower price, we guarantee this. We pay Ehud a small percentage for introduction to you; you make your own profit. But if you do not sell fifty percent of project in six months we finish business and we make arrangement with another agency.'

'So, how many apartments are you proposing for the Sunny Beach site?'

'Not Sunny Beach exactly, but near. We will call it Sunny Beach North. We make a project with eight hundred apartment.' The man sat back with a proud smile. 'Is good, no?'

'Yes, that's big, but it's the kind of scale we need. What's the average price?'

Ehud unfolded some papers. 'In Euros? Average is just over forty thousand, prices start at thirty thousand and some small amount of penthouse and larger apartments at fifty thousand. I think maybe you can make the same margin you make in Budapest, no?'

Tom was happy enough at what he was hearing; all the figures stacked up and these guys didn't seem to care what profit he made as long as he moved the project on quickly. He looked around the room at his new partners. 'So, maybe we can see the project, get an idea of the layout and location, and we can start to do some business.'

***

The seafront café was a pleasant place to sit and relax after the hectic pace of a very long day. It wasn't up to the standards of the Costa del Sol, with its red plastic chairs and painted concrete floor, but the view from the terrace over the long sandy beach was spectacu-

lar. Tom loosened his tie and raised the cold beer in salute to Ehud
Mamzer. He was beginning to like the Israeli; the man was nothing
like his noisy and boisterous cousin in Budapest. He exuded calm;
he seemed to be completely unfazed by the chaotic environment in
which he did business. This was a man in control of his situation,
and he inspired confidence.

'So, to business.' Ehud raised his drink in response. I tell you how
it will be, it is not for negotiation. We both need to make profit, I will
be fair, I don't have a problem with the level of your profit.'

'You probably know from Amir that we will want to make a
substantial margin from this development. The market will stand a
much higher price than what's on offer, but we'll have to make the
market. There isn't a market for this stuff anywhere as we stand.
Scorpio must create it.'

'I understand all this. I don't have a problem. I want five percent
from the sale price of every apartment, paid when the contract is
signed and the first payment made.'

'That's a lot of money Ehud; we're the ones doing all the work. In
any case, we would prefer to pay you half at that stage and half on
completion; that way you stay interested.'

'Make it two thirds at the start and the rest at the end and we
have a deal. For that I will take care of all business here for you, all
problems that arise. I know from my cousin that you have great potential for selling; he was foolish in my opinion to get maybe a little
greedy with you. I believe that we can make a great partnership for
several years; we can make a lot of money here. That is between us,
you understand; I do not want to be disloyal to my cousin.'

Tom extended his hand. 'Ok, we have a deal. We can work out
the exact details over the next few days, but in general I think that
we have a good arrangement.'

'Ok, Tom, I think that you and I understand each other. We can
work well together.'

'So how did you learn Bulgarian?' Tom was curious at the Israeli's
command of the local language.

'In my home, from my grandmother. She was Bulgarian, my
grandfather was Romanian, all from this area here. My grandfather
was from Vama Veche, just across the border, and my grandmother
came from a small village close to the border, is not now any village there.'

'I've never been to Romania, but I'm going there tomorrow. I can't get a flight from Varna; I have to go to Bucharest. I think I need to get a taxi to Constanta and a train to Bucharest, is that the best way?'

'I can take you in the morning; I collect you from your hotel at eight. I bring you to Constanta to the train and you get to Bucharest tomorrow afternoon for your flight no problem. With taxi will be difficult, is better if I go with you across the border. Maybe we find some business in Romania when we are there?'

'Are there possibilities?'

'I don't think so, realistically. I don't have a problem to pay people, you know, people with influence have to be given some small present if you want to do business. Problem in Romania is you don't ever know if you pay the right person, maybe you pay ten people and still not get the one who can make things happen. In Bulgaria at least I know who to pay.'

Tom was intrigued. 'So how did you end up in Tel Aviv?'

The Israeli smiled sadly. 'You have one week? Is the story of many families in Israel; we are from Hungary, from Romania, from Bulgaria, from Poland. We are driven from these places one, two generation back, to our homeland in Israel. Now we come back to make business here, we come to places where we know how things work.'

'Seems that you have a handle on how things work here anyway.'

'Yes, is not difficult when you know the place, is impossible for a stranger. When the Russians came, they put the most stupid persons in charge, and this system replicates itself you understand. So now with what is called democracy, still the most stupid persons control the towns, is easy to do business with such idiots.'

'So the other developers, in Sunny Beach and these places, did they all make their money from government contracts, like Petar? Is that how they get big enough to get into major developments like this?'

'Some, not all. Many of them make their money from the triangle.'

'The triangle?' Tom was puzzled.

The Israeli thought for a moment. 'Sorry, wrong word; excuse my English, the pyramid. They make their money from the pyramid.'

Tom was still lost. 'What is the pyramid?'

'A few years ago, when Bulgaria got freedom from Russians, everyone wanted to be a capitalist. Some smart people, mafia types, they made a pyramid scheme, you know, every person puts in one hundred dollars, then they have each to get another ten persons to put in a hundred dollars and so on.'

Tom had heard of the concept. 'Only the people at the top can ever benefit. We had a scam like that in Ireland, it was aimed at women, called it 'women enriching women' or something like that.'

Ehud took a sip from his drink. 'It is the oldest trick in the book as they say. I see many such scams on the internet, as little as one dollar you have to send and they promise that you will get back one hundred thousand dollars in six months. Of course many people still fall for it.'

'So what happened in Bulgaria?'

'It was different here, much more serious. Almost everybody in the country was involved, and everybody's savings were sucked into the pyramid. Even the banks did not escape, the national bank collapsed. Also the farmers, they put the money that was for the seeds into the scheme, and there were no crops the next year, there was actually a famine. It was crazy, really crazy.'

'So a few people made a lot of money.'

'Of course, the usual story; the people that started the scheme made a lot of money. There were about twelve developers that came out of that scheme. Now they are just about six.'

Tom nodded. 'Amalgamations, mergers?'

The Israeli smiled sadly. 'No, they are dead, the others are dead. They kill each other, now there are just six. It is necessary to be very careful in Bulgaria, Tom; do not try to make business without friends.'

**

The Lada cruised along the country road, speeded through towns and villages by the ever present Nikolai, the cheerful motorcycle policeman. The sun was shining and the countryside looked its best under the hot sun. The road ran through rich farmland, with large fields of sunflowers and corn that reached right to the edge of the road. The road itself was shaded with rows of nut trees, their trunks whitewashed to a couple of meters from the ground.

'Your family comes from near here? It's a very nice part of the world.'

Ehud lanky frame was hunched over the wheel, his eyes on the road as he flogged the old car along. 'Is beautiful this time of year, but in winter…'

'It gets cold?'

'Yes, very bad winters, sometimes the Black Sea freezes, ice.'

'Hard to imagine now, it reminds me of Spain when I look at the blue sky, although the fields are green and beautiful. Spain is a lot more arid.'

'Maybe you can make this a marketing idea. Call it 'New Spain'. Sell Bulgaria like an alternative to Spain, you know, for holiday all year round.'

'But it's hardly Spain really; if it gets very cold here in wintertime, we can't really call it the New Spain.'

'Look, Tom, in three years maybe we are already finished working here, maybe less. We make a lot of money, we can retire or go someplace else, and the buyers maybe will have a property that they will enjoy for holidays in summer. Is beautiful in summer, as you can see. It will not be a problem for us if they are complaining then; we will not be working here then.'

'I guess so, Ehud, 'buyer beware' as we say in the business. It's just our job to sell the stuff; it's their job to look where they're going.'

The car slowed as they approached the frontier. Nikolai slowed and motioned them to stay behind him. He would get them past the Bulgarian border police; that would be half the battle in getting across this notoriously slow border crossing.

The border post was like something from an old cold war spy movie. A huge concrete structure spanned the roadway, and a line of cars and trucks was pulled in along the side of the road. A rusting red and white barrier blocked the thoroughfare, manned by a policeman who looked bored and disinterested.

Their escort blipped his siren and the policeman raised the barrier and allowed them through. The motorcyclist pulled off the road and entered a police compound, waving them on as he slowed. Ehud drove past through the no-man's land to the Romanian crossing.

A smaller queue waited at the Romanian side. They parked the car at the back of the line and they both got out and stretched their legs. A line of people waited at small hatch where Tom could see a large policeman with a bushy moustache just inside the glass.

'Give me your passport. You have some small euros notes?' Ehud spoke quietly out of the side of his mouth.

Tom turned his back to the window and opened his wallet. 'How big?'

'Maybe two twenties, you have this amount? Not bigger.'

Tom passed the two twenties surreptitiously to the Israeli. The tall man folded one note into each passport and approached the window. He slid the documents in through the hatch and Tom saw the officer examine them, and heard the bang of a stamp being applied to each one. In a moment Ehud was back. 'We go, all is ok. Welcome to Romania.'

The English tourists in the queue were indignant. 'We've been waiting here for an hour, these locals get preference, it's not right.' The woman was speaking loudly to her male companion, deliberately loudly enough for everyone to hear. 'What do we have to do to get into the bloody country? What's the problem here?'

Her pleadings fell on deaf ears; the policeman closed the hatch with a snap and went away from the window. Ehud put the Lada in gear and moved off through the now raised barrier. He looked at Tom and ventured a wry smile.

'She complain and complain but nobody is interested, maybe even she makes more delay for herself.'

'Cash is king here so.' Tom was impressed by the way that Ehud had eased their way across the border.

'Yes, but I told you last night, you have to know who to pay. That is the problem in Romania; maybe you pay, and pay again, and you still not find the person who it is right to pay. Here is simple, just one stupid policeman who makes small increase on his salary; if you want to make business however it is more difficult. You have to know who to pay.'

Tom sat back in silence and took in the sights on the road north from the border. Although they were in a different country, the style of buildings, the rusting steel and concrete fences in the villages, all bore the same stamp as the environment in Bulgaria. They slowed as they passed through a small seaside village.

'This is Vama Veche, from where my grandfather comes; his home was here along this road, but the house is no longer here. It was just here I think.' Ehud slowed as they left the village and pointed out a spot to the right hand side of the road where some flat land stretched to the cliff tops. The place was pretty, with stunning views out over the Black Sea.

'Vama Veche is a very much loved seaside town, for holidays, very traditional holiday village. It was a place where many dissident gather for holiday, intellectuals, but was tolerated by communists. You understand the word dissident?'

'Yes, of course.'

'It never made developments like other seaside towns, but maybe in the future it is possible. I have made application for the return of our family lands here; maybe we will succeed, maybe not. If we succeed, maybe we make a project here, what do you think?'

'Looks nice, and anything is possible. How far are we from Constanta?'

'About half hour, you will see.'

He speeded up the car again and headed north; huge cranes loomed on the horizon. The sight looked to Tom like a shipbuilding facility; it reminded him of the gigantic cranes in Belfast.

'This is the big shipyard of Mangalia, was belonging to the state, now belongs to the Koreans. It was an important place for ship building in the old days; they still build ships but now I think it is mostly for repairing.'

They crossed over a big bridge and Ehud pointed out a dockyard on the left. 'This is the naval dockyard, the Romanian navy. If we look at this place maybe ten, fifteen years ago we are spies.' He laughed. 'Was nothing to see really, just some small ships.'

Ehud seemed to be very relaxed in Romania; he knew his way around and he was a mine of information on the places that they passed. 'Here is Efforie Sud, next is Efforie Nord, they are important resorts on the south side of Constanta. On the north side of course is Mamaia, biggest resort in Romania, very busy in summer.'

'Any business possibilities for us in any of these places?'

'I think not. Prices of land are too high, and we don't have information from the right people. I visit here maybe every month; I am always looking, maybe in time we will make a project here. We will see.'

They slowed as they hit heavy traffic on the outskirts of Constanta. The city limits were defined by a small ship, probably a decommissioned patrol boat Tom reckoned, that was mounted on concrete supports beside the highway.

Ehud joked as they passed the marooned ship. 'Was a big storm maybe, bring the ship so far from the sea. You want some lunch before the train? There is time.'

'Ok, that would be good. You know someplace?'

The Israeli turned down a side street and drove through several back streets; the surfaces of these minor roads were badly rutted and potholed. It seemed as though the authorities in Constanta only maintained the roads that were on view to passing motorists; the locals had to put up with a lesser standard. He skidded to a halt in a grand cobbled square that was surrounded by some old and attractive buildings, as well as a few derelict sites.

'This is the square of Ovid, you know of Ovid, the poet?'

Tom had a vague recollection of the name from his schooldays. 'Yes, I know of Ovid, can't say I know any of his poetry off by heart though.'

The Israeli laughed. 'Me neither, just I know there was such a man and he had a connection with this city.'

Ehud ordered a pizza and Tom asked for an omelet. The food arrived quickly and they ate in silence for a while. It was tasty and filling, and they followed it with two coffees. Ehud looked at his watch and pushed back his chair, dropping some notes on the table. 'Let's go, we must go to the train now.'

The station was not far away; Tom waited on the platform while his companion bought a ticket at a tiny window. The train pulled in, exactly on time, and Ehud showed him how to read his compartment number and seat number from the small pasteboard slip.

'We talk soon, Tom, have a good trip. I hope that we make a very successful business together.'

'I hope so too, Ehud; thanks for all your help.'

CHAPTER TWELVE

'Tough trip?'

Tom stretched himself back in the front seat of the Mercedes. 'It was tough, Tania, but thanks for coming out to collect me; I'm too wrecked to queue for a taxi.'

'You had to go round the houses to get home.'

'Yes, Bucharest, then Prague and on to Dublin, and I had a three hour train trip from Constanta to Bucharest as well.'

'Sounds like a long day.'

'It was, left the hotel at eight this morning Bulgarian time, had a long road trip to Constanta, and the taxi from Bucharest station to the airport took another hour, just made the bloody flight.'

'You'll have to plan ahead a bit for the next trip, that's too much of an ordeal. Anyway, fill me in on the details; I only got the bones of it from you on the phone.'

Tom recanted the details of the arrangements he had made with Ehud and the Bulgarians, and the potential he could see in the project near Sunny Beach. Tania was amazed at the possibilities.

'I knew that Bulgaria would be good, I just had a feeling about it. If we can do another Kover Amber on it, and with eight hundred apartments, we'll make a bloody fortune.'

'I don't think that will be the end of it either; they have another project in their own backyard, same kind of size, called Kukovo, but the Sunny Beach North job will give us a great start. If any of our competitors try to get in behind us we'll have a second string to our bow, so we won't have to worry about product for six months at least.'

Tania drummed her fingertips on the wheel as she waited for the lights to change. 'Is it wide open out there, could someone like Harry go there and get a break like we got this week?'

'Are you worried about Harry? I don't think you have to. I'd be more concerned about some of the others, maybe some small outfit that wants to get big quickly. It's very difficult to do business there, it seems to be a bit of a mafia setup; I heard some stories of developers killing each other to gain an upper hand.'

'Killing each other? You mean literally? Dead bodies?'

'Yes, seems like they are involved in some kind of natural selection process. Only the fittest will survive and all that.'

She pulled up outside Tom's apartment building. 'Be careful anyway, Tommy baby, don't get yourself killed for my shiny things. Are you not inviting me in?'

'Not tonight, Tania, I'm about ready to drop. See you in the morning; we have a show to run.'

'Ok, if I'm not wanted. Don't you want to know about Turkey?'

'Of course, forgot about that, how did you get on?'

Your contact Omer, he came over and we hammered out a deal; we'll be selling the villas tomorrow. The site is right next door to the Blue Apart Hotel, and we'll be doing as you suggested, two years rental guarantee at five percent. He keeps half of any rent on top of that and we get the rest. He seemed happy enough, I think that the project was going very slowly for him, we maybe threw him a lifeline.'

'Well done, boss, now I'll leave you and get some sleep.'

***

Tania was in her office when Tom arrived; he dropped gratefully into the chair across from her desk and peeled open his coffee.

'Sorry, would have brought you one, didn't think you'd be in this early.'

'No problem, Tom, I had some already. No, I had to come in, I'm working on something.' She pushed back her chair and looked at Tom. 'I have something I want you to do for me.'

'Within reason.'

'You know the way that Murtagh is always on the TV talking about foreign property? He's something of a pundit I suppose you'd call him.'

Tom nodded. 'He is because we made him one. That jackass knows nothing about the overseas market; anything he comes out with is what he got from us.'

'That's what I'm coming to, we made him what he is; would you agree?'

'Sure.' Tom wasn't clear on what his boss had in her mind. 'Only because it suits us; he's out there plugging all the spots we're doing business in. It's free advertising for us.'

'It is, but it's also free advertising for all our competitors; twenty four at the last count.'

'I'm sure you'll get to the point in a minute, Tania.'

'It's very simple, Tom, I want to go on TV, not just once but every week if possible. I want to be the choice of all the producers whenever they need an expert on foreign property. I want to be known as the leading foreign property expert in the country.'

Tom didn't know whether to laugh or say nothing. He looked at his boss; she had a serious look on her face, there was no doubt that she was in deadly earnest about this latest plan. He wasn't so sure about the wisdom of her idea though; it seemed to him to smack of vanity rather than common sense.

'I don't like it, Tania, if they throw questions at you that you can't answer....'

'That's where you come in, Tom; I want you to write me a synopsis of each market and to predict the kinds of questions that might be asked. Also, from today I want you to stop doing the radio slots; I'll do them from now on as well.'

'Ok, suits me very well if you can manage it.'

'Another thing.' Tania leaned forward across the desk. 'We need to up the ante a bit, let people know in no uncertain terms that we are the big guns in this business. From now on we don't do property shows, or property expos; this weekend's show is advertised as an 'investment seminar', that's what we will call all our shows from now on.'

'Ok, I go along with that. I like the sound of it actually.'

'So, get going and prepare me for the TV show tomorrow, I need a briefing document in two hours.'

'If you think it's wise, Tania, but I still have my concerns.'

'Don't worry about my ability to perform live on air; I'm well able to do that. What other worries have you got?'

' Murtagh. If you put him off side, lose him his bit of fame, we'll make an enemy of him.'

' Murtagh will do what he's told; at the end of the day we spend five grand a week with the Globe group, that's enough clout for us to call the shots.'

Tom didn't see it that way; if Murtagh got mad he might start being a journalist, start questioning things. All that they needed was someone to ask a few simple questions and the whole overseas property market would come crashing down around their heads. Still, there was no stopping Tania Sherry when she got the bit between her teeth.

'So how do you propose getting on the TV? You can't just ring up the stations and tell them that you'll be taking over from Murtagh from now on.'

Tania smiled smugly. 'I didn't tell you; that's all sorted. Mickey Macken, the racing guy, he's promised to get me on the business show tomorrow, and on the property show on Tuesday. I'm going to be billed as Doctor Sherry, the property doctor.'

'Mickey Macken! That jerk? How do you know him?'

'Don't be so judgemental, Tom, he's not at all like people think; he's a lovely man. He was in with me on Wednesday while you were off enjoying yourself in Bulgaria. Can you believe this; he's going to buy ten apartments from us in our next project? You see, I'm working hard selling apartments here while you're off on your travels.'

'I meant to warn you about Macken, Harry and Walter had an episode with him a few weeks ago. I was going to tell you about it at the time but it slipped my mind.'

'What kind of an episode?'

'He did the same thing with them; he booked ten apartments and then went off touting them among his hangers-on and cronies. He has to get a grand per apartment of a commission, insists on it, but no sign of a deposit or anything. When Harry pressed him for deposits he got stroppy with him, more or less said that he had lots of power and could make things difficult for Sunspots.'

Tania pondered this new information for a moment; then she brightened. 'But he's getting me on TV, that's something. Anyway, what harm if he doesn't have customers for the bloody apartments, maybe we can use it to our advantage.'

Tom had the feeling that he was playing catch-up again. 'I'm sure you have an angle Tania, what are you thinking?'

'I can wind Macken round my little finger; I suggest we make him the front man for our advertising campaign in Bulgaria, make it look as if he is endorsing the project, or even almost appear as if he's the developer. That way, people will have a lot more confidence in it, you know, he's a very famous name in sport and all that.'

'But how will you persuade him? Harry found him very difficult.'

Tania smiled knowingly. 'You know that I can get what I want when I want, Tom; I'll take care of Mickey Macken. After all he used to be a jockey, didn't he? I'm sure he hasn't lost the knack.'

***

The Bulgarian business was going well; for a place that nobody had ever heard of a few weeks before, suddenly everyone was an expert on Bulgaria. The Scorpio team had shifted three hundred apartments to small investors who were excited about the prospect of a guaranteed rental return on their properties, and the newspapers were full of information on this emerging economy. Tom's contacts within the newspaper business were providing almost all the facts in the marketplace, and Tania was now a regular contributor to a succession of radio and television shows.

He reached for the remote control and turned up the sound. The well-tanned breakfast show presenter was finishing off an interview with a woman who had several elderly greyhounds to re-home; the piece featuring Tania and Mickey Macken was just about due.

'So, coming up next, we have two experts on the overseas property market and the fantastic opportunities that are to be found for Irish investors in beautiful Bulgaria. Join us after the traffic report when we will be talking to Doctor Tania Sherry and our own Mickey Macken about the superb value that is to be found in that part of the world, and be in with a chance to win a trip to Sunny Beach. See you after the break.'

Tom flicked on the kettle again and made another cup of tea. The traffic was getting worse by the day; the booming economy that was driving the overseas property business was also grinding to a halt as more and more people got jobs and bought more cars to add to the numbers already crowding the roads. It was time to get to the office, but not until he had seen how Macken would handle this slot.

The traffic report finished and the programme returned to the studio where Tania relaxed on the couch as though she owned the place. Macken sat beside her, his short legs dangling over the edge of the brightly coloured sofa. He looked self conscious in his casual attire; Mickey preferred the tweedy look that went with his more usual racecourse environment.

'So, Doctor Sherry, welcome to the show, and of course Mickey Macken, no stranger to the viewers.' The presenter was treading carefully; this had the potential to become a serious piece, not what was expected this early in the morning.

Tania gave her broadest smile straight to the camera. 'Delighted to be here, Anto.' It seemed to Tom that her breasts had got bigger; she was showing a lot of cleavage and the camera operator was making the most of it.

'So, Doctor Sherry, you own the largest overseas property company in Ireland, and of course we see Mickey here on our screens a lot, promoting your developments in Bulgaria. Why Bulgaria?'

Tania never stopped smiling. 'Well, Anto, as you know we sell beautiful properties in Spain, but unfortunately not everyone can afford them, so we had to look for an alternative where Irish investors could get real value for money as well as the fantastic weather that they have come to expect in Spain.'

'So is Bulgaria similar to Spain, climate wise?'

'Yes, Anto. Beautiful climate, fabulous weather, and of course when they join the EU all the property will double in price. It really is too good an opportunity to miss, and investors have been voting with their feet for the last few weeks since we launched our project at Sunny Beach North. This is the only game in town, Anto, when it comes to investment overseas; welcome to the New Spain as we say.'

So, Mickey, would you say that Bulgaria is a good bet? It is a good each way shot, great weather and great investment?'

Macken grinned at the camera. 'Better than a safe bet, Anto; you get your money back and lots more with it, and a guaranteed return of five percent for the first two years after completion. This is the bet that never loses, Anto. No fallers or non-runners here, Anto.'

'Excellent. That's the kind of news that we love to bring to our breakfast viewers. Looks like everyone who can scrape up a few bob should get to your investment seminar at the weekend. And if you want to win a trip to Sunny Beach, text your name followed by the word Scorpio to the number on the top of the screen right now. Calls cost one euro per text, network charges may vary.'

The camera zoomed out to show Tania and Macken on the couch, Tania was still smiling broadly and Macken swung his short legs to and fro. The presenter leaned towards Tania; Tom had a terrible moment when he thought that she would let him have a piece of her mind for staring at her cleavage, but her smile never wavered.

'So, Doctor Sherry, thanks for coming in this morning, and we'll see you at your investment seminar at the weekend, details in all the national press?'

'Thank you, Anto, anyone who wants to make some money from foreign property needs to be well informed; we have an investment seminar every weekend, get there early for the best choices and before prices get too high.'

'We're having a lovely week here this week, nobody would ever go abroad if we had weather like this, but of course we don't, so that's where you come in. So, what's the weather like in Bulgaria right now; is it as nice as here?'

Tania looked flustered; she glanced down at her notes. The smile never wavered but it was beginning to look strained. The silence seemed to Tom to go on for ever, but eventually she looked straight at the presenter. 'It's like here right now, but nicer.'

***

Tom was leaving the car park when he got the first call of the day. He clicked the phone into the cradle and answered on hands-free.

'Good performance, Tania.'

'Fuck you, Tom, you left me out on a limb there, you know I've never been to bloody Bulgaria. Why didn't you brief me about the weather, the stupid prick nearly caught me out.'

'Come on, Tania, how was I supposed to predict a low ball like that? Anyway you finessed it ok, nobody noticed that you were lost for words for a second.'

'Not good enough, Tom, you're pulling serious money out of this company every month; I'm not paying you that kind of money to half do a job. I don't need another slipup like that, ok?'

Tom sighed. 'Ok, Tania, next time I'll try to predict the fucking future.' He punched the phone into silence.

It rang again; Tom swore at the instrument. 'Fuck off, Tania, I've heard enough shit for one morning.' He pressed the green button.

'Tom, Tom.' Ehud's voice was excited, panicky. 'Bad news, Tom, big problem for us.'

The tone of the Israeli's voice startled Tom; there was clearly something badly amiss. He pulled in to the side of the road and plucked the phone from the holder. 'What's wrong, Ehud? What's up?'

The Israeli was slightly breathless, as though he had been running. 'Sorry to call you so early, but this is very urgent, my friend.'

'What's wrong, Ehud?'

'Is Andon, he is dead. This morning, half hour ago.'

'Andon, the mayor, the developer?'

'Yes, Andon.'

'What happened, was it a car crash?'

'No crash. One bullet, in the head. He step out on the balcony for cigarette, bang!'

Tom almost dropped the phone. 'Fuck. How? Who killed him? Why?'

'Some persons, you know of who I speak, they do not like that we are making so much business so quickly I think. They do not want another big developer in this area. Maybe if we had started with the Kukova project it would have been better.'

'How did it happen?'

'They invite us to meeting on their site this morning; they tell us that they want to buy us out of our development, to amalgamate all projects in that area. Andon says no way; we don't need to make a business with them, we doing ok. He walks out on the balcony for his cigarette, then we heard rifle shot from one of the buildings across the street. He is dead; one shot through the head, looks like was a military person, good shot, very good shot.'

Tom felt sick in his stomach; this was the worst possible outcome. 'So what happens now? What about the sales we've made? Will Petar be able to finish the project?'

'Sure, Petar will finish, but they will take over the project anyway, we will have to pay them some money to stay in the game.'

'Money? How much money?'

'They say ten percent. Is not for discussion you understand. They know how much we are making, they want us to make money so we will keep selling, so we have an incentive.'

Tom felt a slight sense of relief, but he was still shaking. 'So they take ten percent of the price we are selling at?'

'Exact. You make less, but still a lot of money.'

'So you'll be taking a hit as well?'

'Of course, but is better than what Andon takes.'

'So what do we do now?'

'We do nothing. We continue as before but I think we forget about moving on to the Kukova project for now, look for something else away from here, away from the coast maybe. Maybe we look across the border in Romania, or maybe in Sofia, I don't know right now, I need to think.'

***

Tania was white faced. 'Jesus, Tom, this is fucking serious stuff. What kind of shit are we in?'

'We're not in any shit as far as I can see; apart from having our margin trimmed a bit. These guys are relying on foreigners to buy this stuff; nobody in Bulgaria can buy these properties, especially at these kinds of prices, so they won't do anything to spook the foreign companies working there.'

'But if this ever gets out? We won't sell another apartment.'

'It won't get out. Only you and I know about it, it won't make the papers here, don't worry about that part of it.'

Tania took a few deep breaths. 'So what do we do now? Do we just continue as if nothing had happened?'

'That's the plan. Just keep selling and pretend that all is normal. Ehud reckons that he'll come up with an alternative away from the territory that these guys control, and we can ease ourselves slowly out of Sunny Beach North and into the new location. We can keep selling on the coast, but at a reduced rate, and concentrate our sales on somewhere where we are getting the full margin again. It'll be ok, we'll be fine.'

'What about the man that was killed? Was he one of the guys you met?'

'Just on the first day; he was the Mayor. Nice kind of fellow, mild mannered, well spoken, probably corrupt as hell but he didn't deserve to be shot like a dog.'

Tania went to the cabinet and took out a bottle of vodka and two tumblers. 'Do you want one?'

Tom shook his head. 'I could use one, but I'm trying to stay on top of this problem, so I'll pass for now. Thanks.'

Tania poured a large vodka and added some tonic. She sat down heavily and drank half the contents of the glass. 'So what do we do next?'

'We haven't much choice, just continue with this week's show; keep the sunny side out and keep selling. Ehud is working on getting an alternative, somewhere away from there altogether, and I'll go out there on Sunday night or Monday morning and get that end of things up and running.'

'Ok, be careful, Tom; don't get yourself shot out there.'

'No real danger of that, Ehud reckons that they won't touch a foreigner. It would bring too much heat on their heads, and anyway they need foreigners to generate the cash flow for their own developments.'

'That makes sense, but be careful anyway.'

'I'm touched by your concern. By the way, nobody else needs to know about this, not Andrew, not Macken, nobody. Ok?'

'I don't know why you have such a set on Mickey, are you a bit jealous of him?'

'Don't be daft, Tania; just don't give him any idea that anything is wrong. Say nothing, ok?'

'Ok, Tom, maybe you're right.'

***

'New car?'

'Yes, I think is better than the old one, will get me out of trouble faster maybe.'

Ehud grinned as he opened the door of the BMW. Nikolai started up the engine of his motorcycle and headed out along the airport exit road and the Israeli followed behind.

Tom clicked on his seat belt and settled back in the comfortable leather seat. 'You're coming up in the world, my friend, very impressive motor.'

'Is better I think to have a good car in this country, anyway we are making money, Tom, a lot of money.'

'We were anyway, Ehud, not so sure about now; will we get paid for everything now that these guys are in charge?'

'Maybe not the last payment, but this is normal anyway in business here, so nothing new. No, they are starting to do big business with the English agencies, the big ones, and they do not want to give an impression that there will be problems. I think we are in best position, we will be mostly paid. Maybe the companies that come after will get less, or nothing.'

'Any more Irish companies sniffing around here now?'

'Almost every day, some agents are coming, but they are mostly small and are not getting local prices like we do. They are paying full foreigner prices and then they must get commission on top, so they can not compete with us.'

'Anyone we know?'

'From the list you gave me, only one. Mister Simpson was here last week, spoke to Uspeh Developments in Varna and made a deal, but only for approximately forty apartment. He will not be paid for his work; Uspeh will not pay, I know these jerks. Nobody will be paid, not the constructor, nobody.'

Nikolai indicated left and headed out of the city. Ehud opened up the BMW and they raced along the road, the motorcycle siren clearing them past lines of trucks and slower cars. At the outskirts of the city the policeman slowed and waved them on to pass him.

'So, where are we heading?'

'To a place called Malko, is in the mountains.'

'You think there is a market in the mountains for property?'

'No problem, already the English are buying ski property in Bansko, is selling almost as well as the coast. If we make the thing with the rental guarantee, we can sell a lot of this kind of product.'

'So is the skiing good in Malko?'

'Sometimes, I guess so, sure.' The Israeli laughed heartily.

'So not too good then?'

'Is not our problem, Tom, sure there is skiing there, not like Austria or France you understand, but you can ski for sure.'

'I guess so, Ehud, we're only selling the apartments, not the snow.'

'Exact. Most important thing, Tom, can we make business in Malko and can we get paid? This is all that is our concern. After that, if buyers want to buy, they should make their own enquiries about the quality if the snow.'

'Anyway, they'll have a guaranteed return.'

The Israeli laughed. 'Very good, Tom. Yes, they will have a guaranteed return.'

* * *

'Ok, guys, we need to get this strategy together before the weekend. This is a new departure for us; ski property is a different ball game.' Tom opened up a new flip chart and pulled the cap off a marker pen. 'Any ideas, any points that will help so move this stuff?'

Andrew was hesitant. 'I've never been skiing, but maybe we need to sound as if we have all skied a bit, maybe even in Bulgaria?'

'Good point, Andrew, sound like we know the product.' Tom scribbled on the chart. 'Trevor, will you get on the net after this and pull down as much info on Bulgarian ski holidays as you can?'

Andrew was becoming more enthusiastic. 'We could say that Malko is thinking of applying for the Winter Olympics.'

'Many a true word was spoken in jest, Andy, that's a good line.' Tom wrote 'Winter Olympics' on the chart.

'But we can't really say that, can we?' Trevor was new, and was still learning.

Tom laughed. 'We can't say that they are applying, not unless slush-boarding is a new event in the Olympics. Nothing to stop us saying that they are thinking of applying; they may well be thinking about it. Nothing wrong with saying that.'

'Thinking of' is a good phrase. 'Covers a multitude.' Andrew was in creative mood. 'We could say that one of the budget airlines is thinking of flying there.'

'Nice one, Andrew, sounds good. It works everywhere else.' Tom wrote 'Budget Airlines' on the page.

'Joining the EU shortly.'

'Thanks, Trevor. Tom marked 'EU, prices to rise' on the top of the list.

'Biggest problem I see is that this skiing business is a short season, what happens with the places for the rest of the year?'

'Good point, Trevor. We can just say what they say in France, that you can rent to walkers and hikers and all that.'

'But that never happens, does it?'

'It could possibly, if they found renters themselves. It happens in some places, although on a very small scale. Maybe Bulgaria will turn into a hikers' paradise when they join the EU.' Tom wrote 'Hikers' on the chart.

'Guaranteed rent of course.'

'Thanks, Andy.' Tom scribbled.

'So who pays the guaranteed rent? Is it all the year round?'

'We guarantee it, Trevor, but we have contracts with tour operators.' Tom didn't believe in telling the sales team everything.

'And can we show these contracts to the buyers?'

'Commercial confidentiality, Trevor, that's why we have to underwrite the guarantee ourselves.'

'Prices rising at twenty percent a year.'

'Thanks, Andy. Yes, we'll be putting up the price of the next phase by twenty percent, maybe even more if the demand is strong.'

**

'We need to be in more places, Tom, we're the biggest and we are going to stay the biggest.'

'I don't see the point in being in countries just for the sake of being in countries; we only need to be in places where we are making money.'

'Look, Tom, you don't get it, this is about more than money. We're the big operators here; everyone else is trotting to keep up.

We have to be breaking new ground all the time, breaking into new markets.'

'Ok, Tania, but let's keep our eye on the ball as well. Bulgaria and Spain are making the money for us; the others are just window dressing. We've only sold a dozen French leasebacks in the last month, not worth our while being in that market at all, and neither of us has ever been to France.'

'Not true, I was at a match in Paris once.'

'That doesn't count; I mean we never even looked at the developments we're selling in France.'

'We never went to Turkey either, and look how well that did for us.'

'I don't like taking those kinds of chances, Tania, I would honestly prefer that we at least had a look at anything we sell; we need to be sure that it exists.'

'Are you getting timid on me, Tom? I thought you had a lot more bottle than that.'

'I have plenty of bottle, Tania, I just don't see the point in trying to be in so many different territories when we can do very well in two or three, and do them properly. What's with this global domination stuff anyway?'

'I don't think you'll ever understand, Tom; Scorpio is my baby. I named the company after my star sign, and I want the brand to be universal. I want it to be respected. This isn't just about the money, Tom.'

'It is for me. When the money stops, I'm gone.'

Tania pushed two printed pages across the desk. 'Well if you're so concerned about checking out the facts, why don't you get on a plane this afternoon and check out the latest offerings?'

Tom scanned the printouts quickly. 'Montenegro? The Lebanon? Are we not scraping the bottom of the barrel here?'

His boss laughed. 'If people want it, we should supply it. What's wrong with those locations?'

'We discussed Montenegro weeks ago; it's a crazy place, complete lack of law and order. They don't even have their own currency.'

'Crazier than Sunny Beach North?'

'Ok, ok, I'll go to Montenegro this evening. So what's the story with the Lebanon?'

'I'm very excited about the Lebanon, everyone knows where it is because our soldiers served there on peacekeeping duties. It has such a romantic air about it too don't you think? Cedar trees and all that kind of crap.'

'So where did you come across these two offerings?'

'They emailed us, looking for us to represent them in Ireland. I reckon that the word is out that Irish buyers will buy anything, anywhere. The Lebanese came through your Israeli friends. All the contact names are on there, I reckon if you go to Dubrovnik and drive down to Montenegro it's the best way. You can fly back to Rome from Dubrovnik and on to Beruit, do the whole circuit before Friday.'

'You're a slave driver, Tania Sherry. I don't know why I do it.'

'You do it for the money, Tom. Have a good trip.'

CHAPTER THIRTEEN

'Are you with the group?'

Tom looked at the woman with the walking stick. She was dressed in an old-fashioned manner that made her look older, but he guessed that she was really no more than fifty. Her mostly brown headscarf matched the thick plastic frames of her spectacles, and she had the eager look of the very devout. A large wooden cross hung from a leather thong around her neck, and her walking stick was emblazoned with small shields and badges that told a history of many pilgrimages.

'Group? What group?'

'Father John's group, he's the leader. That's him over there; oh he's a wonderful man, a very holy man.'

Tom looked in the direction of the leader. A plump red-faced man in black clerical garb was holding court to a group of excited middle aged women and a few slightly nervous looking men. Like the woman in front of Tom in the check-in queue, Father John also wore a wooden cross around his neck, and he repeatedly tapped the ground with an even more decorated walking stick.

Tom turned his gaze back to the woman. 'No, I'm not with any group.'

'A solitary pilgrim so, you must be very experienced to do it on your own, I'd say you're a priest, or maybe a monk. You should join with us, there's safety in numbers and we can pray together.'

'Madam, I'm just trying to get on my flight, I know nothing about any group or anything else.'

'But this is the plane for Medjugorje, why would you be going if you're not with the group?'

'I'm going to Dubrovnik, I know nothing about Medjugorje or any group, or Father bloody John or anything else.'

'Oh my God, I'm in the wrong queue, sorry, sorry, where do I go now? Father John, Father John, Help me please!'

The priest tap-tapped his way across the departures area, followed by his flock. 'What's wrong, dear?'

'I'm in the wrong queue, Father; where do I go to get on the plane?'

The stout priest looked up at the screen. 'No, you're fine, dear; that's the right place.'

'But this man says it's not going to Medjugorje.'

'I didn't say that.' Tom wished that the whole lot of them would get out of his face. 'I just said that I wasn't going to bloody Medjugorje, that's all.'

'No need to swear, young man; show some respect for decent Christian people. It's ok, dear; you're in the right place. This is your flight, don't worry.'

She glared at Tom. 'Why would you try to put me wrong? May God forgive you; are you a Protestant or a Muslim or what's wrong with you?'

Tom ignored the woman and eventually she checked in and joined her group. He gratefully took the boarding pass from the woman at the desk and headed for security, moving quickly to get there before the straggling line of pilgrims that trailed behind Father John.

He had an aisle seat in the front row and he boarded late, waiting until the rush had subsided before heading down the airbridge. The plane was chaotic, with some of the cabin staff trying to get the pilgrims to sit down so that they could get the flight under way. This was proving difficult; Father John was moving up and down the aisle, counting his group and checking their names against a list. It was clear that someone was missing.

Eventually she arrived; it was the pious woman that Tom had encountered in the check-in queue. One of the cabin stewards rushed her to her seat and they closed the doors and started on the announcements as the passenger apologized to nobody in particular. 'Sorry, sorry, were you all waiting for me? I just went into the toilet and said a rosary that we'd all be safe, I didn't think anyone would mind; we all need prayer, especially at times like this.'

The captain apologized for the delay as he taxied out to the runway. His voice was quickly drowned out by the rising sound of prayers being recited by Father John and his group, a sound that swelled in time with the rising roar of the engines as the airbus accelerated down the tarmac. Tom caught the eye of the young stewardess who was sitting across from him; she raised an eyebrow imperceptibly and smiled slightly. It looked as if this might be nothing out of the ordinary on the Dubrovnik flight.

The sound of hymn singing woke Tom; they were making the descent over the Adriatic. He was grateful for his front row seat; at least he would be off the plane and through passport control before Father John and his followers clogged up the place.

The driver was waiting at the barrier with Tom's name written on a sheet of paper. 'Welcome, Mr. Murphy, I am Vladimir. I hope you had a good flight, come this way please.'

Tom followed the young Montenegrin to the waiting Jeep and they drove south from the airport, away from the city. The road was busy but the traffic was flowing freely, and they reached the border in just a few minutes. The border post looked to Tom like a temporary measure, just a few shipping containers painted in United Nations Blue, and a scattering of blue-capped UN personnel keeping a watchful eye on the cars and trucks that passed through the police control. He showed his passport to the border policeman, who stamped it and passed it back with barely a glance.

One of the men in the blue berets approached the jeep and motioned Tom to get out of the vehicle. He looked at the driver for reassurance; 'Is this normal?'

'It's ok, they check a small percentage of persons; they are UN police observers, no problem with them.'

Tom got out of the car and walked towards one of the blue containers with the policeman. He was surprised at the Irish accent when the man spoke to him.

'Just checking, sir, I noticed the Irish passport when you handed it in. Is the purpose of your visit business or pleasure?'

'I'm on a short business trip, I'll be back tomorrow.'

'Be careful in Montenegro, sir, what nature of business are you involved in?'

Tom wondered at the questioning; maybe the guy thought he was an arms dealer or something. Anyway, he seemed friendly enough, and he was Irish as well.

Tom smiled. 'Nothing illegal; I'm in the property business.'

'This isn't an official comment you understand, just one Irishman to another. Just watch your back, there's a lot about the property business in Montenegro that's dodgy and even downright dangerous. Are you carrying a lot of cash, did your contacts tell you to bring cash to buy the property?'

'No, nothing like that, I'm just an agent, no cash involved.'

'That's ok; I see lots of guys lately with briefcases full of money, maybe not all of it legal, heading down to buy land and sites. A lot of them lose it, and don't ever see any land in return, so I warn them when I see them to keep their eyes open.'

'That's decent of you.' Tom warmed to the young policeman. 'What else is dodgy about Montenegro, what kind of things go wrong?'

'Land ownership isn't as straightforward as you might think, for one thing. A lot of land was taken from its owners during the war, not just in Montenegro but in Bosnia and Croatia as well, and if we get to a restitution process in this region then the title to a lot of it may be worthless. People that buy certain property here may have to give it back at some stage if the rightful owners come back.'

'But if it has title, from the town hall say, it will be ok?'

'Not necessarily, a lot of the town halls are crooked, paper may mean nothing if it comes down to a court case in the future. Look, I'm no lawyer, I'm just an observer here, but I'm saying to you what I say to a lot of people in your shoes, just be careful. Not everything is as it seems in this part of the world.'

The man handed back the passport and Tom got back in the jeep. Vladimir raised his eyebrows. 'Problem?'

'No, no problem, just a routine check.'

They drove for an hour and crossed the neck of a narrow fjord on a small open-decked ferry, then headed south along a winding tree-lined road that hugged the coast and gave views over some rocky shoreline and the occasional small beach. Ten minutes later the driver pulled off the road into a small town and stopped outside the only hotel.

'I have booked you a room here; you can eat here also, or there are two restaurants by the shore. I will collect you at seven in the morning as you asked; we will meet my boss and the other promoters of the project at seven thirty.'

Tom dropped his bag in the room and walked down to the small beach. A few cafes and a pizza restaurant were open for business, as well as a shop selling what appeared to be pirated CDs. The latter advertised its wares by blaring the music loudly through a pair of massive speakers, almost drowning out the sound of the two musicians playing in the small bar next door. A couple of small shops sold postcards and an array of inflatable plastic beach toys, but the people wandering up and down didn't appear to be spending any money.

The waiter in the pizza place almost grabbed him and showed him eagerly to a table. The choices were limited; just pizzas and basic pasta dishes. Everything was cheap but there was nothing to excite the palate; Tom ordered a pizza and a bottle of imported beer and sat taking in the view as the sun set over the small bay.

It was a pretty place, no doubt about that, but would Irish buyers buy apartments here? That was another question altogether. It was a bit off the beaten track, no real reason for anyone to visit the area, but then again that could change. If a project was well packaged, maybe with a bit of guaranteed rental attached, then buyers might be tempted. It would never be Spain though; the place would never be another Costa del Sol, no matter what happened over the next few years. This was the backwoods, even allowing for the fact that it was a summer destination only.

The Irish policeman's advice worried him a little. Was it really that bad? What kind of problems would be down the line for buyers if the UN or somebody started getting back land for its rightful owners? Tom had heard about the so-called ethnic cleansing, where people were forced from their homes and lands during the civil war. What if they all came back and wanted to move into the apartments built on their lands? Would Scorpio have to compensate them? He didn't know, but stranger things had happened.

He didn't like the direction that Tania was taking the business lately. Ever since she started appearing on the TV she was different; it was like she believed her own hype about being the Property Doctor. All this madness about more and more new markets, this was all crazy stuff. What was the point? They were doing fine in Bulgaria and Spain, why divert buyers to crazy markets like Montenegro? At least in Spain and Bulgaria you were reasonably sure of getting paid, and the buyers stood a good chance of owning something; down here, you couldn't be sure of anything.

The waiter brought the pizza and Tom started to eat; it tasted better than it looked, it wasn't too bad. He ate most of it and ordered another beer.

He lay awake for a couple of hours; it was hard to sleep with the racket from the music shop. He didn't really want to be here in this small village in Montenegro; he had plenty to do back in the office and he wasn't convinced of the usefulness of trying to set up business links here. He thought of the trip tomorrow, on to Rome and then to Beirut; that all seemed pointless too. Why did she want to have a presence in all these places? What was this global domination stuff about? Was she just trying to outdo Harry and the bicycle man and all the other pretenders to the overseas property throne? Tom didn't have answers, but the whole thing was starting to annoy him.

He thought about his own situation. He was making a lot of money; he could quit now and never have to do another day's work if he wanted to. He knew that his job involved walking a very thin line between legality and downright deceit; he didn't have a real problem with that but he knew too that some day it might all fall down around his ears. It was a constant niggling concern that all his customers might come looking for their money back when they realised that they had bought so much rubbish. He wasn't overly worried about it, after all he was technically just an employee of the company, and the buck stopped with them. Maybe it was time to think about where this would all end though, to consider his strategy in the longer term.

Eventually he drifted off to sleep in the narrow bed. The blaring music started at dawn and he got up and showered; there was no point in trying to lie on with that racket. The breakfast was much as he had expected; some soggy cereal and some hard bread and curled slices of cheese. The coffee was strong and tasty though and it woke him up, so that he was alert and ready to go when Vladimir pulled up outside.

'Good morning, Mr. Murphy.'

'Good morning, Vladimir. Where are we going to this morning exactly?'

'Not too far from here, it was a big hotel in the old days, now it's closed, empty. My bosses want to renovate, make from it an apartment development, they will meet us there.'

They drove down a side road that led them along the side of a cliff; the road ended at a tunnel and Vladimir shifted into first gear and turned on the headlights. 'This road is not used any more; it will need to be renovated also.' The jeep lurched along the rutted road through the rocky tunnel.

They emerged into the sunlight in a small bay, a pretty place with a little beach and a dilapidated concrete building perched on the steep slope above it. Two other four wheel drive vehicles were parked in the small car park and a group of heavy-set men stood around, most of them smoking.

The older man reached out his hand. 'Welcome to Montenegro, I hope that you had a good journey.'

'Yes, thank you.' Tom was reminded of the policeman's advice when he looked around at the group. Apart from the man in front of him who was well past middle age, the others looked strong and fit, and had the appearance of former soldiers. They all shared the same tight military style haircuts, and they stood with feet apart and with hands behind their backs as if they had just been told to stand at ease. He wouldn't like to be here if he was carrying a briefcase full of money, it would be pretty nerve-wracking.

'This is our project, Mr. Murphy. It was a hotel as you can see, a very fine hotel in the old days but not so good now.'

'Nice site right enough.' Tom liked the look of the little bay with the waves lapping on the small beach. It was idyllic.

'We will make here a project with sixty five apartments and a small restaurant and a bar; my associate will show you the plans in a moment. It will be a top development, luxury apartments, all with a view to the sea. Very nice. Do you think that you can sell such a project in Ireland?'

'It's possible, depends of course on the price and the specification, but everything is possible.'

'This is what I have heard; in Ireland you can sell anything, it is a rich country, a lot of money there. Come, let us go inside.'

One of the younger men unlocked a side door to the building and pushed it open, stepping aside to allow the others to enter. In the hallway another thick-set man placed a basket on a table and motioned to the others.

'In the basket please.'

To Tom's shock, the other men all produced pistols of varying shapes and sizes from inside their jackets. He felt weak at the knees; the policeman had warned him about trouble, but what on earth was going on? Surely they hadn't lured him here to kill him, what would be the point of that?

It all seemed surreal, and Tom wasn't sure for a minute if he was dreaming, but then one by one the men deposited their guns in the basket and walked on into the building. The older man placed a small silver pistol carefully on top of the other weapons and motioned to Tom.

'Your gun please, Mr. Murphy. It is not considered civil to bring your gun to a meeting.'

Tom stammered with relief. 'I, I don't have a gun, I didn't bring a gun, really.'

The older man looked surprised. 'The other Irishmen who were here had guns; please do not take this as any kind of disrespect, but we must check, you understand. Max!'

The thick-set man stepped forward and frisked Tom quickly and efficiently; he had done this before. 'Is ok.'

'Sorry to doubt you, Mr. Murphy, just routine, I hope that you understand.'

'No problem.' Tom was still in shock at the display of weaponry; what had he got himself into here?

He followed the boss to what must have been the hotel restaurant, a large room overlooking the bay. A round table stood in the middle of the room, and one of the other men was unrolling papers and drawings on to it. They sat down and Tom busied himself looking through the plans; he didn't want his nervousness to show in front of these people.

'So, Mr. Murphy, you think you can sell these apartments to your investors?'

'Maybe, depends on the price and how much interest we can generate in Montenegro. What is the situation with the site, the hotel, are you the owner?'

The older man said something in his own language, provoking a ripple of laughter from the men around the table. 'Owner? This is a word that means different things in different countries; it is enough to say that I can make all decisions about this property.'

'So the title, the legal ownership, can be transferred properly to buyers in the project?'

'Of course, everything will have the stamp of the town hall, will be absolutely legal, is absolutely not a problem.'

'I think we can probably generate some interest in this, but I will have to talk it over with my associates, look at the figures, you know.'

'We have many other lands, properties, if you sell this one there will be many others. We can make a lot of business together.'

Tom ventured a smile. 'And you are the owner of all of them?'

The boss laughed and clapped Tom on the back. 'You are beginning to understand my country; we will work well together, I am sure.'

The trip back to the border seemed to pass quickly; the police waved the jeep through without a glance and the signs for the airport appeared almost immediately. Tom turned to the driver.

'I have a lot of time to kill before my flight, could you drop me in Dubrovnik maybe, and I'll get a taxi out to the airport later?'

Vladimir shook his head. 'I am sorry, I do not like to go inside Dubrovnik, is not a good place for me, but I will leave you at the taxi place at the airport, you can get taxi to the city.'

'Are there problems in Dubrovnik?'

'No, no, not for you, not for foreigner, but for a Serb like me, it is not a good place. I would like to help you, but I don't feel good about going there. I hope that you understand.'

Tom waved goodbye to the driver and took a taxi to the gate in the huge city wall; he walked through the arch and down the main street and sat at a table outside a busy café. The coffee was good and strong and the shady cobbled street was crowded with strolling tourists. He ordered some lunch and called Tania.

'Back in Dubrovnik, just marking time until the flight to Rome.'

'Any joy? What was the project like?'

'The project was fine, very attractive site, but they're gangsters; do you know I was the only one at the meeting without a gun?'

Tania laughed loudly. 'We'll have to get you a little gun, can't have you letting the side down. Question is, can we make a margin, and can we be sure of getting paid?'

'Yes to the first, and probably no to the second.'

'Then we shouldn't waste any more time on it, it would be nice to have it on the books though. Maybe we can put it up on the website and say it's all sold or something.'

'I think we should just walk away from it, Tania; forget about the bloody country, it's a dangerous place.'

'What about where you are, Dubrovnik, that's a separate country isn't it?'

'Yes, it's in Croatia. Why?'

'Any business there?'

'Looks great, a very attractive city, a lot more relaxed and lots of tourists.'

'Then have a run around the streets and find an estate agents office, do a deal with them on split commissions, anything at all, just to get a foot in the door in Croatia.'

'Tania, I have only an hour here.'

'Then don't waste it. Goodbye, Tom.'

***

The Boeing nosed up to the terminal at Fiumicino and the seatbelt sign pinged off; Tom stretched himself and headed for the door. There was plenty of time, but he had never been to Rome and wasn't familiar with the layout of the airport buildings; there was always an anxious few moments until it became clear where the gate for the next flight was located. This time it was easy to find, only a short walk from where he had come in. The queue was already starting for the Beirut flight; all the passengers were being checked and having their hand baggage screened.

It had been a stroke of luck meeting the Englishman in Dubrovnik. A hundred yards from the café Tom had pushed open the door of an estate agent's shop, pleasantly surprised at the modern layout and the professional looking setup in general. When he asked the young woman at the counter whether she spoke English, she asked him to wait and went back and brought a young man in a smart suit to meet Tom.

'Hello, I'm Graham, how can I help you?'

'Tom Murphy, Scorpio investments, can I have a few words?'

Graham had moved to Dubrovnik to be closer to his wife's family, and had used his experience in property sales in England to open a new agency in the city. It was doing well, selling property to locals and foreigners, and he was interested in Tom's proposal.

'The commissions are small, so half of any commission isn't much, but its all cash flow and we'd be glad to do business if you can give us reasonable volume.'

'What would you call reasonable?'

'Two or three sales a month would be good.'

'I think we can manage that. If you can get an exclusive project, where nobody else has access to it locally or otherwise, we can both make additional margin and we can probably do a lot better than that.'

Funny how things sometimes fell into your lap when you weren't really looking; he had just gone into Dubrovnik to pass an hour, but it had turned out a lot better than the experience in Montenegro. He shuddered at the memory of the basket of guns and the man who laughed at the notion of ownership of property. Life with Scorpio was never dull, that was for sure.

In spite of his tiredness, Tom was excited at the prospect of seeing another new country. Even though he was only on the plane, the atmosphere was different; there was already a feeling of being somewhere exotic. Many of the passengers were in Arab dress, and the babble of languages was different from his usual experience. He was looking forward to seeing the Lebanon.

At the aircraft door Tom's first thought was that he was walking through a stream of hot air from the engines, but as he descended the steps it became clear that this was a sweltering night. He walked across the tarmac to the terminal and joined the queue at the visa desk. The policeman leafed through his passport and looked him in the eye, comparing his face to the passport picture.

'Purpose of your visit, sir?'

'Business.'

'How many days you want to stay please?'

'Until tomorrow.'

The policeman stamped the passport with a large square stamp and scribbled something on it.

'That will be ten Lebanese pounds, sir.'

'You take euros?'

'Fifteen euros, sir.'

Tom passed over the money and retrieved the passport. The queue at immigration had almost cleared and he passed quickly through and headed for the taxi rank outside. The taxi wasn't air-conditioned and he sweated in his shirt and tie; the cool lobby of the Monroe Hotel was a welcome relief. He leaned on the long white counter and passed his credit card to the receptionist; it was late and he was very tired and not in the humour for small talk. The porter seemed to sense his mood and said little as he brought Tom's bag to the room.

The swimming pool was inviting and he dived in and swam a few lengths and tried to focus his mind on tomorrow's work. The man who was meeting him was a local 'fixer' who had been recommended to him by a friend who had worked for one of the television companies; Mr. Haddad would get a foreigner around safely and probably save him a lot of money in the process. He had the contact details for a development not too far down the coast, at Tnen Kalset; the owner of the project was a Lebanese Jew called Ami Yemen, a distant connection of the Mamser family. At least the devil you knew was better than a complete stranger; Tom was still shaken by his encounter with the gunmen in Montenegro.

The swim refreshed him and he headed out to look around the neighbourhood. The area around the hotel was neat and clean and the buildings were mostly new with white plastic windows and doors, but a few blocks away the character changed and the shops and cafes were simpler and had more of an Arab feel, shabbier, older and with thickly-painted metal window frames. Light glowed from a small single-storey café in a side street, and the noise of conversation drifted out through the open windows. The café had its name over the door in large Arabic writing, and two large white menu panels on either side of the door were covered in more of the same script. The place was brightly lit and still had quite a few customers, so he pushed open the door and went inside. The floor was tiled with large terracotta tiles and the cafe was furnished with a mixture of bentwood chairs and plastic garden furniture, but it looked clean. A glass display case held a selection of Arab sweets, and a large stainless steel tray of what he recognised as baklava, the sweet pastry made with nuts and honey.

He ordered a beer and the waiter brought him a cold bottle of Laziza.

'Is without alcohol monsieur, is this ok?'

Tom wondered whether this might be the rule in the country generally, but he decided not to ask the question. Anyway, the beer looked good and cold in the glass and he wasn't really bothered whether or not it contained alcohol. He raised the glass to the waiter.

'That's fine, thank you.'

He supped the beer for a while, taking in his surroundings. The café was lively with several men in traditional garb enjoying snacks and sipping tea and eating mezzes, small dishes of food that they ate with hot pitta bread. A group of men around one table was playing a noisy game of backgammon. The atmosphere was very welcoming and non-threatening, and Tom relaxed and called for another beer.

He became gradually aware of the woman at the table by the window; she stood out with her western dress. She was engrossed in the book she was reading, pausing every now and then to take a sip from a tall glass filled with a cloudy liquid. The book was an English one and he recognized the cover; he had browsed through it in the airport bookshop a few days earlier.

The woman caught his eye and smiled; he raised his glass in salute. 'Long way from home, aren't you?'

'No further than you.' He was surprised at the Irish accent; Tom had assumed that she was English. He walked over to her table. 'Do you mind if I join you?'

'Feel free. Are you on holidays here?'

Tom shook his head. 'No, just here for a day or so, small bit of business. You?'

'I'm on a long holiday, heading through all the holy places from the biblical times. Just taking a month out from the rat race.'

'Finding yourself?'

'Something like that.'

She had a nice smile and as he spoke to her he realized that she was not as old as he had first assumed. Her hair was flecked with grey, but her skin looked young and she was probably no more than in her early forties. 'So that's why you're reading 'the Battersea Park Road to Enlightenment'?'

The woman threw back her head and laughed. 'In a way, that's what attracted me to the title, but it's a good read in any case, it's very funny.'

'I looked at it in the airport bookshop last week; I was going to buy it. Its all about tantric sex isn't it?'

'Trust a man to take that from it. There's one chapter on that topic, the rest is about various alternative approaches to life. I'm enjoying it anyway.'

Tom was intrigued by this strange woman and her laid back approach to life. He extended his hand. 'I'm Tom by the way, would you like another drink?'

'I'm Pauline. No thanks, I'm fine; I'm heading back to my hotel shortly.'

'Just out of interest, what's that stuff you're drinking?'

'It's Arak, it's a liqueur made from anis, you dilute it with water and it goes cloudy like that.'

'Is it alcoholic?'

'Yes.'

'I wasn't sure of you could get alcohol in this country.'

'You can, mostly wine, but a lot of these cafes don't have it. I think they just keep a bottle of Arak for the foreigners, this is a Muslim neighbourhood and there probably isn't much demand for alcohol. The hotels do all the imported beers anyway.'

'Are you in the Monroe?'

'No, nothing so fancy, I'm in a small place just at the end of the street. It's cheap and clean but a bit basic.'

'Trying to stay in touch with the people?'

She laughed again. 'That sums it up I suppose, I find that big hotels are a bit impersonal, fine if you're looking for a comfortable bed but a bit isolated from the country and the populace.'

Tom nodded agreement. 'I know what you mean, sometimes I wake up and I'm not sure what country I'm in. A lot of the big hotels are the same no matter where you are.'

'So you travel a lot?'

'Quite a bit, but only for short trips.'

'So this is a short trip as well?'

'Just tonight and tomorrow. How about you?'

'I've been here in Beirut for a few days; I came across from Cyprus on the truck ferry. I'm heading down to Tyre tomorrow, then across to Syria for a few days and on down to Israel. I'll be in Jerusalem in about ten days; I'm really looking forward to that.'

'What's the attraction of Tyre, is it a big place?'

'It's a small city, but it's been there for ever and it has the most Roman ruins in the country. There are also a lot of sunken ruins, Roman and Phoenician, just off the coast. I'd love to see those, it would be amazing to float above them and see them that way.'

'So how do you go about that, do you go scuba diving?'

'You can, but I'm just going to go snorkeling, apparently you can see them pretty well, the water is clear. It should be fun.'

'How are you traveling? Have you a car?'

'No, I don't think I'd like to drive here, it's a bit mad. I'm using the buses.'

'It's probably simpler, right enough. The buses are ok, are they?'

She smiled. 'Usually, yes. Sometimes they're very crowded, but everyone is very nice to me.'

Tom thought for a minute. 'Tyre is south of here isn't it?'

'Yes, about two and a half hours on the bus, not that it's very far but the bus goes around the houses a bit I think.'

'We're going to a place past Az Zahrani in the morning, I think it's near enough to Tyre, do you want a lift? It might be more comfortable than the bus.'

'Who's 'we'?'

I have a driver who is taking me down to a small place about ten kilometres south of Az Zahrani, I'd be glad of the company if you want to come along.'

She looked Tom up and down and smiled. 'You look safe enough; I'd be delighted to accept your offer.'

Tom finished his beer and stood up. 'That's fine then; we're leaving at eight, so if you want to drop by the Monroe I'll meet you in the lobby about then.'

She closed her book and put it in her large handbag. 'Thanks for that, I'll see you in the morning. And don't worry, I'll be on time.'

***

Tom slept well and was up early for breakfast in the hotel restaurant. The day seemed to be mercifully cooler; the staff had the sliding glass door open and the soft tinkle of ropes on hollow aluminium masts drifted in from the marina. It all seemed a long way from Tom's image of the Lebanon as a country that was recovering from a civil war; this place had all the relaxed atmosphere of any Mediterranean country, but then again maybe the day would tell a wider story.

The Irishwoman was waiting in the lobby when he went to check out. She was dressed for comfort in a long blue summer dress and leather trekking sandals, and she carried a new-looking rucksack.

'Traveling light?'

'Yes, I have everything pared down to the minimum. When you have to carry it on your back, you get ruthless about packing.'

Tom picked up the rucksack and carried it outside to the waiting car. It was surprisingly light for a month's trip. Pauline seemed to read his mind.

'It's no problem getting washing done. It would be impossible to pack a month's supply of clothes, so I only really have enough for a week, but I stop and launder everything when I start to run out.'

Tom was beginning revise his earlier estimate; the morning was warming up quickly and this looked as if it would be another hot day. The Mercedes was cool, almost icy; Haddad believed in keeping the air conditioning turned up to the full. Tom put the bags in the boot and they settled into the back of the big car.

It was farther than it looked on the map; they were on the road for more than an hour even after leaving the city limits of Beirut behind them. The countryside was dry and arid, with little in the way of vegetation but scrub and thorn bushes. Here and there the blue Mediterranean came into view on the right hand side of the road, small towns clustered along the shore nearer the city but even these became less and less as they moved south. A lot of old ruins could be seen in places, it seemed to Tom that the developers had been working here since biblical times.

Where the land was flat the road passed through several large orange groves; the dark green leaves of the citrus trees making a marked contrast to the arid landscape. In a gap between two orange fields a man tended a crop of wavy green fronds, directing irrigation water along the furrows between the plant rows.

Tom wondered aloud as to what type of crop was being cultivated.

'Its cannabis, marijuana.'

'As in the drug?'

'Yes, the same. Apparently they grow a lot of it here, I'm not quite clear if it's legal or not, but it's grown openly anyway.'

'This country is full of surprises.'

He was glad of the company for the journey. Haddad seemed to be a man of few words and was content to drive and listen to the radio, and Pauline's conversation shortened the road.

'So what do you do when you're not finding yourself?'

She laughed again. 'I'm a saleswoman, I sell insurance. How about you?'

'Me too, I sell property, overseas property.'

'Are you good?'

Tom smiled. 'I'm the best in the country, numero uno. How about you?'

'I was the top seller in the company last year and I'd probably be top bitch again this year if I hadn't taken the month off.'

Tom was surprised; this woman didn't look like she was sharp enough to have that killer touch. 'So, what's the trick, how do you do so well?'

She smiled serenely. 'It's easy once you know the secret?'

'The secret?'

'Yes, it's simple, it's staring us in the face. Once you know the secret, you can do anything.'

Tom smiled. 'So there's an actual secret? Here's me thinking that it was something you were born with.'

She turned away from looking out the window and looked Tom in the eyes. 'It's so simple really; you just have to tell the truth. Everything else follows on from that. Truth, that's the secret.'

'Truth!' Tom laughed. 'I thought that the basis of selling was to bend the truth a little, or a lot. Basically I always thought that sales people lied for a living. I mean, we gild the lily all the time, make things look attractive; I would have thought that truth would kill any sale stone dead.'

She shook her head. 'I found a few years ago that if I told the truth about a product, customers appreciated it and bought from me. There's always one good product and several bad ones, and if you steer the client away from the rubbish they will not only buy from you but they will recommend you to their friends.'

'Truth, that's a novel concept in selling.'

'I apply it to my life in general. For instance I stopped dying my hair, my hair tells the truth about me, I'm going grey, but why worry? Truth sets you free.'

Tom was dubious. 'I couldn't see truth working in my business.'

'Try it, you'll be pleasantly surprised. You'll feel better too, it will take away all that awful pressure of the whole thing falling down around you, the idea in the back of your mind of all your unhappy customers coming looking for you.'

Tom laughed. 'I know what you mean; it doesn't bear thinking about sometimes.'

'So it does bother you, you know, that maybe you're not always doing what is right?'

'Sometimes, I suppose. I mean it's hard to get away from the fact that people don't always buy what's in their best interests. But then again that's their problem, isn't it?'

'Is it? If your conscience is constantly niggling at you, it will destroy you eventually; maybe you need to look at what you're doing.'

The car slowed and turned down an unpaved road towards the sea and pulled up at a rough graveled parking lot beside a rusting metal fence.

'We won't be very long if you want to wander a bit, or feel free to stay in the car if you prefer. It's getting hot out there.'

'I think I'll take walk down by the shore, dip my feet in the sea, but I'll keep an eye out for you and I'll be back when you're ready to move.'

Tom got out of the car and walked to meet the businessman. Ami Yemen was small and wiry, his sallow skin tanned almost black by the hot sun. He was friendly enough, but he was all business and dispensed with any small talk. He stood beside his BMW in white shirt sleeves, seemingly oblivious to the sun that was beating down on his bald head. The car was parked by the small harbour; the few dilapidated buildings in the background seemed to lean on each other.

'Welcome, this is the project that we call Tnen Kalset. Here we will build a marina with three hundred berths, and also a hotel and

two hundred apartments. You think you can sell these apartments to
Irish investors, Mr. Murphy?'

Tom looked at the surroundings; the inlet was attractive and
seemed to be a natural deep harbour; the buildings were prime can-
didates for demolition, they would fall down themselves if left for
much longer. It might have possibilities.

'Maybe, depends on the price. Nobody has sold Lebanese property in Ireland yet, but there's always a first time.'

'Yes, I am told that in Ireland they will buy anything, they are
hungry for investment, but not always with too much knowledge,
no?'

'I'd say that that's a reasonable assessment.'

'I also hear from the Mamser family that you have a system to
encourage them, you make a price that includes the rent for some
time, is that true?'

'Yes, we would need to make allowances for that in the pricing.
Do you have a pricing schedule worked out?'

'Yes, but let us go to the town and find someplace to have a drink
in the shade; you are feeling the heat, no?'

'That's an understatement. How do you manage to deal with it?
It must be well over forty right now.'

'You get used to it, but for foreigners it is not easy. Follow my car
please and we will talk in more comfort.'

'I have a lady with me who wants to take the bus to Tyre, can she
get a bus from there?'

'No problem, the place we are going is actually at the main bus
stop; she can wait in the cafe.'

The café was air conditioned and had several tall glass-fronted
fridges filed with an array of soft drinks and a few shelves of bottled
beers. Tom recognized the Laziza brand and ordered one for himself.
He bought an orange juice for Pauline and Yemen ordered a coffee.
Haddad stayed outside with the cars; the engine of the Mercedes
was running and he seemed happy to remain cocooned in his cool
environment. Pauline recognized that they wanted to talk business
and she took her drink and her book to another table.

The design was very straightforward; there really wasn't any better way to build this project other than what was on the drawings.

All the units made the best use of the view across the marina and out to sea, and it promised to be a very attractive development.

'We have a customer for the hotel as soon as we find an operator for it, but that is not too much a problem, anyway it is my problem. As soon as we have deposits for approximately half the apartments we can find the project finance for all, for the hotel, the marina, all.'

'That seems like a pretty good target, are the banks happy to lend on a project here?'

'Not the banks exactly, but we have big investors who will do it.'

'Investors from Israel?'

'Of course.'

Tom took a long draught from his beer. 'I think that we can sell this project, Mr. Yemen. Of course I'll have to look at the figures and all that, but in principle I like it. Give me a week and I'll give you the full picture, the pricing that we need to sell at and all those kinds of details.'

The Lebanese rose to leave. 'Thank you for your time, Mr. Murphy, and I look forward to talking with you in some days. Would you like another beer before you go?'

Tom had just been considering that possibility. 'Thank you; yes I wouldn't mind another one.'

Yemen paid the man behind the counter and brought Tom back his beer. 'Don't get up, enjoy your drink, and we will talk soon.'

Tom sat back and savoured the cool beer. It was good to stop moving, to sit for a little while and rest from the heat of the day and enjoy a cold drink in the quietness of the small café. The last few days had been a hectic whirlwind of activity across several countries, and he was glad to just relax for a while. Haddad would wait; he seemed happy enough to sit in the car and listen to the radio.

He picked up his drink and walked back to Pauline's table. 'You don't mind if I continue our chat?'

'Of course not, and thanks again for the lift. I'll be in Tyre in twenty minutes from here, your driver says that there's a bus every hour, so I don't have too long to wait.'

'So you think I should start telling the truth?'

'Absolutely. It will change your life.'

'It just goes against the grain of everything I ever learned about selling. I mean, we create a scenario that makes the customer think we are their friend, that we have their interests at heart. That's how we get inside their guard.'

'But there's no conflict between the telling them the truth and getting them the best deal, is there?'

Tom laughed at the idea. 'You've never worked in the overseas property business.'

'It doesn't matter what you're selling, in my view. If you believe in the product it's far easier to be convincing about it.'

'A lot of what is sold in this business isn't great value, to be honest. It ranges from middling to absolute rubbish.'

'You see, you're starting to tell the truth now. I bet you never told that to anyone outside the business before now.'

'You're right. I'm not sure why I told you.'

'That place we stopped, it's beautiful. I gather that you're going to sell property there. It shouldn't be hard to sell that and tell the truth as well. I mean, it's a fabulous location, and anyone who buys it will see that as well.'

'Depends on the price though, doesn't it?'

'I always heard that something was worth what someone was willing to pay for it, no more and no less. Any buyer that gets a place there will love it though.'

'I guess so, I wouldn't buy there myself, but I could see how others might be tempted.'

The woman stood up and gathered her belongings. 'I have to go; the bus will be here in five minutes. Thanks ever so much for the lift, the car was lovely and comfortable.'

'It was very nice to meet you, Pauline, have a good holiday.'

'And you mind yourself, and remember what I told you, truth sets you free. Try it.'

She turned and waved as she joined the crowd of people filing on to the ancient bus. Tom waved back and got into the front of the Mercedes. The car was cold, almost too cold. Haddad sat upright and put on his seatbelt. 'We go?'

'Yes please.'

The driver paused as he faced the car out of the dusty parking lot. 'We have plenty of time; do you want to see other places?'

Tom looked at his watch. 'Is there anything else to see around here?'

'Not really, but if you like....'

'Where does that road go, if we turn right?'

'No place, at the junction over there the right turn goes into Tyre, straight on goes to the border with Syria; you can go all the way to Damascus if you have time, but who would want to go there?'

'And the other way?'

'Back to Beirut.'

'Ok, let's head that way, back to the airport.'

***

The show was starting to fill and Andrew was panicking. 'Did you see Tania, Tom? There's a TV crew here.'

'Leave it with me, Andy, I'll find her.'

Tom called Tania's private mobile number; it answered after two rings.

'Something urgent?'

'The place is hopping, Tania, are you far away?'

'I'm in the hairdressers; what's the panic?'

'You were in the hairdressers yesterday.'

'I'm in the hairdressers every day, Tom, I have to look my best for my media appearances. You don't want my roots showing, do you?'

'There's a TV crew here, doing a piece for the evening news about property, do you want me to handle it?'

'Tell them to wait for an hour.'

'Don't be daft, Tania, these guys want to get in and out and get the item done; they won't hang around. Is the hairdresser far from here?'

'I can't get there in less than an hour. You'd better do the piece yourself, but be sure to mention me.'

'Ok.'

The camera crew looked bored; they wanted an interview and they had a list of questions already written in big letters on a pad on the clipboard that the young assistant was waving about. 'Can we speak with your spokesman Mr. Murphy? We need to get this in the can in the next ten minutes; there's a statement from the agriculture minister due in half an hour and we have to cover it.'

'Ok, I'll do the piece for you; Doctor Sherry is detained in a meeting and won't be here for an hour.'

The cameraman clicked the legs of the tripod into place and focused on Tom as he sat behind the desk. The assistant wasn't happy.

'No, not there, over here in front of that big display, the pictures of the Spanish things.'

The cameraman raised his eyebrows; he moved his equipment and resumed focusing. The reporter peered into the lens and squinted at her image on the tiny screen as she touched up her makeup; she began to read the page that the assistant was holding up behind the camera.

'We're here at the Scorpio Properties investment seminar, and we're looking at the phenomenon of Irish people investing abroad. Hold the fucking thing up where I can see it, Meghan.'

The assistant sighed in an exaggerated manner and held the clipboard higher, and the reporter started again.

'We're here at the Scorpio Properties investment seminar, and we're looking at the phenomenon of Irish people investing abroad. At a time of unprecedented wealth in the country, is it the right strategy for us as a nation that we should invest so much of our hard-earned cash abroad? I'm here with Tom Murphy, sales manager of Scorpio Properties. What's your view, Tom?'

Tom was tired; it had been a long week with all the travelling and he wasn't in the humour for all this nonsense. For some reason, the words of the girl he met in the Lebanon kept interrupting his thoughts. 'Tell the truth, it will set you free.'

He looked at the camera. 'It might be a good strategy, and then again it might not. Maybe it's not for everybody.'

The reporter was thrown by his answer, but she stuck with her list of questions. 'So, where is the best place right now for an investor, what will give the best return?'

'Hard to say. Spain maybe, that's still doing ok, more or less.'

'And Bulgaria, Scorpio is the biggest Irish company operating in Bulgaria. What about these ski apartments in Malko, in Bulgaria, how do you rate these as an investment?'

Tom was still stuck in truth mode; he was finding it hard to lie to the reporter. Maybe the woman was right; if you told the truth then people would trust you and buy lots more from you. He looked back to the reporter.

'They're all right, I suppose; if you like skiing they're fine.'

The reporter was in a dilemma; this wasn't going according to the script, but she had to get the minister's statement and time was passing. She decided to stick with the list of questions on the pad. 'So, overseas investment is definitely the way to go for us as a nation, it's the best strategy for personal and national wealth creation going forward?'

'Not necessarily, but some of it is probably ok.'

'Thank you, Tom. And there you have it. This is Kerry Miles here at the Scorpio Properties investment seminar, and now it's back to you, Jerry.'

***

What the fuck were you thinking when you said all that shit? Have you lost your fucking marbles?'

'Don't you see, Tania, if we tell people where the bad stuff is, we can sell them the good stuff and they'll trust us, we'll have an edge on all the other outfits.'

'I really think you've lost it. What good stuff for fucks sake? Surely you of all people know that ninety nine percent of what we sell is absolute shite?'

'Not all of it, Tania, be fair.'

'Tom, you know yourself that we have puffed up the prices of everything we sell by a huge margin. If any of our customers were to try to resell anything we sold them, assuming they could sell it at all, they would lose half their money. You know this; you were the one that created these rental products.'

'They're not all bad, some of them are ok.'

'Some of them are worse than others, you mean.'

'Well yes, I suppose so. Malko is absolute rubbish, I'll give you that.'

'Of course its rubbish, but it's the place that's paying you and me a shed load of money every week; it's still our big banker and the mafia doesn't have a slice of it either. You need to keep your focus and start shifting it again; that news report is going to do us damage.'

Tom sighed. 'Ok, I admit that it might have been an error of judgment, maybe I'm getting cynical about the whole thing.'

'Maybe it's time that you weren't involved?'

'What do you mean?'

'Maybe you've come to some kind of a crisis, losing your bottle for this game. I can manage fine without you, I can do the business with Mickey as the front man, and Andrew can manage the sales, he's doing most of it anyway.'

'You want to get rid of me?'

'Now that you put it that way, yes. We've been having one disagreement after another the last few weeks. Yes, let's just call it a day before we start having a war with each other.'

'Just like that?'

Her voice softened a little. 'No, Tom, not just like that, but let's say you stay with us for the rest of the show this weekend, and I'll give you a very generous severance payment, just to show that there's no hard feelings.'

'How generous?'

'I'll give you the entire take on this weekend's show, the whole nine yards. Every penny of profit we make between now and Sunday, and everything we made this afternoon, it will all be yours. You just have to sign a contract that you'll stay out of the business for at least two years; I don't want you working for Harry again, or even for someone like Simpson.'

Tom felt a sense of relief. It would all be over; no more looking over his shoulder and worrying about having it all crashing down on him. He was still shocked at how things had turned out, but maybe it was all for the best.

'Tania, you have a deal. I'll give it my best shot tomorrow and Sunday, and then I'll walk away. You can do what you like with it all after that.'

* * *

It had been a hell of a long day. Tom's heart wasn't really in it, but he knew that he had to get as much money on the meter as possible in order to give himself a good paycheck. He still had a feeling that if he could somehow tell the truth to people, he could convince them to buy the better projects and ignore the rubbish like Malko, but that strategy didn't seem to be working. Business was down on previous weeks, and the people who did come to the show had all seen the piece on the news the night before. They had questions to ask.

'Are you sure that this place is worth buying?' The woman was suspicious of the sales pitch.

'Of course, madam, we wouldn't be selling it otherwise.'

'I saw you on the news last night; you didn't seem too enthusiastic yourself. You said it was all right if you liked skiing yourself.'

'But that's true, I would like to think that buyers would buy there with a view to getting some use out of it sometime.'

'Use it myself? Do you really see me on a pair of skis?'

'Why not?'

The woman snorted. 'I can hardly walk with my weight, not to mind ski. Anyway I have no interest in going somewhere that's that cold; I'd rather go somewhere warm.'

'Then can we interest you in something in Spain? It's warm there.'

'I thought that Bulgaria was warm.'

'It is, but Spain is warmer still.'

'I don't like it too hot. I get a rash.'

'Then maybe you'd like something in Sunny Beach North; we have a few left there, and it's close to the beach.'

The woman rose from the chair. 'I'll think about it, I'm not so sure at all.'

Andrew caught Tom's eye from across the room. He tapped his watch; it was time to call it a day. Tom gathered his papers from the desk and stuffed them into his briefcase; one more day of this, then freedom. It felt good in a way, but he would miss it too.

The girl with the buggy and the little boy was talking to Andrew as he was trying to close the door. She wore blue jeans and a leather jacket, and the boy was trying to wriggle his way out of the straps in the pushchair. Andrew let her pass and she strode purposefully towards Tom.

'Sorry, we're closed for today.' Tom had enough, he wanted to catch up with the lads in the Willows and get a couple of pints inside him.

'Don't you remember me, Tom?'

She looked familiar; was it was the blonde girl that he had sold the yellow car to back in City Auto, the girl he had met in the club before he went to Spain? It was, yes. She was a stunner right enough, looked a lot better in normal colours; at least she had got out of her yellow phase. 'Amanda?'

'Yes, at least you remembered that much.' She sounded angry.

'Sorry, I never contacted you, a lot happened.'

'Not as sorry as me. I saw you on the news last night, that's how I knew you were here.'

'Oh, I see.'

Amanda unbuckled the little boy from the buggy; he stood up quickly and tried to run around the room, but she grabbed him under the arms and lifted him up to stand on the desk. She burst into tears as the little boy looked curiously at Tom.

'Tommy,' she sobbed, 'I want you to meet your daddy.'

Chapter Fourteen

'Well, fuck me.' Walter had a way of summing things up. 'This has been quite a few days for you, Tom, talk about a blast from the past.'

'I'm still in shock to be honest. I don't mind about losing my job, I was beginning to get tired of working for Tania, but Amanda turning up with the kid, with Tommy, that was a shock for sure.'

Harry put the tray of drinks on the table. 'How do you feel about having a little boy? Is it a good feeling?'

'After the initial upset, I'm fine about it, really. He's great actually, a lovely little fellow. Yes, I'm delighted if the truth be known, but it'll take getting used to.'

'Did you get to spend some time with him this evening?'

'A case of not having any choice. She shoved him into my hands and said that she was going for a walk, first time she was able to leave him and be alone for the last couple of years. She came back though after half an hour, just before I panicked altogether.'

'You did well to mind him, did he make strange with you?'

'He did at first; I didn't know what to be saying to him. I just sat him down in my chair and sang songs to him, tried to teach him a few nursery rhymes and that.'

'Imagine, Tom a daddy. Here's to Tom, and little Tommy.' Andrew raised his gin and tonic.

The others raised glasses in salute. 'Best thing ever happened to you.' Walter spoke for them all.

'Thanks, guys. My head is still spinning with it all. I need a good night's sleep.'

Walter laughed. 'You can forget that from now on, you'll have a little alarm clock jumping on your chest every morning now. Andy was saying that they'll move in with you, your girl and your son?'

'My son.' Tom pondered the words. 'My son, yes. Amanda's just renting that small flat, my place is big, so we're going to give it a try, take it as it comes for a month or two and see if it works out.'

'I don't want to be a party pooper, Tom, but you two hardly know each other really. Do you think that an instant arrangement like that can work? Are you not rushing things a bit?'

'I think I'm about ready to try the settled life, and having a kid changes the picture too.'

'But you only met her a few times, and you know nothing about each other.'

I know that, and it may not work out at all, but I fancied her from the first time I met her, and we really hit it off when we spoke this evening. After she had taken out a few years of frustration on me first that is.'

'So you are both willing to take a chance?'

'Yes, we both know it's a bit of a long shot, but there's Tommy to consider as well; I missed out on his first couple of years and I don't want to miss a minute of the rest.'

'So where are they now?'

'She's gone home tonight; give us both a chance to get over the shock and get Tommy to bed. I'm going to give her the keys tomorrow and she'll move some stuff over while I'm at work. I'm a bit nervous about it, but I'm looking forward to it in another way. I'm too long living on my own.'

'That's true.' Andrew sounded wistful. 'You were getting crusty, set in your ways.'

Harry laughed. 'That's good, coming from you, Andy. What was that about you leaving Scorpio, Tom? I missed that.'

'Tania sacked him.' Walter couldn't resist the jibe.

'She didn't sack me; we agreed to part the ways.'

'You want to come back to work for me? That door is open still.'

'Thanks, Harry, but she put a clause in my payoff that bars me from working in the business for two years.'

'I don't think this business will exist in two years.'

They looked at Walter in surprise. 'It's true; I really think we are just riding the crest of a wave here, this will all evaporate as quickly as it grew.'

'You could be right.' Harry was inclined to agree with Walter. 'A lot of the business is based on expectations of price rises when places like Hungary and Bulgaria join the EU; if those rises don't happen fast, if they take a normal kind of timescale, people will get disillusioned and the market may well fizzle out.'

'Rise?' Walter laughed. 'If they hold their own it'll be a miracle, particularly in Bulgaria. We're looking at big losses there anyway no matter what happens with EU membership.'

Tom smiled. 'You don't care Harry; you never intended this as anything but one last fling, a retirement fund.'

'True enough, Tom, I did better than I ever thought possible to be honest, but I'd like to think that Walter's job would last a few years more.'

'Don't worry about me, Harry. The last couple of years have been good to me, set me up well. I think we all did well on this caper really.'

Andrew raised his glass. 'Amen to that.'

'So, what makes you think it will all be over sooner rather than later?'

'I just have a feeling, Tom.' Harry was in a mellow mood. 'My gut instinct is that we've crested the wave, that's all.'

'Any particular reason, or is it just a feeling?'

'A few things. One thing that will kill it is bad press; if a reporter starts to dig too deep in places like Bulgaria then the shit will hit the fan. That guaranteed rental thing you started has run riot lately, everyone is adding rent on to prices, and a lot of the small guys aren't doing the deals you did over there. They're adding margins and rent on to prices that are already way above the market.'

'True enough, a lot of the developers know what we're getting for stuff, and that's the kind of prices they're quoting to small agencies, so they have to add their margins and rent on top of that again. It's getting completely crazy out there; I've seen places sold lately for a hundred and twenty grand that are worth no more than thirty on a good day.'

'The whole business is getting really mad in lots of ways.' Andrew smiled at the thought. 'Tania even has a load of dentists signed up as agents, they persuade patients that they bought great value from Scorpio and then they pass their details on to us to close the sale. They get a commission for every contact that delivers a sale.'

Tom nodded. 'That's true, she went in one day to have her teeth polished, and she signed her dentist up to send clients to her. After that she went around on several of them and she has about six surgeries on her list now. It's mad all right.'

Walter laughed at Tania's latest stunt. 'It's getting a bit crazy when you can't have a tooth pulled without someone trying to sell you a place in Bulgaria.'

'I know. Anytime you visit a lawyer, or an accountant, you're in the firing line as well. It's probably gone beyond sanity right enough.'

Walter smiled. 'So maybe you didn't mind being sacked?'

'I wasn't sacked, I left. Anyone for another pint?' Tom waved his empty glass at the barman and pointed around the table at the others. 'Everyone for the same again?'

They nodded.

'As regards the bad press thing though, I don't reckon that any reporter will dig very deep. This industry is one of the biggest advertising sectors in the newspapers right now. I know we're spending up to fifty grand some weeks, and there are more than thirty companies in the market at this stage. Ok, some of them are small, but it still adds up to a lot of bread.'

Harry shook his head. 'Doesn't mean someone won't go after it. Murtagh is already trying to dish the dirt on Budapest, talking about foreigner prices and local prices and all that stuff, seems like a direct reference to the job you sold in the gypsy district. His editor has sat on it so far, but it's only a matter of time before the talk starts.'

Tom carried the drinks down to the table and collected the empties. 'I think I know what's biting that little shit.'

Walter laughed. 'He wasn't paid enough dropsy?'

'Nothing like that, he got plenty; it's more that he's pissed off at losing his crown as mister overseas property. Since our Doctor Sherry started getting the TV slots, Murtagh has his knife in her. I did warn her at the time but she was hell bent on being seen as the world's leading property expert. No talking to our Tania when she has the bit between her teeth.'

'What have you done, leaving me in the hands of that woman?' Andrew sounded worried.

'Don't worry Andy, she doesn't know how to handle you, you don't dance to her charms.'

'I'll miss having you there all the same, Tom, all joking apart. It's been great.'

Tom chugged back the rest of his pint and stood up. 'I'm heading off, lads, have to clean up the flat and put all breakable stuff up on high shelves, little boy coming to live and all that.'

***

It would soon be over, and no harm. Tom sat back and watched as the young couple walked over to the lawyer's desk with their deposit cheque. That sale had been easy, he hadn't even pushed them; they were so convinced by the rental guarantee in Malko that they had bought two units. Like taking candy from a baby really, lambs to the slaughter. He felt suddenly tired, weary of the endless round of exhibitions and long flights, and the blur of hundreds of people passing his desk, all of them convinced that they were on a path to riches.

It wouldn't be anything of the sort though, he knew that. Give it four years at the most, two years to build the projects and another two years when they got back their own rent, minus a handling fee and maybe some tax. Then the shit would hit the fan. It might take a few months more, but gradually the realization would dawn on them that there was no crock of gold, no magic formula for getting rich in some foreign place. A few would do ok; the people who had bought from Harry in Spain had already done well, and even the early buyers on Montana Fea were selling on at small profits. Harry had sold some good stuff in Budapest too, downtown in good areas, but Mamser's rubbish in the Renaissance quarter was always going to be rubbish, no matter what you called it.

He sometimes felt a small pang of conscience when he thought of the people that had bought at high prices in Bulgaria, especially in the mountains where the snow was intermittent and where not many people went to ski. What would happen to all those places? Would they fall down eventually, vandalized during the long closed season when the slopes were green? Would people just sell out at a fraction of what they paid? Maybe local people would someday live there, attracted by the knockdown prices and the mass exodus of foreign owners? It was hard to tell.

He felt sorry for them all in one way, but in other ways his conscience was clear. After all, it was greed that drove them to buy these places, nothing more. They all had homes already, just trying to get rich quick without having to work for it. They all knew about buyer beware, it was up to them to check out the facts, but they didn't. It was their own fault.

'Penny for them, Tom.' Andrew had wandered over; it would soon be time to close.

'I'll miss it all, Andy, but maybe now I'll get a life. Is it nearly time to pull down the shutters?'

'Give it ten more minutes, and then we'll call it a day. It wasn't a bad weekend anyway, we did well.'

'We did fine.' Tom was happy enough; his final paycheck would be a good one. It would have been better if he hadn't lost it a bit on Friday, but it was ok. He wouldn't starve.

His mobile rang; he was surprised to see Andrew's number appear. He picked it up and pressed the button. 'Andy, where did you disappear to?'

'I'm out in the toilet.'

'Are you ok?'

'I can't come in, she's here; I can't face her.'

'Who's here, what's wrong?'

'That bitch, my uncle's wife, she just walked into the room. I covered my face with a folder and ran out. Oh, Tom, I can't face that woman, I can't come back in. I feel sick.'

Tom looked across the room to where a blonde woman was perusing the displays. She looked to be in her late fifties or early sixties, her skin was very tanned, almost leathery, and she was dressed in cream trousers and a white top with sparkling crystals on it. Her hands and arms were festooned in expensive gold chains and rings. So that was old Milton's wife, imagine that!

'Look, Andy, it's ok, I'll get rid of her. You go on home and I'll lock up the stuff.'

'Thanks, Tom, you're a pal, I'll talk to you during the week; I'll give you a ring.'

Tom stood up and walked over to the woman. 'Can I help you, madam?'

She smiled a cold smile at him. 'I have some funds; I'm looking to invest in property.'

'You've come to the right place, madam.' He led her over to the desk. 'What level of spend did you have in mind, madam?'

'About three million, maybe a little more.'

Tom swallowed; he tried not to let the surprise show on his face. The bitch was spending Milton's money in a big way.

'That's a lot of money.'

'I know. I saw you on the news. I thought you were very honest; you didn't come out with the usual sales talk. That's why I came to see you.'

'Oh, thank you.'

'My husband and I live in Spain, you see. He doesn't come back here at all; I only come home to see my mother, she's getting on a bit.'

I bet she is; she must be fucking ancient. Tom kept the thought to himself. 'So you want to invest a lump sum, maybe get an income from it?'

'Yes, that's the idea. Retain our capital and draw an income as well.'

So that when the old goat pops his clogs, you'll be sitting on a fortune that his relatives can't get their hands on? Tom wished he could say out loud what was on his mind.

'So what's the best place for this kind of money?'

Tom pondered his situation. He looked over to the door; Amanda waved, and Tommy strained to get out of the buggy to run to his daddy. The room was empty except for the salesmen and lawyers who were writing up their records. Somebody turned off the air conditioning and the place was suddenly silent.

'Mama, there dada.'

'Yes Tommy, that's daddy.'

'Mama, Critopher Wobin was bold.'

'Was he, love?'

'Mama, Critopher Wobin catrated the puttycat, mama, he catrated the puttycat.'

She tried to keep a straight face; Tom smiled back at his family. Everything seemed to be turning out for the best; Amanda was a lovely girl and as for Tommy, well, that kid was something else. It wouldn't be easy to start a new life with someone who was practically a stranger, even if she was the mother of his child, but the next few months would tell him a lot about the realities of family life, whether the actuality would match the dream. He was looking forward to it, to this new challenge and this new way of living.

He looked back at Mrs. Milton; she waited for his response. It wouldn't be right to take their bloody money, even if Milton had screwed him when he closed the shop. Maybe the woman in the Lebanese cafe was right when she said that telling the truth gave you peace of mind.

He looked back at his son. Then again, there would be school fees, and maybe if all went well little Tommy would have a brother or a sister. They would have to be fed and cared for, and that city apartment mightn't be the best place to bring them up. A big house in the country would be nice, with a big garden where they could run and play. Then they would grow up quickly, the kids would need houses themselves, it would be endless. This caper could be expensive.

The woman was looking at him, she repeated her question.

'Where would I go with that kind of money?'

'You'd have to be very careful, madam, that's an awful lot of money and you'd need to be sure that it was invested wisely.'

'I know that, I'll get one shot at this and it has to be good.'

Tom wavered. This woman was putting her trust in him, and he would have to live up to that trust. He would have to tell the truth, to follow the advice that Pauline had given him. She had seemed very content with her life, so it had to be the best way forward. You couldn't live for ever in fear of all your unhappy customers coming back to haunt you, it was better to be straight and honest and to leave all the dodgy dealing behind, to make a new start. He thought of the old Englishwoman in Pueblo Alto Blanco; he felt an uneasy stir in his stomach when he pictured how she had looked as she sat on the steps and wept at the loss of her life savings.

On the other hand, a three million sale this weekend would put well over a million in his own pocket, and that was serious money in anyone's language. Taking a small amount from a lot of people was not such a problem, but taking that much money from an old couple would be too much, really. How could you live with something like that on your conscience? Then again, he had responsibilities to his family as well; it was all very difficult sometimes.

He looked at the woman sitting across from him; this day wasn't over yet. He turned on his most sincere look and leaned across the desk. 'You're a serious investor and you're obviously a smart woman; there's no point in wasting your time with some kind of sales pitch, so let me tell it like it is. The very best advice that I could give you would be to put your money in the same place that I put mine, madam. Tell me, did you ever hear of a place called Malko?